Shapes the Sunlight Takes

JOSH WAGNER

Asymmetrical Press
Missoula, Montana

Published by Asymmetrical Press, Missoula, Montana.

Library of Congress Cataloging-In-Publication Data
Shapes the sunlight takes / Josh Wagner — 1st ed.
ISBN: 978-1-938793-81-3
eISBN: 978-1-938793-82-0
WC: 90,969
1. Literature. 2. Fiction. 3. Coming of Age.

Cover design by Colin Wright
Formatted in beautiful Montana
Printed in the U.S.A.

Publisher info:
Website: www.asymmetrical.co
Email: howdy@asymmetrical.co
Twitter: @asympress

ASYM METR ICAL

For Mom and Dad

Si las moscas fabrican miel
Ofenderán a las abejas?

—Pablo Neruda

Shapes the Sunlight Takes

0

ABOUT AN HOUR AGO I saved the world.

That was down there, under the pale lamplight where feeble bones and dotard eyes still overtake the quiet streets of our town. But from up here on the ridge, where the canyon drops off a thousand feet and I can feel the heat from ancient forest fires, the buoyancy of a Pleistocene glacial lake, the footfall of the reptile and the ape, the soft white glow of my mother's headlights—here it's all different. Here it's all golden starthistles spilling through night's dark gash. Like I'm looking through his eyes. Glossy brown eyes that have only just begun to see. I can smell wet bear grass and dry clover, and I can feel his breath, sweet and heavy on my shoulder like the wind stirring through the cloaked pines.

It's early June and there's snow falling in the valley, but up here my skin is tender and warm.

I was born under the stars and reared in the shadow of a volcano and raised beside the ocean, and when I was seven I got separated from my mother in Los Angeles and I wandered alone down Hollywood Boulevard past the Chinese Theatre where I saw the tongue of a man with a bleach-white face eating fire, and sometimes I wonder whether I ever found my mother again or if I just walked through the gates of the theatre's golden pagoda and entered a new life in the cinematic shadow of these mountains and the swift indecision of alfalfa fields.

I'm fifteen. I'm bleeding. I bellow and bend, inhaling the future and exhaling the past. I am one more sentence in the primal contempt between the virus and the cell, the clash of the cross and the spiral. Everything I say is some kind of lie, told to outlive the stones that will outlive me.

My mother calls my name from out in the woods like some hoary witch trying to summon me into the world. I picture her at my age, dreaming of one day having a daughter, trying on names, manifesting her future.

In the gypsum sky one star after another goes out. I can see snow. Like really see it. And I can see his footprints trailing into the trees.

I think I might go to jail for this.

My arms stretch out to the clouds. My fingers uncurl and her breath rushes in.

Mirielle.

1

MY DESIRE FOR MIRIELLE STARTS in the space between her eyes and unfolds like dark calligraphy toward each of her ears. Her eyebrows kindled this fire, but I didn't fall in love until it became clear just how much she hates them. Brooks has found her hunched over in her locker, tweezing around the edges, curating rogue hairs. Mirielle sees her eyebrows as a grotesque and savage wilderness, but I see a reticulate interior, an Amazonian paradise, scars of shadow on a face of otherwise pure light.

Today she and her friends sit in the grass in the Yard—as in the schoolyard—like something straight off the cover of a college brochure. There's the low-hanging tree branch, the serene, soft-focus skyline. Notepads and textbooks scattered around like fallen fruit. Cream-colored sweaters. Knock-off designer jeans from Target. Ultra-tiny purses. Label tees. Bridgett Marrowgold, the oh-so-perf future supermodel-in-training, holds an apple just so, its waxy skin sweating in the sun. Rae Stryker, decked out like Janis Joplin, fiddles around on a rosewood guitar. I've been watching for ten or fifteen minutes, composing their conversations and taking mental snapshots as they pose immaculately on behalf of whatever subterranean gods oversee wasted teenage potential.

Bridgett leans into Mirielle's shoulder and without deviating from her scripted girlish laughter she whispers, "Maggie Andrews is such a total cunt." Mirielle's smile does not falter. Parted lips ripe and delicate, nearly translucent. She stares at clouds. I follow her gaze and I see a narwhal, a pomegranate tree, a smartphone.

"What's that hippie shit you're playing?" Gail Langley asks Rae Stryker. Gail has short hair, neo-punk; total bitch.

Mirielle narrows her eyes when she smiles. Her hands never drop below her hips and her arms refuse to dangle. They hug her ribs like she's trying to keep the stuffing in. Oh god, the moments when her fingers rake the nape of her neck, when she stretches her back and presses her face to the sun! Or when her arms settle around her waist. I'm crazy about midriffs and hers is like the Platonic ideal of all midriffery. When she walks she's an aspen in the fog. Something about her smell makes time flow backwards. I love that her breasts are small—they're even smaller than mine. And, by the way, this is the one and only reason she doesn't have guys crawling all over her. High school boys aim as deep into the bra alphabet as they can, but don't know how to deal with the unquantifiable face of the sublime. Exotic eyebrows, for instance. But I've seen older guys, college guys—the way they look at her—they can see.

"Did anyone get letters back?" Rae sets her guitar down and pinches the skin where cheek, lower eyelid, and the bridge of her nose meet. She pulls a teardrop as if out of thin air, holds it on her fingertip like a splinter, and then snuffs it out with her thumb.

"I got into the U," says Gail.

Mirielle shakes back her hair, and the sunlight electrifies long candystripe waves of cinnamon and mocha.

"That doesn't count," says Rae.

Hair that visibly refracts the sunlight.

"Weren't you trying for Berkeley?"

Hair that pauses at the apex of the toss before descending back onto her shoulders, each strand a parachute.

"Fuck that. California is screwed, my brother says. They won't even have water in five years."

"Doesn't he live in L.A.?"

"He's moving to Mexico."

Rae has a torn tear duct. Years ago, while she was quarantined with the chickenpox, one of the blisters exploded at the bridge of her nose and spread into her right eye. She scratched at it so much that it ripped open the puncta of her lower canalicular duct. Now whenever the duct fills up it drips. Persistent saline jewels cling to the corner of her eye, and she destroys each one with a habitual swipe of her fingertip.

Bridgett takes a bite of her apple and drops the rest into a brown paper bag. Today for lunch my mother packed a turkey sandwich with sprouts, a bag of almonds, a box of Craisins, root beer, and a tampon. It's like this every day. She thinks I am deliberately not getting my period to ruin her life. Some girls just take longer. I'm cool about this. I'm not as desperate to become a woman as my mother wishes I was.

Bridgett reaches into her purse and grabs her phone. She flips it open, checks something, and then closes it again. She says, "I'm so totally moving to Paris after high school."

"Paris is dirty," Gail says.

"College is a scam, that's what my brother says."

I have never seen Mirielle's left knee. She tore her anterior cruciate ligament skiing two years ago and it still hasn't healed, so there's always this brace, whether she's in skirt, shorts or bikini.

The enigma of that knee haunts me. Does it look just like her other knee? Is it smaller? Misaligned due to the accident? Is there a birthmark on the cap?

"You could be a doula," Mirielle says, looking back at the sky. How is it that her hair has yet to fully settle?

"A what?"

"Like a midwife, but you don't need medical experience or training."

"What do they do?" Bridgett asks.

"It's mostly, like, emotional support." Mirielle stretches. Her shoulder blades kiss. She has this way about stretching like she's getting ready to tell you a secret or something so surprising that her body has to find the right shape first.

"Doula, you said?" Rae is already Googling it.

"They pay you for this?"

"It's a good way to live abroad."

I listen from across the courtyard, my spine pressed into the hollow of a tree. I'm like a pair of binoculars held by some dryad looking through me. I have these moments, these vibratory sessions, when my consciousness seems to draw away from the back of my skull and I perceive things as if through someone else's eyes, like I'm floating above my body. They're too far away for my actual physical ears to hear anything. What I gather comes in glimpses and secret codes delivered directly to my brain. I fill in blanks. My mind works with a holistic map of possible realities. Interpolation of human chatter and behavior is no big deal. I know to a reasonable margin of error what Mirielle will wear next Tuesday.

Rae reads: "Doula comes from Ancient Greek meaning 'female slave'. Nice."

"Uh, no thanks."

"… call themselves labor companions and birthworkers." I suspect Rae is on Wikipedia.

When I picture Mirielle in my room she wears a dozen pearl necklaces and a short black skirt. Her thumb stretches the waistband down ever so slightly until I can see lace licking her right hip. Her knee brace is on. I can't get rid of it even in my imagination. But the Velcro has come loose and the top edge hangs slack. Her feet are bare. She walks toward me, curling her toes. I'm immobile on the floor except for the conspiratorial twist of muscles around my lumbar spine. The ache of my longing constricts my breath with the playful hesitation in her steps. I love how she takes forever—how she wrings out every delicious second until she's hovering over me, her hair done up all messy with a few stray locks falling between us, drifting across my face, tickling my skin. I feel her fingertips on my neck. Her breath on my eyelids. She has rings on every finger. Red nail polish. Silver hoop earrings. No mascara. Bare lips.

Sheldon Dawn walks past the girls and gives them a casual nod. Rae stretches out to steal a high five, which mutates into this complicated architecture of fist-bumps and mirroring gestures that all take place between Sheldon's steps without breaking his stride. I have no clue how other kids even learn this stuff. Is there a class? It all reminds me of how they wouldn't even know my name if I ever tried to go over and say hi. Maybe Bridgett might. She does her homework and knows one or two shitty facts about everyone in the school.

Mirielle and her friends are seniors. They're all so beautiful and delusional and enviable. Gail is a virgin who only sucks cock. Rae is sleeping with three guys right now, and they all know each other and know about each other, though none of them seem to care. How does she do that? Bridgett has been true-love-gaga over the school's star halfback since fifth grade. They went to prom last year and wear promise rings. I'm the only one who knows he's fucking Megan Chase. Mirielle has never had a boyfriend. Unless you count Derwin Richter, but even with them there was never any talk of it being official. Derwin took off three years ago. Now he's somewhere down south I think. That's what Brooks says. He's Derwin's little brother. Mirielle dated Mark Fleischer off and on last winter and is sort of seeing Steve Chambers right now, but she's never had a like-really-for-reals boyfriend. This is a good sign.

Rae is still staring at her phone. "Did you know babies are sometimes born kneeling?" She flicks a tear off her cheek. "*The baby is in a kneeling position, with one or both legs extended at the hips and flexed at the knees.* Creepy!"

"Your eyeball is creepy," says Gail.

Going over to say hi is not an option. Better to stay invisible. I used to wake up an hour early to try and make myself look at the very least like an average teenage girl. I tried makeup and different hairstyles and hats and all kinds of clothes. I don't do any of that shit anymore. I cut my own hair and I don't care if it's ugly. Beauty is for the weak. Now I dress like I want. There isn't a thing I could put on that would hide the fact that I'm a freak. My left eye is huge. My nose is crooked. My lips are thin. There's this long scar running between my scapulae and down under the left claw of my false ribs from a Mitral valve procedure when I was thirteen months old. I have this cuspid that's like twisted around the vertical axis—it's almost backward. Yeah, a backward tooth. My father's weird ears. I can't not realize this. And I know it doesn't matter, but it doesn't matter that it doesn't matter, you know? How can people not be insecure about this stuff? Maggie

✸

Andrews, for example: dog-faced, but she walks around like she's Mila Kunis.

Brooks is on the west end of the Yard, kneeling in front of a fire hydrant. He crowns it with pebbles and blades of grass in a lattice pattern. I'm his only real friend. Brooks is blonde, quiet, occasionally bruised. He has this one piercing blue eye that never seems to move. His other eye is brown. Brooks gets pushed around and teased, but he's just small enough that no one is too rough. I think people are scared to break him. Brooks loves video games, magic tricks, dissecting analog electronics, and listening to music no one's ever heard before like Lowercase, Glitch-Opera, Danger Sound, Alexander Scriabin, and this spooky German jazz band who always perform in total darkness. Brooks was born a century too soon. The future will be populated by people like him: people who manifest their dreams, who can scream down mountains.

"Autistic individuals display many forms of repetitive or restricted behavior such as stereotypy," Rae says. "That means repetitive movement, such as hand flapping, making sounds, head rolling, or body rocking." Now she's reading about autism. She's been link hopping: doula to midwifery to breech births to autism. How do I know this?

Gail looks up with feigned concern. "That sounds a lot like your guitar playing, Rae. Should we be worried?"

"O snap," Bridgett says. Mirielle smiles crane-necked under a fresh sunbeam, still trying to find whatever she lost in the clouds. She closes her eyes. Parts her lips. I feel my vertebrae melt.

"Bitch," says Rae.

"Nickel-hooker," says Gail.

The yard fills up as kids trickle back from lunch. My biology teacher regulates their flow over by the double doors. He catches my eye and smiles. I think I'm smiling back. I'm Mr. Larson's star pupil because on account of my mother got me started on anatomy & physiology in the womb. I swear to god she used to jab around her belly, pointing to organs and reciting their Latin names. When I was a toddler she gave me a stack of anatomy coloring books. I learned to read from *Gray's*. For me, 'Head, shoulders, knees and toes' was 'Cranium, scapula, patella, hallux'. My mother wants me to be a doctor, but I'm going to be a DJ. I expect she'll hang herself when she finds out—that's if my preference for women doesn't get her first.

Maggie Andrews walks up behind me. I don't even have to look. I can smell her lunch breath. Feel the quivering of her impossibly tight rust-red curls. She's a couple feet away but when she talks the words sound like they're coming from inside my ear.

"You might as well just rub one out right here in the Yard," she says, and that's all she says at first, just hangs on it, waiting to see what I do.

Something happens at the base of my occipital bone. I am livid, paralyzed. The hairs on my arms do their thing. If I could make Maggie Andrews not exist… "What do you want?" I whisper, or maybe I don't. Maybe I just mouth it. I'm shaking so hard that even pressed against the tree I'm having trouble staying on my feet.

"She's hot," Maggie says, closer. Expecting me to turn around. I could die. "You want a piece of that or what?"

"What are you talking about?" This I know I say.

"Everyone knows," she says.

No longer lucid, no longer with my consciousness spread out across the Yard—I have retracted fully into my body, which itself seems to shrink and compress. I itch everywhere. Fingernails dig into the palms of my hands. My cheeks burn; my eyes squeeze painfully into their sockets.

Maggie Andrews is a sophomore. She's always it seems like she's out trying to ruin someone's life. With my eyes shut and I can see her twisted little bitch face, her shitty bitch freckles and her extensive gums and her huge drooping bitch tits that she thinks are like secret weapons or something.

"You're a little creeper, Lexie," she says. "Spying on her all the time."

"So what does that make you—spying on me?"

"You know what? Okay. Fine. You asked for it, you smart-ass dyke."

I feel her brush by but I don't open my eyes. This time she really is right there in my ear with a whisper: "I wonder what she'll think about your little crush."

I have a vision here, just a flash, of forcing a lead pipe down Maggie Andrews' throat. What happens actually is it takes all my effort just to keep from crying—a pathetic little hiccup laugh is my attempt to cover up. I can barely get out the word: "Don't."

"Like she doesn't already know. Like it isn't so totally obvious to everyone."

"Oh my god, please." I reach for her. Actually reach out to touch Maggie Andrews on the arm.

"I'm doing you a favor." She's somehow already walking away. Toward Gail and Bridgett and Rae. And Mirielle.

All I can do is I just stand there and watch Maggie Andrews take her determined steps, disrupting the brochure tableau and the harmony of Mirielle's hair. Each step further tears down my perceptive stage. I can no longer hear their conversations over the blood pounding in my head. Gail is the first to notice when

Maggie reaches them, and she nudges Bridgett. Rae's guitar sounds like radio static.

I see what comes next like I'm reading a comic strip panel by panel. I should be running, but I feel like if I step away from this tree I will collapse and fall through the grass and slip between the molecules of the earth and out into the void to drift along like a stray thought looking for a mind to ride. Rae and Bridgett and Gail all squint up at Maggie Andrews, and now Mirielle has turned her head because Maggie just said something. She's talking and they're listening. Gail glares at her like she wants to throw a brick, which would be awesome. Bridgett now pretending not to care or even notice she exists, but Mirielle gives Maggie Andrews her full attention until all of a sudden she glances past her arm and now Mirielle is looking directly at me. At my face.

Now, of all times, now my muscles regain their autonomy and fortitude and my reptilian brain is like *Go!*, but of course this would be the worst time of all possible times to run or even to move an inch in any direction. But I have to move. The body won't stay still. So my right shoulder slumps and my left arm wraps around my stomach like that's a cool kind of pose, and I sort of turn my chin up and pretend I'm checking out the leaves on that tree over there.

In my peripheral vision I see Gail doubled over laughing her ass off and Rae has put her phone away and is peering over her red-tinted sunglasses and even Bridgett has this amused-yet-detached smile going on. The only change in Mirielle is that the skin between her eyes has scrunched up into a turtle's neck and her head has cocked a few centimeters to the side.

By the time Maggie Andrews turns around and points at me —I guess just to verify that yes that is the weird girl who lies in bed late at night wishing she could peel off your knee brace an inch at a time—and Mirielle gets up and starts walking toward me, by this time I'm not even really here anymore. My body is here. My body, which wants to run but has been given strict orders against it and is now being approached by nothing less than the primordial manifestation of my unquenchable desire, is most definitely *here*. But my mind is up in the branches. I'm staring at a fresh sprig jutting out of the knotty elbow on a low limb, thinking maybe I'm doing my best to pretend not to notice that she is seven feet away and closing.

"Hey, um, hi," Mirielle says—and trust me even this sounds succulent coming from her. "Your friend said you wanted to talk to me?"

At this point the terror is almost funny. It's pathetic how funny the terror is. Hilarious. My conscious mind, somewhere high above, would laugh if it were still connected to a respiratory system. I can't look at her. When I finally point my face in her general direction my eyes drop. Now I'm watching her knee, finding some strange sanctuary there. I notice a white tag folded up and tucked into the brace's upper edge.

"She said that you said that you—" Mirielle stops a foot or so away. Her skin releases this sun-baked girl smell that when it hits me it's like a miracle my knees don't buckle, "—want to make out with me."

This is what I hear first, before Mirielle says what she's about to say. Then when she says it for reals, I hear: "—want to be my girlfriend."

But she doesn't actually say that either. What she *really* says —and what takes me fifteen seconds to backtrack and reprocess —is, to my eternal relief: "—want to join our group."

I notice Maggie Andrews snickering in the background. Gail

pantomimes fellatio behind her back. I'm still processing what just happened.

"Look," says Mirielle. "I can totally understand where you're coming from. Totally. And like, I think it's so brave of you to even ask, but, it's just—well, you seem pretty cool and everything, but you're, you know, a freshman. And we're seniors and there's a way these things work, right? I mean, we graduate in a few weeks and then we're gone. It wouldn't even be fair to let anyone join at this point, not even a junior or something. Is this making sense? I hope this is making sense. But I want you to know we're totally flattered, okay? By the thought."

If my jaw has dropped and I am gaping or drooling it's not my fault. I don't even have the presence of mind to focus my awareness anywhere but on her brace and listen to the lilt in her voice, much less to will the muscular contractions required to adjust my body. Fuck you, Maggie Andrews, but thank you at the same time you horrible bitch for not telling her what I'm really feeling, and on top of it all for somehow making Mirielle get up and walk all the way across the Yard to talk to me. To *me*. My skin starts melting, sweating, flushing with relief and oh my god first contact, a thing I never calculated would ever happen. Ever. I should probably be making some sort of reply right now.

"That's cool," I say, entirely unaware as to whether I have just used a nonchalant inflection or an overly excited *that's-so-super-cool* inflection.

"Well, it's nice to meet you," she says. "Your name's Lily?"

"Layla," I say. *Layla?* Where did that come from? Lexie. My name is Lexie. I just corrected her with a name further off the mark than her own mistake. Who does that? "Lexie, actually, is my real name, but sometimes I go by Layla," I quickly recover. I guess. "You can call me Lexie, though. You should."

✸

"Lexie," she says. Not only has she just said my name using her own lips, but now she's extending a hand like I'm supposed to touch it. I think this actually happens. I think we shake hands. In my mind it's more like a smudge where time and space get all jumbled up, and before I know it whatever has happened has happened and she's walking back to her friends. And I'm pretty sure the bell just rang because they're all getting up off the grass and Maggie Andrews is already long gone. Some freshmen who don't know any better sprint toward the doors. Most of the older kids play it chill, working hard to be as late as possible. Bridgett folds her paper bag neatly inside a second paper bag. Rae puts her guitar back in its case. Gail prods her until Rae digs out a loose tear with her middle finger and flips Gail off with it.

I start to perceive things around me again. Brooks continues to place pebble after pebble in precise rows along the various interlocking blades of grass on top of the fire hydrant, and he has not noticed the bell or the hordes of kids trampling past him, swarming toward the door, sucked through like into a whirlpool. He looks so much like his brother today, which has been happening more and more. Pretty soon he'll start growing sideburns. The last time I saw Derwin he was the age Brooks is now. I'm fascinated by siblings because I've never had one and never will. Brooks has two brothers. Mirielle used to have a brother but now she's all alone like me. That was a first, when Jason died, because I'd never known anyone who killed himself before. Sometimes I can tell when his memory flashes across Mirielle's face like an electric shock.

The girls have coupled now, Mirielle with Rae and Gail with Bridgett. My head is loose on my neck, tethered to Mirielle's every movement, and it's not until Gail shrieks, "Oh. My. God!" and points across the Yard, do I fully regain a sense of self. The girls react to Gail's call, looking in unison at a muffin of a bunny sniffing around the edges of its own shadow under the row of nipple-budded rosebushes.

Bridgett's squeal sounds like she's stifling a sneeze. Rae likes to remain aloof to girly delights, but I can see adoration in there somewhere. Mirielle sighs and swoons. She says "Ohhhhh," in a spiraling pitch, and from the raw materials of this audio byte I can almost imagine how her onrushing orgasm might sound. I try, anyway. To imagine. Eyes closed. Lips parted.

Yeah.

2

ONE BY ONE OR IN pairs, but rarely more than three at a time, they arrive with their offerings: Gary Swank with a stuffed dolphin and Edgar Pike hugging a flatscreen monitor and Charlotta Woosher with a bag of—what—fruit? Some kids bring water jugs and old school books, and Cliff Carlsgott brings a broken Sega Genesis. The Patterson twins both had the same idea of their older brother's ex-football helmet and they fight over it all the way up the hill. Some junior I've never met drags a chest of drawers in a wagon and then the wagon goes in the pile, too. They move in from all directions, from the ovular strip of our town's homestead settlement along the river, from the saddle of the central valley, and even way out from the recent satellite suburbs of clone duplexes that punctuate the fringes of what I've heard is by now entirely corporatized farmland. Some kids take the two-lane up Bonzai Trail while others come along the back roads and skirt around the sapphire hills. Moving in time with jowly clouds that drift like a herd toward the wall of pine-coated mountains on the valley's west edge where sometimes you'll get a hundred head of elk coming down in late summer or early fall. On this side there's nothing but acres of treeless hills all the way down to where the river forks again and runs by Highway 15 and across the border, feeding creek beds of clay and roots and small doorways to the insect world. In a week or two they'll open the dams and flood it all.

They all lay their treasures down in a heap at the top of the hill: broken telescopes, lava lamps, dolls, toy trucks, a brass teakettle, antiquated electronics, obsolete computers, and a cactus that goes hotly contested because Richey Buchan said no living organisms, so for a minute it almost comes to a total emotional breakdown because how do they expect Anita to ride her bike all the way back to town for something else—until Sheldon suggests why not go plant the cactus in the field and just bring back the pot.

Mildred Bleens, a math geek who all but begs for the chance to be numerically involved with whatever's going on, whether it's necessary or not, scribbles everything down in a graph-paper lab notebook, lining up names with contributions and who got here first and other tedious details. As soon as she's sufficiently tormented them, Mildred allows the kids to drop their stuff and break away to talk or smoke or throw rocks or dig in the bare earth or dare each other to do something stupid like poke their fingers into anthills. But no one wanders off too far. I brought nothing, same as Brooks, so we stay off the hill, which I guess we would anyway.

We've been here maybe a half-hour, standing in this barren ditch, not exactly watching Clayton Driscoll and his curly mullet show off his kung fu or whatever the fuck he's picked up off the internet this time. Brooks is pissed at me so we haven't exactly been speaking for the last few days. But now we're together in this like holding chamber because the only reason either of us is allowed to be here at all is on account of that Clayton said we were cool. Not that there's anything cool about Clayton, but he's

Sheldon's girlfriend's little brother and that gives him enough clout to let us tag along. Clayton has a lazy eye and dimples and a crush on me. He tolerates Brooks like he's trying to impress my pants off. Tolerating his little heart out. I've never seen anyone put on such a show of tolerance as Clayton. I've been watching the gears work around in that radish of a head as he slowly starts to realize that me and Brooks are on the outs and because of that he's easing his way from tolerance to kind of taking my side, but at the same time trying not to be a dick about it because who knows when me and Brooks will make up again.

The reason Brooks is mad is because last week we were down at the river and he brought up his brother for the first time in a while, so I started talking about old times when Derwin would take us into the mountains or let us watch him play video games or we'd stage a little RPS tournament, but Brooks said he didn't want to talk about it. I said okay, but I miss him too, and then Brooks said since he wasn't my brother that I had no idea how he felt because besides I'd never had anyone close to me just up and vanish. I didn't think that was fair and I said well what about Charlie, but then Brooks just rolled his eyes, so I was like *what*, and he said drop it and I said no. I must've asked him fifty times what's with the eye roll, which then he got fed up and looked at me, like directly at me which he never does, and he said that it wasn't the same as growing up with someone all your life. But then he started going off about how Charlie was probably using me anyway because she was a cult kid and I was easy pickings— his words—and she probably lied better than her parents. But Brooks never even met Charlie. She's the first girl I ever kissed, back when we lived on the coast, and if anything him saying all this makes me the one who has a right to be upset. He just walked away from the conversation after that, and now *he's* the

19

one who's mad. At me. Mad I guess that I pushed him to say something that made him feel guilty, a feeling I don't think he ever gets and definitely doesn't know how to deal with. That's the best I can figure because he won't talk about it. He's distant and quiet. Like, more than usual. Which is a lot.

So when we got here I let him mess around with the Tongue, kind of hopefully as a peace offering to maybe get him to relax and open up, like that will ever happen, but also because he knows about the strange connection between Charlie and the Tongue and it's kind of my subtle way of standing my ground and giving him an out at the same time. The Tongue is a fist-sized glass globe—like a snow globe but without the snow—that my mother bought in Budapest before I was born. She gave it to me when I was seven as part of her lifelong mission to fuck me up. There's a little ceramic castle inside. Dirty vanilla-colored walls and blood-red-roofed spires, strands of painted ivy draping the walls and tangling together under the castle floor. And then the Tongue itself, right? What kind of creep got the bright idea to make a castle with a tongue for a draw bridge? The tongue rolls out through the castle gates, thin and red and stiff at first, but then it flops away from the castle and gets bigger and wider and even more impossibly pink where it presses flat against a good quarter of the globe's inner surface and starts to look a little too real, all covered in slimy little wet bumps. Charlie used to put her tongue against the glass and lick it back, which I always acted like that totally grossed me out. She used to tell stories about it. She liked to call it Castle Tonguesworth but Brooks always just calls it the Tongue, and that's what stuck. Tongue. A word begging to be said out loud.

Brooks has an iPod bud stuck in one ear and the other dangles on his chest like a clip-on microphone. From out here it sounds like a swarm of mosquitoes, which this wouldn't really surprise me. His nostrils flare to the beat. Every few minutes he tears his attention away from the Tongue and looks over Clayton's shoulder and up the creek bed toward the cow pasture and the tall hill with the rocky crown where Sheldon Dawn and Matthew Craig and Richey Buchan have promised to blow up some serious shit before sunset.

"It's called t'ai chi ch'uan," Clayton says, his face squeezing out intense concentration. "That means slow motion time." He holds his flimsy replica Chinese sword parallel to the ground. He slides it centimeter by centimeter in front of his eyes. His free hand is raised in a two-fingered Boy Scout salute, one leg up stork-like as the medial arch of his foot braces against the opposing knee. He wobbles but doesn't fall. "That's the thing. You gotta go as slow as possible. Slower the better."

"Do you have to talk in slow motion, too?" I barely have the patience to deal with Clayton in real time.

"Yeeeeeessssss." He draws the word out for about ten seconds. I walk up the side of the ditch and grab a handful of exposed roots frayed out like electrical wires. Brooks holds the Tongue to the light, trapping clouds inside. He stares at it like it's his only friend. Maybe it connects him with the home he can't remember. Brooks' family is Czech, and he was born there, but when he was a baby his mom divorced his dad and a couple years later she packed up her kids and moved them all to America. She managed to pull it off by getting involved with a TV show called *Life Swap* on the *Free-Incarnation* network. It's one of those shitty reality shows whose gimmick is to have two families trade places. *Life Swap* researchers determine what sort of fabulous and challenging existence your deepest subconscious would rather be living, then they search through their database for another *Life Swap* candidate who matches the specs and also happens to test out as desiring yours, and finally they organize the swap. Sometimes there's no direct match and complicated swap chains need to be lined up between multiple parties. Apparently his mom's inner longing was the small mountain-town life raising her kids alone and working part time at a garden shop. The network coordinates everything—the move, the visas, career training, compensations, neighborhood introductions, lots of social lubricant—and all you do is get on the plane and walk into your new life. The downside of the deal is you sign over that life to be documented for the next 15 years so fans can see how much you suck at adjusting to your new reality. The lesson learned here is I guess you should just be happy with the shitty hand you're dealt. The first three seasons are fairly intrusive, then interest drops off and your story becomes more archival and nostalgic, which is why these days we only very rarely see Brooks with a camera crew trailing behind him.

Sheldon and Matthew Craig and some chubby kid in a pink hoodie covered in sparkly green dollar signs all come down off the hill to tell Clayton to stop being such a nerd and how maybe he could to do something useful for a change. Clayton resists but only until Sheldon says he'll shove that tai chi sword so far up his guts that the top of his head will spark on the clouds, so he drops his sword and starts climbing the hill. Sheldon sits down on the crumbling bank, pulls out a bag and rolls a joint. The fat kid hovers over his shoulder, practically drooling. Matthew Craig sticks his hands in his pockets. I walk up and grab the sword. It's make of polished steel with a dull edge and a lion's face on the base of the handle. The little lion eyes roll back in its head, its mouth a dark oval.

"When are we gonna see some action?" Brooks says, but he isn't talking to me or to anyone really. Sometimes he just throws words out to see what happens.

Pinky puts on a face that I guess is supposed to intimidate. He's got drooping bully eyes and no chin. "Shut up, ballsack," he says.

Sheldon licks his joint shut and twists the tip. Uses his lips to snatch it out of his hand. Talks out of the corner of his mouth. "You little ladies want a hit?"

"I came here for explosions," Brooks says. "But I'd settle for a nip slip."

The paper lights up. Sheldon exhales down the slope of his chest and a cloud of smoke drops between his knees and rolls out along the creek bed. He offers the joint, pinching it with forefinger and thumb. Brooks laughs. "Drugs are for dolts," he says. Sheldon shrugs, pivots toward me. I shake my head 'no'. Somehow he sees this without looking. He takes another little sip and passes it to Pinky.

Matthew Craig watches me for a minute, trying to figure out where he recognizes me from. I'm more than just one of the hundreds of faceless freshmen. We've seen each other a dozen times at the Chestnut Homes Retirement Community, where I volunteer twice a week in order to boost my citizenship profile for college applications. Also to be close to my father, who lives there. Matthew Craig's grandfather Pasha lives there, too. Nobody visits their grandfather as often as Matthew Craig. It's kind of sweet.

"What did you bring?" he asks me. He was a senior last year. Tall, rugged, and blonde. One of town's oh-shit-handles of manliness with a lofty Roman nose and California fashion sense. He's been going 80s lately: popped collar under a suit jacket with rolled sleeves, pomade gumming his hair into tiny waves. Beautiful eyelashes on that boy.

"Nothing," I say. I'm stabbing Clayton's sword over and over into the ground, trying to hit the original slot every time. Always missing.

"You gotta bring," Sheldon says. "That's the deal."

"Clayton didn't tell us."

Matthew Craig gives up on me and turns around, walking a little ways up the ditch. I can feel him fold his arms as his eyes begin to scan the bobbled hills and the criss-crossed fences that work their way across the land in spirals and pentagrams and other absurdly impractical formations for no reason anyone has ever been able to explain to me.

Sheldon squints at Brooks. "What's *his* deal?"

"Deal?" I say.

"Squirrely little dude."

"We could blow up the sword." This suggestion from Pinky.

"Dangerous. I like it," says Sheldon. "What's that thing?" He's pointing to the Tongue, still in Brooks' hand.

"That's mine," I say. I know what's about to happen.

Sheldon licks his fingers and snuffs out the joint and hands it to Pinky, who puts it in his pocket. Sheldon gets up and stretches, reaches out a hand. "Lemme see it." Brooks doesn't move. He's lost inside the castle. Lost in his head.

"Hey kid, hand it over."

I'm powerless. The distance between two or three years is high school's equivalent of a lifetime. Sheldon's a junior. There's nothing I can do. And really it only gradually occurs to me what's going on. I don't see it in real time—not really visualizing it until after I see him holding it the same way he held the joint, giving it a good once-over—a full fifteen seconds after he's already hopped into the creek bed and snatched the Tongue out of Brooks' hand.

"The fuck?" he says.

"It was a present," I say.

"It's got heft."

"My mom."

"I bet she'd soar like a mother," says Sheldon.

"From Europe," I say.

"That a tongue?"

"It's irreplaceable," I say.

"Dude, check this out. Gross."

"Probably one of a kind."

Sheldon makes an arc with his arm, demonstrating the way the Tongue would fly if propelled by a suitable explosion. Pinky trying to get a good look from underneath. Brooks doesn't move. His glare smolders but bounces off the indifferent backs of the older boys. "Give it back," he mutters. "That's what you want me to say, right?"

"Gotta pay the toll," says Sheldon.

"People are dying every day in the Middle East and you think the most important thing to do with your lives is torment some girl over her stuff."

"What do you know, Dweeb?"

"I'll translate it into a language you understand," says Brooks. "Basically, you're dicks. Hairless dicks." This earns him a shove from Pinky. Brooks stumbles backward, barely recovering his balance.

"Make that cunts," Brooks picks up without hesitation. When he finally does open his mouth he kind of lacks the ability to close it. There is no line between bravery and stupidity with him. "Dickless cunts," he says.

"Watch it, frosh," Sheldon says. "Or we'll put *you* in the pile."

"Put you in the pile," Pinky echoes.

"Just give it back," I plead.

"I don't know why Richey wants to waste his M-80s on all this broken junk when we've got so many frosh to pick from."

It occurs to me that I am holding a deadly weapon.

"You think you're scaring us," Brooks says. "Is that what you're going for?"

Pinky rushes him, then stops short in a bluff. Brooks flinches and Pinky laughs with the idiot cackle of a broken alarm clock.

"We'll take this to the pile for you," Sheldon says.

I feel my arm rising, bringing the sword tip up to belt level. Let it sway. No one notices.

"Ten years from now you'll die choking on your own puke," Brooks prophesies to Pinky. Then to Sheldon: "And you'll be paying child support to kids that don't even like you."

Pinky stops laughing. He takes Brooks by the collar, making a mean tough show; puts his breath up my friend's nose. *My* friend. Which means it's *my* job to do something. I hold the sword. Brooks stares down at Pinky's sausage fingers balled up into fists. Pinky starts spitting threats. A few steps is all it would take. Just follow the sword, let it do its thing. I'm mostly angry at myself now. Rage at my own paralysis. There's this voice in my head saying if I try anything they'll kill me. I don't know where the voice comes from, but my body listens.

"Knock it off," Matthew Craig says from over my shoulder. Pinky snorts and gives Brooks one last sneer before shoving him away. This time Brooks can't stay on his feet. He lands ass-first in the dirt.

Matthew Craig says, "That's Derwin's little bro, idiot."

"No way," says Sheldon.

"Let's go," says Pinky.

They climb out of the ditch with the Tongue still a hostage. Sheldon tosses and catches it every few steps. Matthew Craig reaches out to touch the sword blade, pushes its tip down. "Don't show your hand," he tells me.

When they're gone I can finally move. I drop the sword and run to Brooks. He doesn't get up. I ask if he's okay and he says he just wants to sit a while. Part of it is they said his brother's name. Brooks hasn't really heard from Derwin since he took off. A postcard to the family every Christmas and Easter. Derwin's kind of a legend around town. More than just a dropout with a motorbike. I know Brooks, and the last thing he wants is special attention, but he's also glad not to have his face bashed in. Just another reason to love and hate his brother.

I wander alone up the creek bed. My arms shiver. I wish I could cry because of the Tongue and because I might never see it again and also because I can't shake the image of myself standing there like an asshole while they shoved Brooks around. But if I cry it's like they win all over again so I hold it in and keep walking. I move up past a pile of flat red rocks where the ditch widens out and the embankment gradually rises until I'm in a little canyon. Here seven fences converge around a sandy beach that turns to mud at the water's edge. I follow the slope's narrow lane until it traps me in a tangled cul-de-sac of barbed wire that I crawl through, and then suddenly I'm on a small mound next to a lone tree. I stand underneath a wagon wheel of branches looking up through constellations of apple blossom into the filtered sunlight, listening to the swarm-song of bees. There must be thousands here. I'm buzzing with them. I can feel their vibrations inside the hollow of my thoracic cavity. They skip from flower to flower, dipping in and moving on, every one of them desperately in love. My mouth hangs open, inviting them to crawl inside.

Craig and Sheldon and Pinky have made it back to the hilltop where Richey orchestrates his collection of explosives. I can see Brooks back down in the dry ditch, pushing himself up. He walks one way and then the other, then back over to where I dropped the sword. He picks it up. The way he carries it he makes it look heavy, like he can't quite keep the tip from drooping. On the hill Richey spends half his time yelling at people to back off. He needs room to work, but everyone just wants to crowd around and get as close as possible to the action. Brooks climbs the hill. The blade rests on his shoulder. He's going to go up and wave it around like an idiot until someone takes it away and beats the shit out of him. He's going to get the Tongue back. He doesn't care how many bruises it costs him. And whether or not he succeeds, it is this act alone by which he will forgive me and we will be friends again. I will clean the blood off his face and we won't ever talk about what happened.

I sit on a rock at the base of the tree and try to pick out the longest branch I can find. The chorus of bee wings surges and I can feel it in my spine. The hill is so far off, the movement along the ridge so faint, that I don't even bother looking, but I can see it in my head when Brooks reaches the top. What I see in these moments of lucidity is not exactly my imagination. It's not the same as making stuff up. I don't alter details as they occur to me. It's like with the girls the other day in the Yard. I could hear their conversations, but not with my ears. Their intentions, the meanings behind their movements—all clear voices in my head. I knew how Rae Stryker was link hopping; I could see the wikipedia pages like I was looking over her shoulder. They happen all the time, these, I don't know—visions, I guess you'd call them. They've been happening since I was young. The first time I was with Charlie, and since then they've gotten gradually more intense, like they're ramping up to something huge. Usually when they're coming I start to feel some kind of strange physical sensation. One time it felt like I was suddenly wearing a fur coat and another time it was like I'd lost my toes. This time it's bee wings: I feel like there are literal wings growing out of my back. And what's happening now in my mind is I see Brooks' actions playing out like a movie. He's winded but he doesn't rest. Marches straight toward Sheldon who is facing away from him, hunched over Richey Buchan's careful work with the explosives, tossing the Tongue from hand to hand. Pinky keeps trying to lean into Jeanette Andreas' hips, but she's up there to flirt with Richey so she dodges his moves. Richey flicks his lighter and touches the flame to a fuse. This happens just as Brooks and his tunnel vision and forward momentum intersect Jeanette's backpedal dodge so his face almost mashes into her ass. The sword bends and slaps her thigh and then sticks into the dirt and Brooks falls right onto the handle, knocking the wind out of himself. Brooks and Jeanette go down in a pile. I can smell the sparks swallowing up the black powder. Pinky laughs. Sheldon turns around, not quite sure what just happened, but in his confusion the Tongue hits the grass, rolls a few inches, and stops, taunting the sky.

Something explodes and I open my eyes.

3

SITTING ACROSS FROM ME IN the semi-lucid state of impending nap he refers to as the white stage of awareness, is my father—my real father, though my mother will never admit it, will never say the words: "Donald Victoria Estringi is in fact your biological father." Whenever he perks up he asks me about school and what kind of grades I'm getting and whether I have any boyfriends yet, and always he phrases this more like whether I've been knocked up yet, and then he asks if there's any chance I'll make my move before his Rigor mortis flares up or at least, like, in this century.

Donald Victoria Estringi, now confined to a wheelchair, was once a military man. He yells things like *Report, At ease,* and *Fucksack* at more or less random intervals. He keeps his seventeen medals in a dark oak case on the wall. He wears a bolo tie and American flag cufflinks. A different belt buckle every day. He despises gambling and hates to eat anything without utensils. Spends a lot of time talking about the importance of rooting out communism. A wandering hematoma plagues his face. His remaining hair is doily white, parted on the left side and combed over with laser precision. Glasses hang on the edge of his nose like a porch swing, but he prefers not to look through them. He could smell worse for his age.

A couple years ago doctors diagnosed him with Guillian-Barré Syndrome on account of his sudden paralysis, but the symptoms never spread beyond his legs. His psychiatrist suspects psychosomatic hysteria or a very crafty will-to-death. Either way, it's all wheelchair all the time.

I can tell he's my father just by looking at him. Brooks says I have his eyes, but it's more like how the way you can sometimes tell a person is lying just by looking at them. Sometimes he looks back at me like he knows. Sometimes he looks at me like he knows I know. And I know because I know—because I've seen the whole story play out.

I try to hang out with him as much as I can. This helps me avoid having to deal with all the other old people who aren't nearly as much fun, but mostly I do it for the quality time. He's really old and I have no idea how much longer I'll have him around. We usually sit in his little room and play the Chinese version of chess, with pieces you won't find in normal chess like elephants and cannons. The games start out serious and then digress into whatever daily rules fly off the top of my father's head. His moves take up to a half hour when the meditation consumes him. "A true soldier only strikes betimes," he explains. I take these opportunities to help myself to the mini-fridge and read the actual paper-and-ink newspaper, which may or may not make me cool in certain remote hipster circles.

Today my father is particularly spunky. He laughs when he makes a move. He takes one of my elephants with a cannon by jumping off a pawn and crossing the river. I'm pretty sure this is a real rule.

"Walked right into that one," he says. "The master returns without leaving."

I scan the board, fidgeting with the olive green scrunchie

that I stole out of Mirielle's locker a few weeks ago. Stray hairs still coil around the elastic—I take care not to lose a single one. There's a question I've been meaning to ask for the whole hour I've been here. It's a lead-in question on my way to my real question—the question I swear I'm going to ask every time I come to the Home, but never do. This isn't the first time I've used this particular technique. It almost worked last time. I try to sound off-handed, aloof.

"What were the nineties like?"

"A long and tortured decade," he says, scooting his glass of chocolate milk closer to the edge of the table so that his face can reach the straw.

"How about, say, 1996? Was that a good year?" I know that I am not smooth, but he is old and I am desperate.

He takes a long, palsied slurp. "Ninety-six… The year the Ruskies and the Chechnyans really got into it. Operation Desert Strike… Taliban took Kabul… eh… Clinton re-elected."

"Where were you?"

"Sitting on my fat ass, that's where!" He laughs, he sneers, he surveys the board. I know exactly where he was in 1996, the year I was conceived. "It was right after my discharge. They gave me this little shit room in Pest while I underwent six months evaluation and waited for a plane home."

"How about in April? Were you still living there?"

"April? Christ in a deep dark well, how the hell am I supposed to remember April?"

I pick up a chariot and rub it between my fingers. My pieces are black and my chariot's symbol looks like the kind of flag-on-a-stick thing armies once carried into war. My father's eyes follow my hand and then drop back to the board, trying to anticipate what I'm up to.

"Well, it was the start of spring," I say. "Sunshine, flowers, girls in short skirts—"

"Helen of Troy!"

"—birds chirping, baseball, high rivers."

"There's nothing like spring in Bavaria." He digs something out of his left ear. Stares at it for a while.

"But I guess like, what I'm asking is, what were you doing at the time?"

"They stationed me in Bavaria in the spring of '93. Something intoxicating about those years."

"1996, specifically, is my interest."

"Communism already a ghost of the past. The Internet was learning to crawl."

"And, like, how you spent your time."

"There was this feeling in the air that anything was possible."

"Any, you know, special ladies?"

"Talk of eradicating all borders, creating a world currency, microscopic explorations hitherto unimagined. Inner space!"

"Was Viagra around at the time?"

"Was what?"

"Vi—agra."

My father points at the board. "You gonna move that soldier or are you waiting for its value to depreciate?"

"I'm thinking."

My favorite rule is how when the last chariot gets captured, all the remaining pieces undergo a crisis of faith that ends in heart attacks and death unless one of us can sing every verse to the Battle Hymn of the Old Republic without error, which happens, like, never.

My mother literally screams when I refer to Donald Victoria Estringi as my father. She says, "I'll tell you who your father is," and then gives me some bullshit story about a trip to northern Italy and a Milanese businessman who fucked her and split. Tells it like it's the hottest soap opera ever.

"Ah, the nineties," says Donald, drifting into the opiatic grin of old farts. He has excellent teeth for his age. "Optimism was in the air. The dawn of a new era. If I could freeze time I'd freeze it in '91. I was still in Berlin, helping rebuild." There are days I can get him to talk about the dark side of his time in Europe, the two years before he left for the States. The two years before I was born. When he's in the mood he'll say things that give me the creeps, but he lets go only in fragments and gasps. Some seriously crazy shit about the Slovakian forests. Munitions that got lodged in the trees and then absorbed as branches grew around them. Moss-covered hand grenades wedged forever in the bark. Talking trees. An underground network of root systems facilitating human mind control. Donald worked on a base in West Germany through most of the '80s until the Wall came down. Then he took part in some sort of diplomacy through the old Soviet Bloc countries. Eventually they stationed him in East Berlin. I guess sometime around '94 he moved to Budapest on a secret intelligence mission, and there he ran into something that messed him up for good. He says that in Pest there's a hole dug all the way down to the center of the earth. The Nazis started it and the Commies finished it. Somewhere below a pre-fabricated '70s housing project on Szigony Street. Who knows what kind of crazy Area 51 shit they brought back up, but my father must've dipped into whatever it was because he left the army a 62-year-old fountain of virility.

Eventually he got back to the States and ended up here, living on the streets, going off to anyone who'd listen about how an angel saved his life. He spent seven or eight months taking handouts and drinking himself and everyone else crazy. I guess he used to sing old German songs at the top of his lungs and run around telling people's fortunes, offering to give away high-level government secrets for the price of a bottle. According to some other old timers I've interrogated three federal sedans pulled into town and tracked him down in an alley for a nice long chat. After that the checks started coming in and he lived in a condo until he lost the use of his legs, was diagnosed with Guillian-Barré Syndrome, and ended up in Chestnut Homes.

The point is he was in Budapest in '96. And so was my mother, the angel who saved his life.

"My mom must've been pretty back then," I say, nibbling on my lip. "In the '90s, I mean."

"Have I met your mother?"

Evasive, Mr. Estringi. Very evasive. I watch his hands. My mom says a man's lies slip out through his fingers.

I know what really happened. I knew it from the moment I met him. I saw it in like a waking dream, maybe the most intense vision I've ever had. They wheeled him into the room one day and every detail flashed across my mind—as clear as if I'd been there. My mother was single, stupid, recently divorced, on some sort of mid-life crisis backpacking-through-Europe-thing, and wrestling with a biological Big Ben when she and her girlfriends rented a place in Budapest. My father was fresh off his mind-altering experience with the evil experiments of the enemy. While waiting for the army to decide his fate Donald Victoria Estringi wandered into local church confessionals several times a week, looking for some peace of mind. What he had to say drove two priests out of town. The Church of St. Margaret is where they met. Neither had come for the services. She was walking a friend. He was planning to shoot himself in the head and splatter as many dendrites, glial cells, and other bits of brain as possible onto the stained glass.

He brought his issue sidearm along and wore his stripes. He pulled his cap low on his brow and placed the barrel against the patch of the United States flag. My father intended to pass that bullet not only through his brain, but also through the state that drove him mad and the church that could not repair him. He knelt in the grass. Both hands held the gun upside-down, thumbs folded in prayer across the trigger. He snapped off the safety and mentally calculated the angle of trajectory that would shatter the glass on the east side of the nave, pierce Christ's side, tear through the chapel, and exit out the eye of St. George's dragon, binding God and the Devil in 9x19mm of cosmic wedlock.

My mother walked back across the street for a second time just as Donald was finishing his sidearm drills. The friend she'd left at the door had forgotten her wallet in my mother's purse. She went all the way up to the front but was too intimidated to go in. She crept around the side, thinking maybe she could see her friend through a window and signal her. Donald was praying out loud: "To the principalities that swarm the throne of the Most High, obscuring the threefold face, the tri-part blade, the blender of consciousness, the hole at the center of the galaxy, the flesh around which this tiny shroud of the universe drapes… To the cocksucker who stole my marbles, to the first and the last, to the tooth and the scapula, to the purity of love which can by no means find further expression—not with his creation devouring him like a goddamn pack of wolves—Oh, infinite spirit of the holy intractable neon mainframe, I release thee from this chamber of blood and pulp into which thou hast haphazardly submerged thyself. This tomb of a head, this labyrinth of a body, this rotten cage of meat." He took a deep breath. His lungs rattled.

My mother, who'd heard it all, took a step backward. Her impulse was to take three more and pretend she'd been around the corner when the shot went off. Then, wrenched with pity, she changed her mind. "Excuse me," she said, touching his elbow. "Don't do that."

Donald Victoria Estringi neither lowered the gun nor squeezed the trigger as he caught my mother's eye. Her hair a mess; her fashion sense less than spectacular; the skin under her eyes, like her breasts, starting to sag—she must've seemed like an angel to him. She took the gun out of his hands and crouched down to embrace his ancient frame, the great sobbing hulk in his uniform. She knew what she was doing. A man returning from the brink of death is not something to waste, and she soaked up every drop of emanating life force that old Donald had intended to launch out the back of his skull, but which he now redirected into a physical, mental, and emotional flowering not unlike the rapture of the Buddha or the resurrection of Christ.

Some people hate that part of the story, but it's my conception and I'll describe it however I want.

4

PENDER WALSH, THE BOY WITH the biggest ears in the whole school, is last in line, with Brooks in front of him and me in front of Brooks. In front of me is a girl I know only from gym class, and in front of her another couple dozen of the desperate and the hyperactive and the confused, and from the smell of things, we may be stuck here for hours. Gossip percolates back from the head of the line, announcing an explosion in the kitchen. There's Sloppy Joe everywhere, they're saying. I've seen three janitors march by already, mops at their sides, filing into the kitchen like a SWAT team. Everyone's complaining and cracking jokes and generally freaking out at the prospect of starving through the second half of the day. Everyone but Brooks, who, of course, has his face stuck in some book. He always reads while he waits. Sometimes he even reads while he's walking. I've seen him trip a million times.

"What the crap?" says Pender, directing his comment over Brooks' shoulder and straight into my left tympanic membrane. "I'm dying of hunger. Literally dying. To death."

You're not the only one, pizza face, I think, and I really want to say, *Why don't you eat your own face, pizza face*, but instead I turn and look at all the happily satiated pre-kitchen-disaster kids gathered in the oblivion of lunchroom tables, nibbling on potato chips and fruit snacks, pre-kitchen-disaster Sloppy Joe dribbling from between the hemispheres of sesame-seed buns. This lunchroom is a hive. A swarming slippery complex of open mouths. Younger kids cluster up to whatever charismatic junior will tolerate them; some sit by themselves, slopping up their food or tapping bland rhythms on the laminate tables. Phones everywhere flung open, delivering silent messages like pheromones, most texts confined to this very room. If I had any friends I'd see if someone wanted to share. I guess I could go give it a shot, right? Go make a friend. Say hey, friend, you aren't going to let me starve, are you? But I don't step out of line. I'm staring at Brooks' forehead, trying to will him to look up for one goddamn second and notice the crisis we're in, when all of a sudden, in a pair of heels that tap almost musically upon the linoleum, the girl who stalks my dreams steps into the line behind us. I have never seen Mirielle in the lunchroom. Seniors don't eat here. They have the right to leave campus at noon and go downtown and get a sandwich or a hamburger like normal humans, and if they don't want to leave they eat in the Yard, but no self-respecting senior ever comes down to the cafeteria. Like ever. So it has to be a sign that today, by some gem of fate, Mirielle is here, right behind us.

First thing I think is I can't let her find out the kitchen has exploded and that the line is never going to move again. She finds this out, she's gone. Second thing is I have to figure a way to move two places back in the line so that I can stand beside her. We're not talking a mere brushing of the shoulders in the hallway here. This would be a persistent position beside her radiant skin, for a socially acceptable reason, guaranteed to last as long as the line does, which apparently is forever. My knees start to shake just thinking about it. It's a weird compulsion, wanting to stand next to someone. A little bit like when you're cold and your body kind of wills itself to go stand by the fire. It's the romantic equivalent of that. It feels like an outside force commanding me to stand next to that one, then get inside her, then share identities, then slide out the other side transformed, a new hybrid, more complex, leveled up, holding onto a bit of each other forever. Sometimes I think wanting someone is really about wanting to be them. To know what it's like to be Mirielle when she's alone, to experience making her stupid decisions, to think the train of her thoughts and feel all the little peculiar things like breathing and heartbeat and eye twitches and lower intestinal gurgling and chills and the way she paws at the hair behind her ear when she's nervous. There's something bigger than lust at work here. Bigger than me. Bigger than both of us.

Somewhere way back in the depths of the kitchen there is a great queen chef. She is fat and middle-aged and wears a hairnet and smokes a dark brown cigarette that she ashes into her stained apron's front pocket. But she doesn't cook. Instead she writes a series of trashy romance novels. Every morning she decides what her workers will prepare and what the children will eat, and then she goes back to her heaving bosoms and throbbing members. And as she hacks out these scenes on what I'm guessing is some prehistoric typewriter in the back office she maintains a telesthetic bond with the cooks and the servers and the dishwashers. She imposes her characters on them, her dramatic, overwrought scenarios, and sometimes they fall in love and sometimes they repress it but either way it all ends up in the food and when the food finally reaches us kids we eat it and our gonads glow. It's trickle-down lust radiating through a prism, splintered into hundreds of little Fabios and Daphnes. Once the infection settles in we can't help but turn our heads and search around the room for someone delicious. We stalk each other online and send messages cryptic and overt, and scheme maniacally for the mere chance to stand beside the ones we want, even if we don't know what we'd do if we got them.

The clock on the wall reads 12:26.

Brooks is no problem. I could cut in front of him and he wouldn't care. But Pender is another thing. Pender is a pubescent little twerp and he's as horny as the rest of us and there's no way he's going to give up his chance to spend a few seconds next to two goddesses of the senior class. I can smell her skin even from here, even over the Lysol, grease and sweat saturating the lunchroom air.

"Pender," I say, getting his attention. My only chance is he hasn't noticed them yet.

He faces me, eyes wide, his mouth stretched like a frog face that makes his neck muscles flare out. "I know, right?" he screeches. "Her boob might totally touch my arm."

Pender, who has no concept of volume control, is a tiny little twerp, a freshman with a splotchy round face. His body is wormy is the only way I can describe it. I don't think he ever washes his hair. And of course, there's the ears.

"Gross," I say. I try to remember everything I know about Pender. Can I bribe him? Can I blackmail him?

"Brooks," I say, and nuzzle up. "Whatcha reading?"

He doesn't look at me. "Bester. Short stories."

"You realize this line isn't moving."

"So?"

"Get Pender to cut in front of me."

Still not looking up. "What for?"

"Because."

"Will that make the line move?"

"Just do this thing for me, okay? Do it."

I know I've won him over because of the clucking sound he makes with his tongue.

"Pender!" says Brooks, still managing to keep reading.

"What?"

"Come here."

"Why?"

"Come here before I kick your ass." Brooks has never kicked the slightest suggestion of ass in his life and I doubt he ever will. He's even shorter than Pender, and it's not like Pender has any basketball scholarships in his future.

"What do you want?" The little twerp is practically screaming.

Glancing at immobile Pender, torn between the radiant female field in which he basks and the voice of peer authority, I kind of just want to grab him by his wee cock and drag him out of my way. Mirielle's back is to us, attention pledged to Rae who's laughing because Gail's been moaning on and on about some boy named Flanagan from out of town who she made out with last month, but then who was recently caught in the Quad licking the chess captain's nipples. All very traumatic for Gail, I'm sure.

"Pender," Brooks says with level tone, finally snapping his book shut and glaring at us through the hanging blonde ivy of his brow. "Move forward. Give someone else a turn."

I see the wheels spinning in Pender's brain. I don't know if they get him very far, but he can feel the deadly seriousness of the situation. Brooks can be a hell of a friend when he puts his mind to it. Without quite knowing why he's giving in, but mostly just because he's a spineless worm, Pender trades me places. Then he pulls out his phone and starts playing *Happy Game* like he made the decision all on his own.

At last I am within the crystal-quiet membrane of Mirielle's outer orbit, completely surrounded by her scent, close enough to feel the warmth of her body. Now what? Her laughter rings like tiny silver bells. Smells like she washed her hair with apple cinnamon shampoo, but there's a hint of peach and lavender. Conditioner maybe? I've never been this close to her for this long before. My eyes are shut and I turn away, putting us back to back. "Is Matt still calling you?" Rae says. I can feel Mirielle blush. Adorable! But wait. Who is Matt? Her comments are brief, restrained. Apparently some new boy has got her all twitterpated. Matt Vorlock? Matt Swain? Gail the blabbermouth won't shut up, but I can still hear the cashmere of Mirielle's breath in the undertones. In my mind she touches my hair, hands me half a smile. I want to have her babies, or for her to have mine. Is that too much to ask? She grabs a fistful of her skirt and drags the fabric up her leg, up above her knee. She reaches down to peel apart the black Velcro of her brace, and—

"Big buddy Brooksy!" comes our great, muddy thunderous surprise. Not quite booming, but unwavering and rising above the yammering crowd, his familiar voice soars in from beyond the enclosure of my imagination and rattles the lunchroom machine. In my periphery I can see fear in Mirielle's eyes, and something else—something more violent than hunger. She's turned her body toward him, turned at the call of his voice leaping over the lunchroom from the double doors where Brooks' older brother Derwin leans with that perfect slouch, one elbow up against the doorframe so his arm just happens to draw back his leather jacket, showing off a triangle of white t-shirt and a tarnished silver belt buckle of a rattlesnake strangling a cactus.

44

I know what she's thinking.

They never broke up because they were never really together. Her eyes used to cling to him like lichen to indifferent walls of stone.

Three fucking years.

When Derwin was Brooks' age he spent five months in a group home for vandalism and aggravated assault after he beat the shit out of Stuart Knox and his car. Derwin had been walking on the side of the road when he saw a squirrel jump out from behind a bush and run into the path of Knox's pimped-out yellow Cadillac. All he had time to do was think, "Don't get hit," three times before the front right tire ground the poor critter into the pavement. Derwin still swears he saw the car swerve and that he heard the engine shift into the intentionality of a higher gear. It was deliberate, in other words. So Derwin threw his iPod at the car, bouncing it off the driver's side window. Knox hit the brakes. Derwin picked up a rock, sinking a crater into the back windshield. Knox opened his door and screamed, *What the fuck do you think you're doing, faggot?* Derwin asked Knox if he licked his mom's pussy with that mouth. Knox jumped out and rushed Derwin, who waited until Knox got close enough, then put his foot in his crotch. The squirrel murderer went down. Derwin didn't stop. Broken bones, concussions, internal bleeding; these are the rumors. Then he walked over to Knox's pimped-out yellow Cadillac and put it in neutral. The car rolled down the steep incline of Casey Street, nearly hitting four or five other cars before smashing into a retaining wall.

A year later Derwin told Brooks to take care of their mom. He got on the skeleton of a 1979 Honda CX500 and drove east. Derwin never touched anything he couldn't fix with a toolbox. Never used a computer. No phone of his own. I think that's what

Mirielle first loved about him. Everything natural, everything macro. At some point before my time bigger is better became smaller is better. Derwin grew up on the other side of that line, inherited an obsession with the Old West and 1950s Americana during his post-Soviet childhood in the Czech Republic. Cowboy boots and Coca-Cola. When his mom moved him and Brooks here it wasn't the America he expected, but he never changed his style. Probably it meant more, knowing he had it all to himself—like a piece of culture that had been sent overseas for safe keeping. As soon as he got out of the group home, Derwin learned to shave with a straight razor and started wearing a leather jacket. Back then it was still way too big on him, but it fits him now, and it's maybe even a little tight in the shoulders. He left home a caricature of James Dean. Ran a comb through his hair and rode away. Now he walks toward us with the kind of swagger that says he's still on the same trajectory, that this lunchroom is exactly where the road had always meant to take him. He's taller than I remember, denser. Same savage black curls. And that tiny vertical scar between his shy green eyes from the fight with a cop. Black snakeskin boots with polished silver tips.

Brooks keeps his head in his book. He's shaking a little, just one leg. He knows who's here but he doesn't know how to deal with it. It's a long time his brother's been gone, a long time without a lot of contact. Derwin ought to expect some resistance after running off the way he did. He puts a little strut into his walk. Kids all over the lunchroom start to notice as he sweeps by. There's something unencumbered in the footsteps of a dropout invading lunch hour at school. He floats so far above the insignificant drama. Everyone can see it. Everyone halfway notices, caught in a mixture of envy and disdain.

He stops a couple feet away. "Hey, little bro," he says, softer now.

A wire of sweat runs from his temple to his jaw. His voice is deeper than I remember, more direct and controlled. I kind of knew he'd come back today. Not like I predicted this one, but seeing him does not surprise me I guess, if that makes sense.

Brooks turns a little but still won't look. Not all the way. Derwin peels off a leather glove. He holds out his hand, fist loosely clenched, offering knuckles to his brother. The hand hovers there long enough that I start to wonder if Brooks is still with us, and then he finally reaches up with his own pushpin knuckles to half-heartedly bump his brother's gesture of reconciliation.

"I saw New Orleans," Derwin says.

"Any gators?" Brooks asks.

"No gators. There was a turtle all covered in swamp slime. Like a little mossy island in a pond."

Brooks grins as their eyes finally meet, then he bites his lip for reluctance sake. But for a second, oh man that grin was everything. I've never seen anything like it on him before.

Meanwhile the conversation between Gail and Mirielle has suffocated. Mirielle's body is still in that quarter turn, just enough where she can pretend not to notice Derwin but where she can hear him better and maybe even catch a glimpse out the corner of her eye. Derwin pretends to keep all his attention on his brother, deliberately not seeing her. The rest of the lunchroom can feel it too—the kids in line, the kitchen workers, everyone watching them not look at each other.

Derwin and Mirielle fell in love on a Saturday afternoon way back when they were freshmen. She was drawing birds in a sketchbook, sitting on a bench by this horrible bronze sculpture of a bull moose with a set of antlers stuck in each nostril. Derwin was on his way to score some weed. He walked past her. She stopped sketching and her eyes drifted over the notebook's edge. She brushed a little hair out of her face in case he decided to look back. He did. She was wearing a purple and red sundress over a black leotard. Silver bracelets. Nylon sleeves covering her forearms.

If you come back here you won't regret it, she thought.

Derwin stopped, only slightly out of sync, and turned around. He rested a cowboy boot beside her on the bench so that his knee nearly touched her shoulder.

"Want a cigarette?" he asked.

She looked out toward the park. "Smoking is a tax on stupid people," she said.

He didn't quite laugh out loud, more of a snort. He pulled a filterless from behind his ear. Lit it with a match.

Derwin pointed at the sculpture. "What the fuck is that?"

Mirielle glared at him from beneath her luscious eyebrows. "Are you supposed to be like a bad boy or something?"

He grinned with a fraction of his lips. "Let's go."

"Go where?"

"Anywhere."

"I'm not going anywhere with you," she said.

His cigarette braced the 'v' of his fingers. He touched both tips to the cover of her book and tilted it toward him. Glanced at her skeletal study of owls.

"Art class?"

"I suck at wings."

The heel of his palm brushed her knee. Their eyes met in a full on optic collision. "You can drive," he said. "I'll draw."

They spent twenty minutes breaking into a Buick only to

find out it had been unlocked the whole time, keys still in the ignition. They cruised up the highway and took a logging road into the mountains. She didn't have a license. He finished four pages of owls before they reached an avalanche that ended the road. He made her stand on the edge of a cliff that hung over a valley of spiked pines and bare maples. He took pictures of her with her phone until they ran out of light. He said, "If I pushed you you'd just fall into that cloud and float away." He told her to take off her bra, and she did it without disrupting her dress, then tied it around his head and laughed at him. She peeled off her nylons and hung them from his ears. They turned up the radio and sat on the hood of the car and shared cigarettes, and when a storm moved in to cover the stars he drove her back into town and did not kiss her goodnight.

Even if I thought it was remotely possible to make Mirielle fall in love with me, even if I was remotely in her league, and even if she swings this way which I am like 99-percent sure she doesn't, the truth is I will never know what it's like to lose her on such a deep level—on the kind of level that she and Derwin lost each other. I'll never feel what it's like to have grafted into her so much that losing her would gut me.

When Derwin finally looks up from Brooks it still isn't directly at her. He smiles at me, which puts Mirielle in his line of sight, but out of focus past my shoulder. He holds out a gloved hand, palm up as if in supplication. His right hand reforms a fist, bearing a challenge I'd almost forgotten.

"Hey, kiddo," he says. "You been practicing?"

Rock-Paper-Scissors is Derwin's obsession. He signed up for a couple tournaments back when he lived here, took second place in one of them. He bought books, watched instructional videos, and attended a week-long workshop two states away. I remember him always working on ways to step up his game. When he was in the group home some kid tattooed a pair of scissors on the anterior region of his throwing arm. Since then he's added new ink, the words, "I" - "always" - "throw" - "rock" stepping down the ladder of his proximal knuckles.

Wordlessly, I accept his challenge. One, two, three. I choose paper to his scissors. Brooks stands between us, hands in his pockets, studying the subtle movements in Derwin's forearm flexors. Derwin stares me in the eye and says, "Now I'm gonna throw rock."

One. Two. Three.

He throws rock. I throw scissors. Dammit.

"There's a tourney next week in Portland," he says.

"That why you're back?" I ask.

One. Two. Three.

I throw rock and he smothers me with paper.

A long time ago Derwin told me: "Unless you're playing a real pro, folks tend to telegraph one way or another. A good basic strategy to start with is people tend to subconsciously go with the move that just beat them, so when you win, try following up with whatever beats your own last move."

I say, "Again."

"I'm throwing paper," Derwin says. He throws rock and crushes my scissors.

"Again."

I swear it's all got to be random luck, but he does tend to win all the damn time.

"Again."

I throw paper, and as my hands connect my eyes cloud over with a milky mist. The slapping sound doesn't fade, but stretches back through my wrists, rattling up my arms and like from one ear to the other. My palms seem to fuse. I feel warmth at the bottoms of my feet. The colors start to change in my periphery. My thighs melt together. I think about Derwin's hands and the palpability of how those hands have held her. How they've touched the hidden nooks of Mirielle's body. His wind-chapped lips have kissed her mouth. I want to reach out and grab them, but I can't move. I want to be the surface of his skin, to steal a memory of a random caress. The words form in my mind: *You are my champion.* They form there long before I know what they mean, and I repeat them silently, hiding each one like a thermometer under my tongue. The mercury rising. Heat elevating from my feet to my knees. Has he touched her shrouded patella? The blood drains from my head. *You are my champion.* Suddenly the vision pulses into a field of translucent silver.

And this is what I see between the cracks of frozen time: Mirielle's swollen abdomen, blue sweatpants stained with soy sauce, a bamboo green room bleached by the morning sun. Her body unfolding. She assembles a crib and pinches her finger between two pieces of wood. A strawberry-shaped blister forms on the tip. Outside there's snow but no wind, and it's the first sunny day in weeks. The thermometer reads 62 degrees, impossible for February. No one is there to tell her to take it easy. In the very first instant she goes into labor all I see are eyes squeezing shut and then I'm outside floating over rooftops, rushing up and rushing out, my consciousness expanding over the choking skies of deforestation and the looming cliff's edge of ceaseless industry and the aftermath of explosions going off in countries I don't know anything about, a quick glimpse of confused bloodstained faces unable to navigate the complex space that connects the red plastic on-switch from a consumer-grade espresso machine in Guilford, Vermont, with fifteen dead and six injured after someone—no one can even tell anymore whether they're bad guys or good guys—incinerates a mall in Kuala Lumpur. Everything running on and running out as the planet shrinks and dehydrates, and somehow any chance this miserable world has left is resting on the fulcrum of her unborn infant. An infant fathered by the man who just challenged me to Rock-Paper-Scissors.

You are my champion.

I know why I'm here now. I know what I'm supposed to do.

This is what it feels like to be born. The thought precedes a rush beneath my skin that's like every vein in my circulatory system bursting and every blood cell seeping into my pores. So much light in the room, I can't take it. All too soon the euphoria gives way to panic. My heartbeat moves to random places throughout my body: my hips, the base of my neck, the bottoms of my feet. My teeth grinding. I feel like prey. They're hunting me. Like every sinister entity in the cosmos has suddenly become aware of my presence, and have turned their eyes to look at me.

Derwin is wagging a hand in front of my face. "Hey, hello? Are you okay?"

"This happens," Brooks says. "She's fine."

It happens, but not like this. Never this big, never this crippling. I'm forcing myself to breathe again, swallowing, then gasping.

"She doesn't look good," Derwin says.

Coming back to my head now. Everything will seem to move more slowly for a minute. I'm good. I'm not. Breathe.

I speak in a dreamy voice. "I threw paper."

"Paper beats rock," Derwin smiles, raising his fist, but I know he's lying.

What happens next is a combination of my vision's drowsy epilogue and the first phase of a brand new compulsion that is at this exact moment starting to take shape in my subconscious. I stumble backward with dizzy steps, and bump into Mirielle. Jolted, she turns, reaching out to catch me. But I don't fall because Derwin's fingers have already got me around the arms. Tethered between them both, feeling their breath cross paths, my senses are a threshold. I am a conduit bringing their eyes into alignment.

"Hey," he says, too gruffly.

"Hi." She's trying to put on a bitchy, who-cares kind of tone, but she falters. "You're back."

They must be whispering.

"For a while," he says.

"Whatever," she says.

Then all I can feel is how much she totally and completely hates him, and how impossible this would be if they weren't somehow cosmically designed for each other. The moment lingers and I still hear their voices in my head. I see his coolness crack. He doesn't even realize how much he wants her, and even if he did there's nothing in the world that could ever make him say it out loud. I become his distraction. "You sure you're okay?"

"I'm good," I lie.

Derwin scruffs his little brother's hair and tugs him gently out of line by the elbow. Brooks jerks back, not with anger or resentment but because this is part of growing up. Derwin gets it and lets go. They say goodbye and my body goes through all the motions. A smile, a wave.

I'm surrounded. They're going to kill me.

Derwin drops a burgundy helmet on Brooks' head. It almost fits.

The line starts to move. Brooks and Derwin are gone. Mirielle and Gail are gone. Pender creeps forward and we follow the herd. A fat woman in an apron and hairnet waddles out with a huge new pot of Sloppy Joe held up with both arms and propped on a hip. The chatter of kids is a raw scrape of sandpaper down the back of my reptile brain. The mass exodus follows the sound of the lunch bell as it slurps back up into the circuitry from which it was born, the hidden mechanisms inside the walls, leaving me huddled and shaking in a corner until someone finds me.

5

"THIS IS A HORRIBLE PLACE to die."

Donald Victoria Estringi and I have been staring at the board for thirty minutes and neither of us has made a move. I'm not exactly sure whose turn it is. I think maybe I just covered his elephant with a little red cloth ear thing from what was once allegedly an old mouse toy for the stray cat that lived with him when he was a spy in Romania. For the past thirty he's been mashing up old stories of his life with plots from recent televisions shows. I'm hardly listening. I'm barely present. I can't get her face out of my head. Derwin's either. Their grown-up versions, faces superimposed.

It's never been like this. My visions tend to be sudden but calm, flowing naturally into and out of my mind. This was a full on assault. Almost violating. Like a deposit in my brain. Like some spy of the spirit world was caught stealing this information out of the future, but somehow managed to get away until, after a long chase, they cornered the desperate bastard right when he happened to be next to my ear, where he shoved the vision into my brain so no one would find it.

I can still feel them searching.

I text Brooks again. He's told me he's on his way a few times now. We've been doing this all afternoon. First he said he couldn't make it, which I'm sure means he's kicking it with his brother and my problems don't mean shit right now. Then he agreed to meet up, but it had to be outside the Home. *It smells weird*, he said. *Old ladies want to touch me*, he said. I bribed him with the promise that we'd sneak around the halls looking for ghosts, which would have convinced him any other day than the one where his brother comes back. So I raised the stakes and said I'd finally show him one of Pasha's books. I think I need to show him anyway because maybe it's going to take one little extra bond of trust between us before I can really talk about what happened. And talking this out is exactly what I need. Brooks can tell me I'm crazy and life can go back to normal.

"I see them carted out in the middle of the night," Donald says. "They snuff it at breakfast like Clem Lancer. Face down in his eggs."

I was there when they wheeled Donald toward the elevator for the last time. They'd decided to moved him upstairs for good so he could be closer to his treatments. The others watched in silence. Instead of turning to say goodbye, Donald raised his left arm and flipped off the room. For the next few days all anyone could talk about were the good old times when Donald would crawl naked down the halls or declare his undying love to the nurses. He hasn't been the same since. He's getting more depressed. Of course the counsellors won't listen to anything I have to say.

"What's a good way to die?" I ask, mostly out of habit. We've been over this before. I check my phone. Come on, Brooks.

"A man should die in battle," my father says. "Airlift me into the middle of a Central American revolution. I don't care which one and I don't care whose side I'm on. I'll fight where I land.

Fight until a bullet gets me. To hell with this sitting-around-waiting-for-the-end shit. I've had it! Complacency is the unforgivable sin of the soul."

Donald looks out his window, where the Tongue sits on the sill. It's been there for safe keeping ever since the day Richey Buchan and Matthew Craig tried to blow it up on top of the hill. There's a maple out there, leaning in with a branch where a sparrow is cleaning under its wing. I mention to my father how there's a law in this state where you can get drugs to help you die. Not that I'm suggesting this. We've had the conversation before. It helps to rile him up a bit. Adversity can bring out the best in him.

"I don't want to kill myself!" He drops a fist on the table and the board shudders. "I want to die! At the hands of a bloodthirsty enemy. Only thus can a man hop the tracks of the gods." He takes a deep breath. "Before it's too late." The bird stops grooming, seems to notice something from beyond the view of the window, then explodes into the sky.

Chestnut Homes started out as the most upscale hotel in the state before its conversion to a sanitarium in the 1930s when sanitariums were all the rage. I guess it was the '60s when the amount of old people in the valley got ahead of the amount of crazy people, or maybe the crazy people just got old. Or maybe they realized a sanitarium right in the middle of downtown wasn't getting a lot of good press. I can walk here from my house in ten minutes when the weather's good. It's a pretty nice place. Red brick with white Roman columns lining the front face where a meticulously manicured garden slopes down toward the hedges on the street. The back of the Home is wilder. A flurry of weeds and flowers staggered between bushes of wax currant and chokecherry and sandbar willow where wide earthen trails lead down to a grove of cottonwoods and ponderosa pine. Technically it's part of the river trail system, even though the river itself is about a quarter-mile west and of course all this is cut off anyway by the concrete wall. My father sometimes has me push him around back there and when we go by that wall he'll make me stop so he can stare dramatically into the past before the inevitable blah blah blah about how much it all reminds him of old Berlin.

"Did you say you're in a band?" he asks.

"No, I just write music."

"You play pinao?"

"No."

"What then?"

"Nothing," I say.

"How can you write music without an instrument?"

"On the computer, Donald."

This answer inspires a deliberate sneer of disappointment. "Contraptions," he says.

A new text from Brooks tells me he's locking his bike up downstairs. "I've got to go downstairs now," I say.

"Just because I'm kicking your ass."

I jump up and kiss him on the forehead. "I told you, I'm not allowed to have favorites. I'm supposed to spend time with everyone." Which technically this is true. If I had a choice I'd hang out with Donald my whole shift, but the nurses make me put in rec room and socializing time and track my interactions.

"Coward," Donald says. "I'll wipe the floor with you next time."

When school gets out I'll add another couple volunteer days to my schedule, so I should be able to squeeze in a few extra hours of dad-time per week. Meanwhile I'm stuck with the rest of the geezers. I don't have any real skills so mainly I bring them meals and hang out and let them tell stories about the old days. There's no verification process, no way to know what they're making up or misremembering. Mostly I just listen. The one thing I can do is believe them no matter how many details change, and try not to look bored no matter how often they repeat themselves.

Brooks is waiting in the lobby by the time I get downstairs. I jerk my head, summoning him into the hall. We walk along the narrow strip of carpet that looks like a trail of coffee grounds under the new UV-emitting bulbs they've been installing to promote the production of Vitamin D. He tells me he brought the camera. I resist the urge to spill my guts right there on the floor in front of him because I know what a shitty listener Brooks can be when his mind is fixated on something. Pasha's room is six doors down. Brooks can take his pictures, the books will appease him, then we'll talk. If anyone can tell me what to do about this kind of thing it's Brooks. He's got a real talent for weird shit. But really what I want is for him to convince me that it's all in my head so I can get on with lusting impossibly after Mirielle and keep things the way they've been. My nice, cozy, unrequited lust.

When we're almost at Pasha's door I tell Brooks to wait while I go in. "Hold on," he says. He pulls off his backpack, unzips, and hands me his Polaroid SX-70 Rainbow Instant Land Camera. I know this because the hipster who sold it to us treated the exchange like an arms deal. Had to go into all the specs. I didn't care, Brooks didn't care. It's the price you pay for not shopping on the Internet.

"Are they here?" I ask, looking around the hall. But I've never seen one. They're invisible to me. Do they know what I know?

Brooks aims the camera at the beige wall. "A nice neutral background," he says. He covers the camera flash with one hand, puts his thumb on the big orange button. With a click, blades of light squeeze out between his fingers. The machine whirs and grinds and chugs. Out comes the milky photo, not yet starting to hatch.

"Do they know we're here?"

"They don't care," he says. "This is gonna take a minute."

Brooks holds the film out and aims it at the crack under Pasha's door.

What matters most I guess is the Polaroid part, because they aren't the kind of thing you can take an actual photograph of. They don't emit, reflect, or refract visible light. It's the chemical processing of the image in their presence that does it. Apparently the electromagnetic disturbance surrounding them can interfere with the chemical reaction of the acid eating away at the opacifiers as the photo develops. So you don't even have to point the lens at them, but you do have to hold the developing paper up in their general direction.

Brooks insists that Chestnut Homes is full of ghosts. Not old people ghosts, though. Residents do die in their beds pretty often, but Brooks says they never stick around—not that he's seen anyway. I guess most old people don't have enough spirit left over to leave behind. First time Brooks saw one in the hall was about a year ago. A little blonde girl maybe six years old, walking into the men's room. He followed her in but she was gone. Today there's four of them, Brooks says, ghost children huddled around on hands and knees next to Pasha's door, ears to the wood, listening I guess to the sound of his scratching pencil. Or maybe ghosts can read long distance through their ears. What do I know about ghosts? Usually when Brooks sees them it's here, which this doesn't surprise me because Pasha's the closest thing to a ghost I've ever seen.

Pasha Luski is seventy-something and never isn't touching a wall. Like ever. He slides around the Home from one wall to another and doesn't step away. Every dinner you'll find him leaning in the same cafeteria corner holding his plate up under his chin, shoveling his food like a machine. The more of his body that's touching a wall the safer he feels, but he can tolerate a maneuver when necessary, as long as at least one tiny bit stays connected. If he ever feels like he might detach fully you can see panic bubble off his skin and like glue him back in place. On rare occasions where he has no other choice, like if he has to get across a doorway, he'll lie down and crawl on the floor. He's cool with this. A floor is kind of just a horizontal wall.

When they moved my father to the second floor Pasha was the only one happy to see him go. My father calls him Chuck for reasons no one will ever understand. He also calls him Stale Lunch, Wallflower, Bolshy Ginger Baby Pants, Sad Harpo, and sometimes it's just whatever pops into his head is going to be Pasha's name for the day. But Chuck is the most consistent—and the one that really gets to him. Because he doesn't know what it means. Pretty much everything about my father drives Pasha crazy, though. His swagger and his dominance over the airspace —shouts in the halls, random declarations of war on visitors, endless Cold War stories about the horrors of bordering forests in the '70s and what he calls the great cover-up of the '90s after the Wall came down. He loves to talk about how the Wall was really there to manipulate some sort of portal into hell, and about leading missions into Poland and other Bloc countries to investigate paranormal reports and to destroy grotesque lingering experiments from Khrushchev's regime. When Donald gets into

Pasha's face he brags about how we won, how we kicked the Soviets to the curb. But Pasha couldn't care less about politics and he doesn't even really identify as Russian. Pasha never says anything and he never fights back.

I creep around Brooks, making sure not to get in his line of sight. Even from out here I can hear the scratch of Pasha's pencil, and from this sound alone I can tell he's started on a brand new notebook for his manuscript. He's up to like a million words. All in these black notebooks of unlined paper that are stacked up in towers in every corner of his room.

"Can I go?" I whisper. Brooks nods, flipping the photo paper around to investigate. I step over what may be the ghosts of four children, slowly open the door, and walk inside. There sits shriveled old Pasha, hard at work. His grandson Matthew Craig has set up his desk so that the back of his chair touches the wall, and he even added a little drafting extension that angles forward so Pasha can sit up straight and rest his head against the wall as he writes. He works the pencil with his left hand, while his right vibrates like an antenna on the desk's surface.

When Pasha isn't sliding around spooking the other residents he's buried in his notebooks. And yeah, I'll admit I've read some of it. Okay, a lot. He either doesn't notice or doesn't care when I borrow one. Most of it is an illegible mess of incomplete or run-on sentences, weird intricate symbols and equations, and botanical sketches or these like hybrid figure drawings such as snails with people faces or aardvarks whose gardens grow on their backs. But every twenty pages or so suddenly there's a few paragraphs of eloquent, uninterrupted prose. Sometimes he writes about himself, but mostly he writes about trees. Specific trees from around town: the old maple on 15th, the aspen grove by the river, a birch he climbed when he was a kid. He describes their personalities and motivations, their relationships to the foliage around them, sometimes little dialogues between two trees or between himself and a tree.

My own personal obsession with Pasha's books started when I stumbled on one particular sentence: *The River Tongue that flows from the Castle Strange.* The coincidence creeped me out so much I didn't walk by his room for weeks. But I got over it, and after that I kept going back for more, searching out lucid passages and stitching them together. It didn't take long before certain images and ideas started connecting and taking shape, and a few weeks later I realized it wasn't just that one sentence talking about the Tongue—there were whole paragraphs related to it. And the craziest thing is that some of these even kind of sort of connected to the story my ex Charlie told me about the Tongue, a long time ago.

I've tried to show the Tongue to Pasha a couple times, but he won't acknowledge it. One time I screamed at him. I was like, "Really? You don't see this?" but as far as I know they sell them in every gift shop in Eastern Europe so maybe that's where he got the idea in the first place, and maybe there's nothing all that impressive about me having one.

When I go into Pasha's room my movements are quiet but casual. He's in some other headspace when he's writing and never notices me. Not that I can tell, anyway. I go to one stack and take the journal third from the top. Pasha blinks at his pages. *See you later*, I think at him, and I imagine him thinking back, *You be careful with that.*

Back in the hall Brooks hands me the camera and reaches for the journal. "Wait," I say. "Until we're gone."

As expected, the photo reveals the beige wall. There is a streak on one side from where he failed to block out the flash.

"Nothing," he says. "I think we need older film. Closer to its expiration."

"What's this?" I point at a dark crease in the bottom right corner. He takes a closer look, compares it to the wall.

"Dunno," he says. "Could be something."

Brooks and I make our way back to the rec room and sit on a couch near the computers. Brooks holds a bag of polished green Pente pieces in his lap. The game box sits open on the floor. I finally let him have the journal. The first page is thick with horizontal lines of graphite so dark it looks like ink. There's one empty white square of space on the lower third of the page with the word "city" written in the middle. I know every page of this particular journal. It's one of my favorites.

I'll let him riffle through a bit and then start blabbing. I've just about worked up the courage.

Today the usuals are in here with us. Terrance and company nearby, huddled around a laptop where the plan of the moment is to get a cat video to load. "Click it again," says Darla Flemming, age 74. Darla's an ex-hippie who still wears a tie-dye bandana and dream-catcher earrings. She has hip dysplasia and arthritis, but she juggles muffins in the cafeteria. Literally worships plants. The doctors call her a survivor. She lived through three heart attacks and a stroke. When she chose not to fight the pancreatic cancer that was killing her, the cancer respected her enough not to fight back. It never metastasized and to this day it seems content to sit around a small corner of her pancreas not doing much of anything. Darla leans on Terrance's shoulder, demanding to see the promised kittens.

"Clicking," Terrance says. "Click click click!"

"Give it a minute. Show some patience." This from Oliver

※

Spoonbowl, age 80, withered and hairless, who's been cleaning his glasses on his shirt for the past five minutes. Oliver has no teeth of his own and is so self-conscious about it that he paid good money to have his dentures antiqued to make them look like genuine yellow old man teeth. He managed a law firm in his day. Ran the whole ship into the ground.

Brooks flips ahead a few pages in Pasha's journal to where all these concentric circles spell out words in Latin. In the center of the page Pasha's drawn a tree whose roots curve together into these octopus-like tentacles that wrap around little contorted human heads. In the background, what I am almost totally sure is a drawing of the Tongue—my Tongue—flows by like a highway or a contrail. It continues on the next page and then the next and it just keeps going in the background of the entire journal until it reaches the back cover where the Tongue finally converges into a slimy tip drooping over the edge of a cliff toward a small beach.

"Huh," Brooks says with each page.

"Here let me show you another thing." I take the book back and start flipping, while Brooks opens the bag of game pieces. He lets them sift through his fingers then closes his fist. "Go," he says.

I close my eyes and wait for a number. "26," I say. No surprise there. He starts to count, dropping the stones one by one onto the carpet between our feet. Brooks can count and talk and listen at the same time.

"There," I say I stop on one of my favorite sketches. An old forest of trees so high their tops go off the page. The forest floor is a network of intersecting deer trails, and all along these trails men in suits have been planted up to their knees. They are evenly spaced, their hands flat at their thighs, they stare straight ahead, expressions neutral. A bird nests in one man's hair. A dog lifts his leg and pees on another.

Behind us Terrance is still clicking that mouse button over and over like he's trying to get a streetlight to change.

St. Vincent's Chestnut Homes recently upgraded their tech after an influx of ex-Silicon Valley types started retiring around town. The administration is looking ahead, expecting a demand for broadband Internet and state of the art LAN topologies, plus labs for hardcore fiddlers and hackers. We've got a few trickling in already, guys like Terrance who were around during the days of CDCs and punch card programming. It does a lot to enhance the quality of life for everyone, though. Old folks email their grandkids, find pen pals, browse exotic photos. Some try online dating. World of Warcraft was big for a while. We have a 24-hour tech support staff. Even a few of the old engineers who once helped develop standards way back in the '70s need to buzz a tech every now and then. Terrance Brown, age 75, was key in developing the world's first Graphical User Interface, but he can't figure out a single-button mouse to save his balls.

I close the notebook with a snap. "Brooks, something happened."

He doesn't reply, waits for me to go on. Game pieces fall from the leaky faucet of his fingers, clacking into their brothers and sisters on the ground. He counts fast and steady.

"Something real," I say.

"How real?"

"Real enough I can't make it go away. I think I'm supposed to do something."

"What?"

"It's weird."

"Weird in a weird way?"

I go back to flipping through the book. "Maybe it's nothing."

Something loud and obnoxious scrapes across the floor, so I do my duty and look up to make sure everyone is okay. It's Oliver, scooting his chair as close as possible to Darla. Were he still physically capable Oliver would have a raging hard-on for her. He leans over, trying to look down her sweater. "These machines never made any sense to me," he mutters. "Call tech support."

Terrance starts pounding the mouse on the mouse pad, which goes slap slap slap. "It's shit," he screams. "Today's programmers are spoiled with too much bandwidth. No one cares about proper data buffer handling anymore."

There's a story Terrance met Bill Gates at a conference and shook his hand and told him that he noticed a few bugs in Windows 95. Then he offered some pretty specific descriptions of where he figured the coders had messed it up. By the time Windows 98 came out a lot of those bugs were gone. Terrance got arrested a few years later for hacking the Department of Agriculture. Just for fun, he says. They pegged him with thousands in damages that he insists only accrued because they tried to stop him, and then put him in jail for ten years. After his parole Terrance was moved straight to Chestnut Homes. The court ruling denies him access to computers, but we live in a state where liberty's a big deal and old folks are still people, and even his PO is like whatever, the guy is so old—so the staff overlooks this little detail.

Brooks finishes counting. "29. Not bad. Okay, speak."

"It's really pretty weird," I tell him. I'm trying to get a little eye contact here. Keep dreaming, right?

"Just say it." Brooks slaps his hands together like he's dusting them off. As if there was some invisible powder on the surface of the stones that he has to clean as thoroughly as possible without rubbing it into his clothes.

"You brought this on yourself," he says. "Whatever. I don't care anymore."

"Yes you do."

"My turn."

"Okay, I'll tell you."

He points to the bag. "Go," he says, and takes the notebook from me. He flips to the back, stares at the drawing of the Tongue.

Oliver's might as well be drooling down Darla's shirt at this point. She knows he's crazy about her, but she likes a man with a good head of hair—someone like Donald Victoria Estringi. Darla appreciates Oliver's respect for pacifism and the Beatles, but the poor bastard doesn't have a scrap up top.

"What's this show about?" Oliver asks.

"The cat is afraid of a tennis ball," says Terrance.

"What's the ball doing?"

"Nothing. It just sits there and the cat gets very upset."

"Don't ruin the ending," Darla says.

"Oh hey, here we go," Terrance says. "No, wait. It stopped again. What is this crap?"

Oliver smears his wrinkled fingers across the screen. "What's all this stuff?"

"Those are comments," Terrance says. "People write what they think about the video."

"Read a few!" Oliver loves barking orders. "While we're waiting."

Terrance leans in a few inches from the monitor, squinting. "ROT—Uh, FLMAO?—what the crap, this isn't even English…. Wait, it goes on. Um… Funny shit bro, it says."

"That's it?"

"The age of fine criticism is over."

I dig a handful of Pente pieces out of the bag, the same way Brooks did. They feel like glass candy.

"Ready?" I say.

"30. On the nose."

"No—I mean, are you ready to hear this?"

"Don't tell me," he says. "I don't want to know."

I start counting. I have to count way slower than Brooks because I can't do it and talk or even think at the same time. When I go to say something I have to pause and try to hold the most recent number in my head. Numbers have always distracted me. I developed a weird relationship with them from a young age. I find the number 44 uncomfortable. Oscillating sequences make me feel like talking to myself: 1010101010101010101... on and on and stuff like that. 188 embarrasses me, and when I see or hear 14 I get this little startled jolt at the base of my spine. The number 9 is me curled up tight and cozy in a warm room. I hunt out 9s when I'm feeling shitty. 27 is lonely and 831 helps me sleep. And of course there's my weird thing with 62.

"Okay, here's it is," I say.

Brooks turns a few more pages. "What is this guy on?"

"Are you listening?"

"No."

I lean into him and whisper, "I have to get Mirielle pregnant."

And now that I've said it aloud, with the sentence hanging in the air, I shrink down and wish I could take it all back. Un-think it, disbelieve it. Stupid. Like I could even tell the difference between a genuine vision and a hallucination. Assuming there's any difference at all.

I brace for the smackdown, but Brooks doesn't say anything at first. He just sits there flipping back and forth between two sides of a page. The unsteady rattle of the mouse fills the silence. "Click it again," Oliver mutters. "Why is it taking so long?" Then he shakes the monitor. He always shakes the monitor. No matter how many times we explain that this is a total waste of time and effort, something deep inside Oliver refuses to be unconvinced that it helps.

The sound of creaking plastic rouses Darla out of a random nod off. She opens wide blue eyes and smiles. Oliver smiles back, trying to emulate the grin of Cary Grant.

"I dreamed about Donald just now," she says. Oliver's smile fades. "I was out in the garden and all the flowers were drooping over like they needed water. But the more I watered them the more they drooped."

Brooks takes a deep breath, gives back a dramatic sigh. "You have to get Mirielle pregnant?" he says.

"Yeah, well obviously not by myself."

"Is this some sort of vicarious wish-fulfillment?"

"Maybe. I don't know. It doesn't have anything to do with me. I mean, it does… I mean, I think I'm supposed to make it happen. Me. For reasons."

He shuts his mouth for a minute. I can almost hear him thinking. Finally he says, "Good luck with that."

"And I know who the father has to be."

"Don't tell me."

"It's your brother."

More silence.

"I mean it, Brooks. I know it's weird."

"When did you decide this?"

"I didn't decide it," I say. "I saw it."

"That's a really specific vision."

I finish with the pebbles. "Twenty-nine, thirty, thirty-one. You're way too good at this."

Oliver pretends to wait for Darla's conclusion with great interest. The kitten video starts to play, but no one notices: Oliver relentlessly transfixed, Darla in a rapture of her imagination, Terrance zoned out on a large clover-shaped mole on the back of his hand.

"That's when Donald showed up," Darla says. "He was walking around carrying a giant backpack like a mountain climber. The bag was full of bees. I could tell from the sound."

"Melanoma," Terrance says.

"Okay," Brooks says. "When did you see this?"

Don't think I don't notice he's not exactly trying to talk me out of it.

"Today. At lunch. Standing between them."

"When you spaced out?"

"Yeah."

The small pile of green stones that has emerged between us looks like the ruins of an ancient city. I shouldn't have said anything. My insides are all knotted up. All at once I doubt everything I've ever said or thought my whole life.

"Mirielle and Derwin?"

"M-hm," I nod.

"He's not staying for long."

"I know."

"He's dating someone."

"Who?"

"He won't say."

"Maybe it's her." Could I be so lucky?

"They hate each other," he says.

71

"No they don't."

"Pretty much yes they do."

"They love each other, too."

"What about you?" Brooks says. "I thought you loved her."

"Trying not to think about that right now, thanks."

"Okay, let's just say for a second that what you saw was real." There's a hint of jealousy in his voice, and something like reluctant admiration and skepticism and pride all mashed together. "Did it feel like a prediction or like an assignment?"

Like it's gestating inside me. Like the world depends on it. "Like fate, I guess? Like I don't have a choice?"

"What if you don't do anything about it? Will it happen anyway? If it's supposed to."

It's a good question. The kind of thing I think about a lot. I tell him I don't know, I just feel like I have to do something. Like if I don't I'll live forever with fear and regret. "And anytime anything bad happens in the world it'll be my fault somehow. Like if I'd just done what I was supposed to do…Ugh. I shouldn't have said anything."

"Stop it," he says.

I already feel the weight of it. In my stomach, in my hips, my lower back. This thick gelatinous gravity swelling around me, trying to fold me in half.

"Do you think things happen for a reason?"

"Things happen because of a reason," I say. "There's a difference."

"You're the most cynical mystic in human history."

"So? You're an atheist."

"I reserve the right to be an atheist. Even mystics weren't afraid to be atheists every once in a while."

"I don't want to talk about it anymore," I say.

"What are you afraid of?"

"I'm fifteen years old. I'm not supposed to have responsibilities like this yet."

On screen the kitten is finally freaking out as advertised, hopping around the tennis ball like a jumping spider. This is now the only movement in the room. I'd think time was frozen if not for that kitten. The others corpse-like until Darla finally says, "He took off the backpack and threw it into the air. And when it came down it turned into a swarm of bees that floated down like tiny umbrellas onto the flowers."

Her words make me realize I've been staring at a drawing in Pasha's notebook without really looking at it. Lying open at the last page Brooks flipped to. No words on this one, only a single sketch of a garden blooming under a radiant sun. Trees and leaves bend toward its light. Bees hover low over flowering jaws. Just like her dream. 62, I think.

"Tell me what it was like," Brooks says.

"Hard to explain."

"Try."

"I felt—I still feel—hunted."

"By who?"

"I don't know."

"And it was real? Like really real? You're sure about this?"

"I don't know."

"You have to know. Don't bullshit me with something fake. You sound like you're trying to convince yourself."

"Maybe I am. It felt realer than us sitting here right now, okay? And while it was happening I felt like...like an electric wire. Like there was this image of Mirielle and she was pregnant and it was Derwin's and it could only happen because of me being there between them."

"Why does it even matter? Why does she have to get pregnant?"

"I don't know," I lie.

I do know. I know. I know.

"Yes you do," he says.

"It sounds dumb."

"Say it."

"They'll have a child. A girl."

"Yeah? And?"

"And she'll be important."

"How important?" Brooks demands. "How important is this?"

I know there's a chance I'm crazy. I know most people don't think about the world this way. Most people aren't so obsessed with their own dreams. I'm probably a total dick. Overall I think it's better not to involve other people in my shit. But sometimes I just can't help it. There's the movements I make and there's the movements made out of me.

"You think it's stupid," I say. Brooks is the only person who would ever take this seriously.

"No," he says. "I don't. And I'll help. You want my help?"

"I have this sick feeling."

"Like what?"

"Like I'm making it up. Like it's a mistake."

"I trust it," he says.

"You trust it?"

"Mostly."

"I don't trust it," I say.

"That's why I do."

The sun in the middle of Pasha's garden drawing is like an eight-pointed star, and in the center of this star is a middle-aged man, limbs outstretched, pressing against the circumference of the sphere. He's wearing a dress that's way too small for him. Long, gaudy locks of hair, flowering eyelashes, and thick, glossy lips. I feel at one with the page, like I'm somewhere down between the lines, creeping around the weeds, hiding in the shadows of small velvet leaves. The sun always watches. I feel hunted and visible and vulnerable and exposed—like the vision is a beacon going off in my head. Like whatever I saw can see me back. What have I become a part of?

From a second console Oliver Spoonbowl has discovered a news site. He jabs into the heavy silence by reading headlines out loud. Something about a proposed bill to define conception at the moment of ejaculation. "Civil war," he mutters.

Brooks grinds the tips of his sneakers into the pile of stones. "D doesn't fall in love," he says.

"Am I a dick?" I whisper.

"People start wars and burn villages for worse reasons," he says. "Tell me what it felt like."

"I can't."

"Try."

"It was like—I don't know…like taking a shower." Not exactly like that. A little. My bones liquified, I lost my skin. I was there in the room with her. I could feel her baby kicking; I felt the snow outside, the heat of the explosion, the groaning of the earth. I could feel everything. Everything.

Brooks reaches out to me with one hand, a rare and impossible moment. I think probably he's my guardian angel, a protector for me, and he doesn't even know it. He'll figure it out the day he either saves me or fails. He'll stand there and finally understand, but not until that last minute. Part of being an angel is you have to operate without realizing that you're an angel.

Their ignorance is the source of their power. Because the only thing that makes anything mean anything is that there's nothing anyone can ever do to change the past. We can't change the past, but we're changing the future all the time and we can't help it.

"I was in love once," Terrance says. "She had this perfectly round mole. Right below her ass."

"A love story," Darla sighs.

"A goddess," Terrance says. "A priestess! She was the Euler of seduction, the Turing of sex."

Oliver nods off, wakes up, stares at Terrance like the man just turned into Abraham Lincoln.

"Never could touch her behind that cage, though," Terrance says.

A groan from Darla. "Oh, please."

"It might be easier than you think," Brooks says to me. "They were kind of retarded about each other, huh?"

"Stubborn, though," I say.

"Maybe all we have to do is get them alone together."

"No problem?"

"I bet she shows up Saturday night."

Saturday night as in the party. As in the big party in the woods party that no one has even considered inviting me to except that Derwin is taking Brooks and where Brooks goes I go. I'm excited but mostly in that morbid curiosity sort of way. I am not star-struck and stupid about the way high school kids waste their time. My prudishness and snobbishness about drugs and alcohol is legendary in my own mind. I have enough experience with my mother's alcoholic ex-boyfriends to know exactly how much fun I'm getting myself into. Will I feel cool stepping out of Derwin's car in front of everyone? So what if I will.

I hear the wall clock chime a fraction of a second before it actually chimes. I'm not psychic, I don't believe in any of that shit. I don't know what it is I'm seeing and feeling but I'm sure it would all make sense if I had more information. I've read that the arrow of time is an illusion we live through, and that in reality the future and the past are just kind of there the same way any part of space is just there. Our memory of the past isn't that much clearer than our best guess about what's to come. Like we're looking out over some hazy field, catching glimpses of the future all the time. Especially young kids, who have so little of a past to distract them.

"I mean this girl was a real professional," Terrance says. "Eye-fucking everyone in the room."

"I want a snack," Oliver says.

"She turned me into a dog. One smile and I was a pathetic little baby."

"Something to chew."

"She wasn't a whore, though. She wasn't a whore."

"What in Green Gables are you talking about?" Oliver says.

"The inexplicable conquest of my reason. I'm an intelligent man, but I'd have killed myself right there if I thought it would have made her happy."

Darla is still shaking her head. "With a dancer! Boys."

"What an ass she had!"

Brooks was supposed to come here and tell me I'm crazy. Instead, it's like he's proud of me, which makes me feel worse. The part of me that thinks I'm making it all up is sick with guilt, the part of me that knows it's real doesn't want any validation—is in fact terrified by the idea. I need to be alone. Probably forever.

"We need a plan," Brooks says. He's flipping rapidly through

Pasha's pages now, not reading or skimming, just browsing the froth of words and diagrams.

"Didn't you ever have girlfriends, Terrance?"

"Sure. Plenty. But what we're talking about here is love."

"Did you talk to her?" Darla says.

"Only ever saw her the one night. A little club in Phoenix. Couldn't say a word. Thought my heart would explode."

"I heard all you old hackers are virgins." Oliver licks his lips. Darla glances at me and Brooks for the first time, like she's concerned that maybe we shouldn't be hearing this kind of shit.

Terrance starts to float out of his chair. "I wonder if she's still alive."

Most of the stories I hear at Chestnut Homes are about long-lost lovers. The one constant is that usually the more intense the love story the less time the lovers actually spent together. Most of the old folks come around to the notion of wasted time. Thirty or forty years of pain and struggle from which the great realization of love only showed up after the lover died or broke things off. After it was far too late. There aren't very many couples in the Home. Loss is love's white gasoline.

"Maybe a grandmother somewhere," Terrance says. "Maybe long gone."

6

CLAYTON DRISCOLL, WHO ONLY AGREED to be a part of this if he got to partner up with me, and who I only agreed to partner up with if we got to change partners halfway through the operation, constructs a tower of coffee creamers on the table of the Town Pump Country Store kitty-corner to Mirielle's house, where we sit face to face, except that my face looks nowhere but out the window. She's in her front yard, dressed in white cutoffs, a twilight-blue sleeveless blouse, sandals, wide amber sunglasses, and of course, the fabled knee brace. Hair up in a pony tail. Skin tanning before my eyes. Her hands glide over the clay model of an owl sitting on the stump of Douglass fir that she uses for a table. She crouches to work, stands to scope it out.

Brooks got intel this morning that Mirielle is in fact now dating someone—some older guy out of high school is the official rumor. We don't know who; we don't know for how long. What we do know is he's probably coming by to pick her up sometime this afternoon. We're here to find out names. I need to know what I'm up against.

"How long are we supposed to sit around?" Clayton asks.

"As long as it takes," I say. Pretty sure I picked that

expression up from some show. It sounds serious, saying it. Like this is a real life mission.

My phone buzzes on the Formica. I swipe the screen, read the words. Nothing to report. All afternoon Brooks and Pender have been tailing Derwin, who I guess is running all over town, so they're not having an easy time. The good news is Brooks already has some idea of what Derwin is up to today, so they manage to keep tracking him down. Brooks says he's got some mystery girl. Is it too much to hope they're already doing my work for me? Maybe that's what we'll find out. I think this every time a motorcycle drives by.

Can we switch yet? is what I text back, because the way Clayton's staring at me keeps getting creepier and creepier, like he thinks eventually it'll get so creepy I'll kiss him or something just to make him stop. How do dudes ever get laid? I pick up the binoculars again, and I'm probably using them more than I would otherwise because it keeps him out of my peripheral vision. They're Pender's, which is how he got to be involved. Mirielle carves a streak into the owl's wing with her littlest finger. It's horrible, the owl. She's such a bad artist. I love that about her.

The next text I get is a group message to me and Brooks from Alex Flight, who we bribed into helping in exchange for Brooks writing his next three English papers. Says Derwin was spotted pulling into Loche's, home of the Pile-o-Burgers burger pile. Then another text from some number I don't recognize, insisting that Derwin just walked out of Denny's. All I can do is trust Brooks has the situation under control.

"Okay so wait," Clayton says. "If we're watching Mirielle for Derwin, why are we also watching Derwin?"

"We're not."

"But Brooks is."

"So?" I'm still hiding in the binoculars. Occasionally I tilt down to steal a glance at her knee brace. "How do you know our missions are connected?"

"Because you keep texting him every five minutes."

"Business as usual," I say. "It's what best friends do."

Clayton's car is parked out front. The only reason we let him in on this is because of wheels. Legally he can't drive on his own with just his learner's permit, but like he gives a shit, and that's the other reason.

Something bright cuts between me and my view of Mirielle—a glare on a window, some car I don't recognize: silver Prius, spotless. The driver honks the horn in two short bursts. Mirielle gets up and waves, jogs lightly to the passenger window and leans in. Whoever it is, it's not Derwin. Even if the car wasn't all wrong, his hair's too short, shoulders too broad. Mirielle hops in, then hops right back out to grab her bag off the porch. She's in again and they drive off. I've already taken fifteen or twenty pictures with my phone.

And I'm up. "Let's go."

"I have to pay for my coffee," Clayton says.

"I got it already. Time to drive."

Clayton's black Camry is older than I am, but it still runs. We manage to pull out in time to catch the Prius at a light, and to his credit Clayton does a half decent job trailing them. I text three pictures of the car to Brooks so he can hand them off to Pender who allegedly has some sort of photo-matching software on his iPad that he can run against public profiles of local friends and friends of friends on Facebook, and if the gods of the internet are with us maybe this car is posted somewhere. The race is on. My binoculars vs. modern technology.

They're driving all over town, not stopping anywhere. I can't convince Clayton to pull up next to them.

"It'll blow our cover," he says.

"Who cares? We just want to know who he is."

"Okay, yeah, but don't you want to know who he is without them knowing who you are?"

Pender's got nothing. Brooks wants the license plate. Says they lost his brother twenty minutes ago on account of Brooks having an aura, as in a seizure aura, which is something that's been happening to him more and more lately. He hasn't had a full-on attack in almost a year, which is good but also could mean he's due, I guess, and that's why he's been seeing the doctor every couple weeks.

Maybe it's him? Brooks says. *He has been known to steal cars.*

Not unless he got a haircut and went to a magic gym, I type back.

K, just follow them. We'll find D.

Fine. Good.

He says, *Sorry, I just kind of froze.*

Hope it was worth it, I text back.

I saw a double rainbow.

We joke but it can be serious. Some kids call him a faker, but I saw it happen once and even if I didn't believe it before, you see it and there's no mistake. I thought he was going to die and take me with him. His mom heard me scream and she ran into the room and put a rag between his teeth. I saw the literal backs of his eyeballs. I thought his tongue was going to rip out of his mouth. He went into this sort of shriek that didn't even feel like sound, more like something alive squirmed right out of his pores and in through mine. Later he told me he had no memory of falling over and thrashing around and biting himself and knocking shit over. Only this floating feeling and a voice that kept saying, Come back to me, come back to me. Which it turns out that's what his mom was saying over and over as she held him down, and this seemed to bring Brooks out of it after a while. He was bruised up and his mouth was cut and bleeding, and if that was fake then he's just one hell of a good faker.

Mirielle and her mystery driver pull up in front of a house I don't recognize. Clayton parks a block away. I tell him to get closer. I probably sound like a bitch, but Jesus, learn to spy.

"They'll get out of the car. You'll see his face."

But they don't. Through the binoculars it's like they're sitting there waiting just to mess with me. Mirielle keeps looking into her lap—probably on her phone. Mystery man slaps his hands on the dashboard to whatever's on the radio. Five minutes go by.

"Come on, go closer."

Clayton sighs and for a second I think here we go, but when he reaches for his keys he hesitates. His lips twitch. He looks at me funny. When his eyes go to my throat it's probably not even intentional. Something shifts in the air and all at once he's lunging at me, and because my body tries to go two directions at once I end up not moving at all. He slips a hand behind my head and the other goes to my knee, and now his lips are pressing against my face. No tongue, just a forceful and breathless jolt. My eyes wide, his in slits. I don't move, my skin turns to stone but my blood is roaring. Random desires fire off in my periaqueductal gray. Like the impulse to strike out and kill and then at the same time some even weirder desire to tear off all my clothes and run back down the road and up the into the hills until I find a forest. *Clayton needs to stop*, is what I'm screaming inside my head, he needs to stop kissing me and leap into a canyon, and then random thoughts like if Mirielle was only a ceramic doll and I stole her and gave her to a homeless person could I get into heaven? I don't know if I'm pushing against him or what. Why isn't the car door opening when I clearly want it to so clearly to stop stop make it stop.

And then it does. Clayton pulls back, leans against his own door now, looking at me in this way like he's studying me or something. He shakes his head. "So it's true," he says. "You heart pussy."

"Fucking. Asshole," I whisper. My hands adjusting clothes for the sake of making sure everything's still attached.

Clayton shrugs. His little playful laugh makes me feel more violent than when he was on top of me. He taps his fingers on the steering wheel. "Nothin' to be ashamed of."

"You think just because I don't want to fuck you that I'm a lesbian? You arrogant prick."

His right hand scratches around in his hair. When I open the door I see something way more predatory flash across his eyes. He reaches for me again, this time just his arms. He's still laughing. Fingers like talons. I tumble out and as soon as I hit the road one knee down I scramble back up, but Clayton isn't coming after me. He's just a far-off shape through the open door. The predator look is gone and now he seems more confused than anything. I head down the street toward the Prius, but they're not even in the car anymore. Great, dick. Great fucking timing you piece of shit I didn't even want to hang out with anyway. And where the fuck are Pender's binoculars?

I hear Clayton's engine kick over and he drives up behind me. The passenger door is still open. My arms are crossed and I don't look back. He's calling my name now, leaning out his window. "Get in the car, come on." When I don't react he puts it in park, turns the key and jumps out. The last thing I want to do is run, and anyway the sense of threat is weirdly gone. Clayton doesn't follow me, just leans against his hood. "Look, really?" he says. "What're you gonna do, walk? I'm sorry, okay? I shouldn't have done that. It was stupid." I stop walking but don't turn and I don't speak. He gets back in and drives up next to me.

He starts complimenting me on my resolve. Says it must be confusing for me. I tell him, no it's pretty fucking clear.

"Get in."

"Not a chance. Anyway they're gone. Great job."

"They'll be back."

My phone buzzes. It's Brooks texting me they found Derwin picking up some mystery girl from Hidden Needle, this bookstore/tattoo/coffee shop downtown.

"So annoyed!" I yell, trying to aim as directly into Clayton's face as I can. Useless. He just smirks and says he's going home. I reach in and grab the binoculars, wedge them under an armpit, and give him overlapping middle fingers like crossbones. He shakes his head at me and puts it in drive. "Hey, at least shut the door!"

Shut your own stupid door. I cross the street and walk to the Prius without looking back and stand there staring at the license plate. I text it to Brooks in case it helps. No bumper stickers. Sure is a clean bumper, though. I open the passenger side door and now I'm sitting in the sacred space previously occupied by Mirielle, shrouded in her lingering perfume. I can see the dusty imprint of her sandals on the otherwise immaculate floor mat. I start to calm down, push Clay out of my mind. Stupid prick. I open the glove box to look for registration or some indication of who owns the car. I take a deep breath. For the first time I realize how much her scent reminds me of the girl who taught me to how to kiss.

Charlie's a girl I met when we lived on the farm near the Oregon coast. Her parents ran the place, kind of a communal land where we grew our own food and I took classes that covered things like neo-anarchist politics and sustainable agriculture with I think maybe nine other kids. Charlie was three years older than me, which at the time made her wildly sophisticated. The first time I sat down to study at a table where she was sitting she slid her coffee cup toward me with two fingertips stiff on the porcelain saucer until it bumped against my hand. Kept those fingers there until I looked up. "Try it out, sugar," she said in the meltingest fake Southern accent. Charlie cut jagged bangs out of her hair, wore way too much jewelry and almost theatrical amounts of dark makeup. Closed her eyes all the time so she could concentrate better on sound.

Charlie never studied, but always sat at the same table drinking the same cup of coffee. Green eyes drawn over a mad smile, listening to everything. Freaked out by sunsets and snails and not much else. The first and only person to pull my hair. She used to bite my lip and talk into my mouth in secret languages. The first kiss, after dark on the bench by the creek, she told me to keep my eyes open. *Try not to blink.* Her eyes slid from my left to my right. *Talk and listen at the same time,* she said. Our words overlapping where our lips touched. Her breath caressing my muscular palate. Her hands firm on my scalp, needles in my hair. My heart smeared out over my skin.

I used to tell Charlie how crazy and ugly I felt, like all the time. I couldn't understand what she saw in me.

I don't know, she'd say. *All I know is I don't see it in anyone else.*

But Charlie never took me too seriously until I showed her the Tongue. Then she told me a story. A story she said she'd heard from someone who used to live on the farm way before my mother and I arrived, before the cult even got started. It was a long story, and as weeks went by she would recall more details and fill in more blanks, and the more she told me the more I wondered if she was just making it up as she went along. I still don't really know, I guess.

So basically the whole thing takes place far in the future long after the collapse of a technocratic utopian one-world civilization organized by this like all-knowing supercomputer network of invisible airborne nano-machines that people were basically constantly inhaling for nourishment, healing, and communication, until one day the whole system suddenly collapsed. The higher functioning organizational center, which Charlie called the Mabingestialbogoblin, up and vanished or disintegrated or somehow lost consciousness, while at the same time the physical—let's call it autonomic—features kept on sort of heart-beating in a crippled coma state. By this point life is basically a shithole for the remaining humans, who had become overly dependent on the functioning system, and now everything is just a dreary struggle to survive on what's left over. Things don't change much for a long time until one day the Tongue shows up. And the Tongue itself is the story's like major antagonist or whatever on account of how first it obliterates towns as it rolls out over the countryside, and then after carving out its territory how it then starts to trap everyone like flies. It's a real life-sized version of the Tongue in my glass globe, which I think I was more surprised that she had a story for it than she was that I had a thing to go with her story. The Tongue is about as wide as a river and longer than anyone can even think about measuring. And just like my globe the Tongue in the story rolls out through the gates of an abandoned castle somewhere on the shores of the Black Sea. From there it slithers across the moat and stretches for miles and miles and just keeps on going all over Europe, crashing through the walls of any hovel or town or ancient city ruins in its path. It tears through Germany and into Denmark then back down through France and all the way around the Alps and across the great Spanish wasteland until it slips into the sea and that seems to be the end of that, but oh hey here it comes back up again in Italy, climbing the cliffs of Sorrento and rolling straight over the ruins of what was once Rome before the Tongue got it. And the Tongue doesn't stop until somewhere down along the Balkan coast, where it plunges through the earth on top of a cliff, drilling deep into a cave on the beach, where finally its tip emerges and twitches around the shore like it's tasting for something lost on the tide. In more ways than one the Tongue is pretty much the closest thing to a river the world has left—with all the fresh water dried up and no one even able to plant crops or anything. But all along the Tongue's edges new vegetable life is sprouting up, which this is unusual on account of how the world is otherwise totally barren and basically post-apocalyptic and has been only just barely inhabitable for however long. As you'd expect, the Tongue's arrival kind of freaks everyone out, but still it's the only place life grows anymore so lots of people are drawn to the fruit trees and all the other crops blooming up alongside the bumps of its slimy edges. Since the whole world is practically starving to death they start harvesting what they can, and the food tastes pretty okay and it keeps them alive at least. But here's the thing: eating this food makes them sort of start to love the Tongue, and I don't just mean admire and appreciate it for making the dead ground grow stuff again. I mean full-on lusty love. They start to lick the Tongue is how this manifests at first. Then they want more, they want to roll around on it and take their clothes off and sleep on it all day and basically just give their miserable lives over to basking in the Tongue. So by midway through the story what we have is a Tongue covered in blissed-out victims that it's sort of dragging downstream toward its tip where it deposits them in the cave and no one knows what becomes of them after that.

Whoever's Prius this is, he runs a tight ship. Nothing but two full matchbooks and a flashlight in the glove box. Floors that get a daily vacuuming. I keep glancing at the door of the house which I'm guessing is where Mirielle and her guy went. I find the registration under the seat. *Matthew Craig,* it says. Pasha's grandson. Holy shit.

I stay in the car for fifteen or twenty minutes. Clayton's long gone. Brooks wants to know where I am and what I've discovered. I kind of hope Mirielle and Matthew Craig come out and find me here. Death by embarrassment, right? But the worst thing about embarrassment is that it doesn't ever kill you. I see the house door open but I'm already out of the car, already walking away. I've left her stollen green scrunchie on the seat and I will spend the rest of the evening imagining the way her face might look when she finds it, wondering how it got there, trying to remember when she last saw it, if it fell out of her pocket or what. Matthew, you seem nice, but I will rip her away from you with my bare hands if I have to. She's mine. And Derwin's. She's ours. And her child's. All of us interbelonging. I don't really care if that means anything to you or not.

7

AFTER SCHOOL, IN MY ROOM, I bounce between instant messaging with Brooks, digging around the internet for audio samples, browsing art blogs, and tweaking my latest track on a pirated copy of Ableton. It will be mission accomplished if I can get the right pitch bend on this sample I found of some girl catching her breath at like the sight of adorable kittens. Then I'll drop it in as a kind of negative space between beats 3 and 4. Even my multitasking has rhythm, for extra practice I guess. Command-Tab is a kick drum. My pinkie is a metronome.

If I had to guess, I'd say over on his side of the conversation Brooks has a movie on, an iPod in his ears, and is reading a book. He may or may not have taped a penny to his game controller's A-button in order to keep up some meaningless task like digging through a mountain. Brooks' handle is *Iaminyourhouse*. Mine is *Wenus*. We believe in handles. We respect the idea of anonymity on which the internet was originally founded.

Me: Come over to the dark side, Brooks.
Brooks: I am purity and light.
Me: And yet the dark side is so very delicious.

Brooks: I taste only 42 thousand grams of heart attack.

Me: The warm comfort of chili cheese guacamole on one side, the tangy delight of barbecue on the other. I am crunching into one right now.

Which, temporally speaking, is a lie. I send the message before eating the chip. Communicating like this gives plenty of leeway when it comes to timing. Crunch crunch as I wait for his reply. Tweak something in my wobble loop that I can't quite make wobbly enough. I wish I could build these from scratch instead of messing with downloads. I need my own damned sampler. Like a real one.

Brooks: I will cry at your funeral.

Me: Your face is a funeral.

Brooks: Your mom's a face.

Me: Behold the mighty mom of face. Tremble and despair!

Brooks: Also, she says you have to come over for dinner soon.

Me: Your mom?

Brooks: Ya.

Me: Cool.

Brooks: Fool.

Me: Drool.

Brooks: School.

Me: OMG, can you believe we're almost not freshman?

I avoid acronyms and shortcuts whenever possible when texting and such. OMG is my one exception. The syllables ring of incantation.

Brooks: And the seniors are almost no longer seniors.

Me: What's your point?

Brooks: Nothing.

This track I'm working on is for Mirielle. The way she talks and moves and laughs and violates her eyebrows; every aspect of her a specific chord, tempo, and dynamic. This morning I saw her pull a wad of green chewing gum off her front tooth and stick it inside a folded corner of a piece of notepaper and then drop it in the trash on her way down the hall. I want to translate all that into a phrase. I want to compose arpeggios out of her sighs. To play her like a live symphony, to make her body tense and relax, to shape the vocal cords around her breath. To find the dials in her eyes, the levels that bend her pitches, the shriek points and sharp intakes and heavy release sliding across her skin, peaking and easing off the volume. To feel her and make her feel me, and to feel the feedback of what I make her feel. An endlessly rising cycle of tension and tonic. To overlay these tones across the beat of her breast.

Me: Having fun with big brother?

Brooks: Yeah, it's been okay.

Me: Find out his mystery girl's name yet?

Brooks: I did! It's Bre.

Me: Bre who? Bre as in GSB Bre?

Brooks: Maybe? I have no idea who that is. What are we going to do about Matthew Craig?

Me: Eliminate.

Brooks: D's really mellowed out. Seems almost peaceful.

Me: How long's he back for?

Brooks: He won't say. Probably not long. Said they might move to Oklahoma.

Me: With his girl? Together?

Brooks: I guess they've had a long distance thing for a while.

Me: They're in love?

Brooks: D doesn't fall in love.

Me: He did once.

Brooks: Also he's coming over to see you.

Me: WHAT? WHEN?

Brooks: Now-ish.

Me: WHAT?!!

Brooks: Wants to show you something.

I knew I should have cleaned up. I smooth out my bedspread, which is second-hand and-baby blue and everywhere I look the Road Runner is just outside Wile E's reach. Here's how I've arranged my room: my head isn't up against the wall while I sleep, but falls in the exact center of the space. From there if fuzzy coils of light could emanate from my prefrontal cortex or amygdala or hypothalamus they would compose a network of electromagnetic fields resembling a nervous system branching outward toward posters of idols, letters, journals, dirty dishes as yet unclaimed by my mother, plastic anime figures, the stuffed Hellboy in a beanbag chair, rocks, dried flowers, empty cereal boxes, broken harmonica, guitar, bathrobe and other fallen corpses of laundry, eyedrops, gum, Chapstick—each object progressing counterclockwise and from floor to ceiling at the angle of the emotional shrapnel if my heart ever exploded in a dream and splattered the walls with my memories.

Me: What does he want to show me?

Brooks: Chill out, pants. He's not that cool.

Me: Three years. What's he been doing?

Brooks: That's what mom keeps asking him. He's evasive. He's different. Quieter and confident.

I remember Derwin as an impulsive angry teenager. Now his charisma feels softer—still engaging, but no longer as impatient, I guess. One thing I remember is he always had something at least interested, if not actually interesting, to say about whatever topic anyone brought up. And he'd talk to anyone. Any social status, reputation, whatever—he didn't care.

He doesn't show up for another fifteen minutes. I spend the whole time in an anxious frenzy. I get up; I clean more things; I move shit around, then move it back where it was before. Every thirty-seconds I check in with Brooks.

Brooks: I love how movies make you feel like it's possible to be awesome all the time by editing out anything that is not awesome.

Me: I think I may be awesome 1% of the time. Tops.

Brooks: Give yourself more credit. We are awesome more percent of the time than we think we are. I wouldn't put you any lower than 9%.

Me: That seems excessive.

Brooks: So what happened with Clayton?

Me: I don't want to talk about it. What are you doing tonight?

Brooks: Homework. Skyquest. Trying not to shake down the house.

Me: I want you to cause earthquakes. Break open the floor. Blow up the world. What'd your doctor say?

Brooks: I'm gonna be a cyborg.

Me: Wha?

Brooks: Vegas Nerve Stimulation.

Me: Vagus.

Brooks: Whatever. It's like a pacemaker for the brain.

Me: Googling it.

The device gets implanted in the chest. A wire runs up to the neck where the vagus nerve is, monitoring brain activity with a steady stream of electrical pulses. Policing it, I guess—like a watchman—and responding to irregularities, then compensating for them.

Me: So no more meds?

Brooks: You mean the meds that don't work anyway? No, I'm supposed to keep taking them. It's stupid. This thing isn't gonna work either.

Me: A guy on this message board says it cured him. Hold on. I think your brother's here.

Brooks: k.

Today Derwin's in blue jeans, sunglasses, and a beat-up cowboy hat. I let him in and there's this awkward side hug moment before I go back to my computer. This is me playing it cool. He falls into the beanbag chair, puts my stuffed Hellboy in his lap.

"I've got to get out of here," he says.

"You just got here."

"River's rising, snow melting on the mountains, flowers blooming in the valley." He still has the mildest hint of a Slavic accent, but he's worked really hard to make his voice sound a little bit country, a little bit rock and roll. "Gonna find a snowline, I think. You in?"

When Derwin was twelve he hitchhiked to a trailhead into the Hobnail Wilderness—three million acres of pristine valleys and alpine peaks that are accessible for only about five weeks a year. He brought a sleeping bag, a .22 pistol, a fishing pole and matches. Wandered maybe 80 total miles all alone before finding an outpost on the Nailhead River. He told me how he woke up one night to a mountain lion staring at him from like seven feet away. It circled him twice and took off into the woods. Derwin waited for light and tore out of there, moving camp twenty miles only to find the same cat in the same pose the next night, hovering over him as he slept. This time he had to fire his gun into the ground before the thing would go away. Said that cat could've killed him easily without even waking him. Derwin figures maybe its mother had cast it off and it just wanted some company. I like to think it was looking out.

"I don't camp," I say.

"It's perfect out there. Nothing like it."

"Sounds great."

"You just gotta get used to it," he says. "The brain starts to reset after a day. Three days in and you won't want to come back. How've you been, kid?"

Well, let's see. The other day I experienced some sort of electrical shitstorm in my central nervous system that caused me to feel like I was seeing through the veil of the universe into another place or time—a place or time directly connected with the genetic potential between you and your ex in a story involving epic global catastrophe, inevitable unless I do something to make sure this genetic potential becomes sweaty, musky, heart-breaking, life-ruining genetic reality—and out of all of this me feeling like it's totally my responsibility to shut down any feelings I have for her in order to make sure the two of you get it on. And soon. And without protection. Like I'm going to have to sneak into your room and poke holes in all your condoms or something.

"Fine," I say.

He scooches himself and the beanbag closer to me with three clumsy bounces. Slugs me in the arm. "What's this you're working on?" My screen is a mystery to him. Derwin may be the only person I know who doesn't even own a phone.

"New song. Hold on, I've got Brooks here."

"Tell that little pecker he owes me ice cream." I lean over the keyboard to tell Brooks his brother says hi. He has already written, *The modern world has made tremendous advances in cultivating our capacity for boredom. Dinner time. Laters,* and logged off.

Derwin leans back into a stretch. I hear joints crackle.

"Nice to have you back," I say. "Bet Brooks is happy."

Derwin jumps up, perches on the corner of my desk, and scruffs my hair. "I missed you guys," he says. "I missed the woods. No woods in the world like these woods. You got a boyfriend yet?"

"Why does everyone always ask me that?"

Derwin launches back into the beanbag. My mother knocks on the door, bringing dinner. Fried catfish. Grudgingly, she hands a second plate over to Derwin. Doesn't say hello. Doesn't acknowledge his return. I wonder if I'll ever have a friend she likes.

"Who was your fish?" Derwin asks.

"I haven't started eating."

"Not how; *Who?*"

"Who?"

"*Who!* I mean when the fish was alive. What kind of fish was he? Did he have any hobbies? Was she a mom fish? Was she good to her guppies?"

I dangle the rubbery filet between two fingers, really looking at it for the first time. "Of what the fuck do you speak?"

He breaks off a bite with the side of his fork, stabs it and holds it up to my face. "When you eat an animal you should honor it by telling yourself the story of its life." Then he closes his eyes, inventing a dinner story in his mind I guess. On my plate: green beans, mashed potatoes, and two filets. Most likely from two separate fish. I suppose maybe they knew each other in their water world. Were they enemies or friends, or did they just have some vague idea of each other through the fishy network? Maybe they swam past one another every day and never could have imagined they'd end up in the same belly at the bitter end.

He stares at my plate. "You done? Let's go."

"Go?"

"I didn't come here to fuck around. I have to show you something."

"What?"

"Show, not tell," he says. "Come on."

"Where are we going?"

"Enough with the questions. Take a deep breath. Enjoy the mystery."

Derwin's driving some beat-to-shit red Chevy from the '80s. Holes in the bed where you can look through and see the rusting axle and whatever's on the ground beneath it. A disembodied pair of plastic legs with stockings up to its knees dangles from the rearview mirror by a silver chain. Two stickers on the tailgate: *Friends don't let friends eat friends*, and *My god can beat up your god*. The engine shrieks and coughs and I can't believe this piece of shit even runs. Bench seat, stick shift, stiff plastic seat belts.

His fan blows only hot air and my window doesn't roll down. The windshield is an execution wall. I notice half of a grasshopper's thorax stuck on the passenger wiper. Derwin drives west past Sheldon's land and into the mountains, up Bane Canyon on a dirt road that winds over cattle guards and potholes and into blue pines that hover in the sunset. The mountain face is close on my right, but over on the other side the road skirts a cliff that drops hundreds of feet straight down. Every winter some drunk idiot slides off into oblivion. After about five miles the canyon narrows and the mountain presses in. The road forks and we go left, cross a small bridge, and after another few hundred yards, stop. Derwin kills the engine, then the lights.

"I've been up here before, fella," I say.

"Whisper." He rolls down his window, tells me to wait a few minutes and let my eyes get used to the dark. He points across the switchback to where the road relapses over the gorge. Up the slope I see a granite boulder leaning over a scramble of dirt and saplings. He's pointing at something on the boulder, but I can't piece it together. Some dark, motionless shape. Really, I can see it just fine, but what I'm seeing makes no sense, and my brain refuses to accept that this thing is actually what my eyes tell me it is until Derwin says the word.

"A bear. A motherfucking bear."

But the bear isn't moving. Like at all. So I hang onto my doubts. It's more like someone took a stuffed bear and put it on the rock as a joke.

"Is it dead?"

"No."

"How did you know it would be here?"

"He's been sitting there for three days. At least."

"Shut up."

"Swear to god!" Derwin takes off his hat, slings it over the stick shift. "I drove up here the day I got back into town. That's the first time I saw him. Right there, just like he is now. He looked at me then, but most of the time he stares at his paws."

"This is weird."

"Like his paws are something he didn't expect."

"This is a joke, right?"

"Like he's just figured out he has paws and still can't believe it."

"What if we get closer?"

Derwin kicks over the starter and crawls to the bend in the road, keeping his lights off. The way his engine screeches like the slow painful death of every exploited child since the Industrial Revolution should scare away any wildlife for miles, but it's like the bear doesn't even notice. We get close enough to see his ears twitch and his muzzle rise, just a hair like a cork floating in water, and for a minute I lose the ability to breathe. The bear stares at the truck. I swear I see him squint, like we're just becoming visible through a fog, or maybe like we're only the possibility of a thing he's trying to imagine. He looks young, a yearling. Is he blind and deaf? I guess bears are high enough in the food chain that even total sensory deprivation would still leave him with a fighting chance. And then, just like Derwin says, he goes back to looking at his paws where they lie, palm up, in his big bear lap.

"I've been back to see every day," Derwin says.

"What if we get out?"

"Of the truck?"

"Haven't you?"

"That's a motherfucking bear out there, dude."

"*The* bear," I say, and the words come out in a whisper like some other self inside me hijacked my mouth to say them.

"What?"

"Never mind. I don't know." I want so desperately to see the bear move. Off the rock, mostly. I feel this desperation for it to run away. That's what bears are supposed to do, right? If the town knew he was here they wouldn't stand for it. We'd all have this feeling inside like that bear better move or else. Bears can't just chill peacefully on rocks. The very fact of a bear just sitting and ignoring us is unacceptable. The papers would be all, *Why won't it move?* and outdoorsmen would say things like, *Only stationary bear's a dead bear,* and the cops and the forest service would be out here with tranquilizer guns, and even though you wouldn't be able to tell the difference they'd feel obliged to shoot him twelve times. Then they'd haul him deep into the wilderness somewhere to get him out of our minds. If a bear's going to just sit there he should have the decency to do it where we can't see.

I pull the handle and the door clicks open. I push it a couple inches and the hinges squeak. The bear does not move.

"Stay inside," Derwin says.

"Okay." I let the door rest, but don't shut it. "Now what?"

"I don't know. Take a picture? You got one of those fancy phones?"

No, because I left it at home. I feel like the victim of the same cosmic agency that makes damn sure cameras are broken, out of batteries, or able to take only low-resolution video whenever aliens or bigfoots come around.

"Should we go?"

"You want a better look?" Derwin says. "I can hit the headlights."

"No."

"Just for a second."

"What will he do?"

"He might look at us."

I hesitate. "No," I say. So far the bear has been mostly shadow, possibly a trick of the forest. "Okay, only for a second."

"Go for it." Derwin gestures to the lever that if I pull it, it will flood the mountain with light. But I can't do it.

"I can't do it," I say.

"Why not?"

I literally cannot force my arms to pull the lever. Like in a dream where you're being chased but you can't run and your legs refuse to move anymore than a slog and the harder you try the slower you go. I wouldn't quite call it fear.

"Right now he's on the edge of real," I say. "But if I turn on the lights he will either be real or he won't."

"Okay," Derwin shrugs.

"You do it," I say, and he laughs. Reaches. "Wait!" He waits. I shut the door. "Okay."

He reaches again. "No, don't," I say, but it's too late. He pulls the lever and every shadow cast by the texture of the hillside leaps away from me. The remaining space is pale and blinding. Then the bear comes into focus. He still doesn't move. He looks into the light. The bear's coat is the color of cinnamon and it's more fluffy than coarse; his face hasn't quite grown out of its cub features. His bottom lip is slack and I glimpse the white of his teeth. Glossy, black eyes swim in the glare.

Derwin kills the lights. Before my eyes can readjust I say let's go. He puts it in first gear and we drive up to a spot where we can turn around. I want the bear to be gone. And I want to see him again. I close my eyes so he can be both and neither. Derwin brings the lights back up and we cruise down the mountain. We start laughing at the same time.

"Did you see that, huh? What the hell, right?"

"I don't believe it," I say.

"Nothing like it. No one will believe a story like that."

"Just sitting there," I say.

"We can keep coming back. See how long he stays."

"Aren't bears scavengers?"

"They like to scavenge," Derwin says.

"That bear was not scavenging. That bear was sitting."

"That bear was lazy."

"Looking at his paws."

"Not much will fuck with a bear," Derwin says. "Wolf pack. Mountain lion sometimes."

"Trying to count. One paw, two paws. Bear breakthrough."

"Bear-fucking-breakthrough!"

We reach the bottom of the hill and take a long straight road back into town. I use this time to bring up Mirielle. Derwin kind of clams up when I say her name. "Was it weird to see her again?" I ask. He shrugs, shifts gears, spits out the window.

"I've got a girl," he says. Then he gets a gleam. "You want to meet her?" My shrug means yes.

Derwin takes a hard right and drives us through a neighborhood I've never been to on the north side of town. He puts the truck in neutral, pulls the parking brake and leaves the engine running.

"Well?" he says.

"Where are we?"

"You know Nate Pavelich?" Derwin says.

"What makes you think I'd know Nate Pavelich?"

"They're playing *Uprising* down there. Right now."

"Your girlfriend's there?"

"She's probably winning. Let's go."

The door to the basement apartment is six or seven steps

✹

down into a wooden enclosure where moths bounce like popcorn off a porch light. Derwin doesn't knock. We enter to a cloud of smoke and sheared green carpet. The cigarette burns on the couch blend with its '70s brown floral pattern. Dishes rise up out of the sink in a kitchen that's all just part of the living room. If I could pick any group to belong to it'd be the GSB. Not that I've ever met or talked to any of them, but these guys represent the coolest of the weird. Most of them just out of high school. They're so cool they don't even have to try. Other cool kids hate them is how cool they are. They know things; they do things. They have a mission. It's intimidating. The rumors are incredible —as in I'm pretty sure they all have to be lies. But just looking around the room I suddenly believe everything I've ever heard.

Most of the light of the room hangs out around an old dining room table where the kids drink wine out of plastic cups and pass around a bottle of some ancient single malt Scotch like it's a bag of corn chips. Nate's parents are loaded and he's used the better part of his trust fund on one of the state's finest and most comprehensive collections of liquor. Keeps it all inside an epic steamship chest inherited from his grandmother. He only ever breaks out a bottle for *Uprising* nights and other special occasions. One cigar makes the rounds. There are no empty chairs.

When we walk in the conversation is going everywhere. "—that's like two hundred and fifty million people for just two percent of all the wealth," is the first thing I hear, and the first person I see is a girl in blue eyeshadow whose black cherry lipstick accentuates strong zygomatic bones. That's gotta be her. Bre Running-Crane. Hair so black it's almost purple. Just the right kind of curvy. Dresses like a boy. She's wearing a couple of baggy t-shirts whose collars frame a black bra strap. Dark eyes behind round glasses. A slight underbite when she smiles. Lips kissable as fuck. Doesn't really seem like Derwin's type, but what do I know? She's talking about how language is hard-wired into the brain but mathematics has to be learned. She's insistent, vehement; stabs the cigar across the table toward Jonas, the guy she's arguing with, who only ever uses three facial expressions and whose voice never fluctuates in pitch or tone. He stares at her until the right space for his counter-argument comes along, then rattles it off regardless of who is listening or whether Bre decides to try and cut him off. More voices meld, some of them intent on the board game that is the object of the evening. *Uprising*.

Only Nate, blondish and dapper, acknowledges our entrance. He's got on a charcoal suit jacket, purple boots and the same kind of plain white t-shirt he always wears. I hover in the doorway and Derwin walks to the fridge, scrounges around for beer. "Drink whiskey," Nate says, licking his pale lips. "GSB."

"Yeah, yeah," Derwin pulls a green bottle out of the door, hovers behind Bre. She glances at him and he sort of awkwardly touches her shoulder. I know what he's doing. He's trying to fall in love. Everyone I know is trying desperately to get something they don't really want.

She says, "You have to wait for the next game. Who's the kid?"

"That's Lexie," Derwin says. "Brooks' best buddy."

Nate has a cousin on the East Coast who invented this game. *Uprising* hasn't really caught on except in some extremely nerd-type circles in New Orleans and Atlanta, but Nate got a prototype and everyone in GSB loves it, mostly because they get to come together over something that's just theirs. *Uprising* is a two-part game, where the first hour or so is spent developing your nation according to whatever government principles you choose, evolving from monarchies to oligarchies to democracies and back again. You're supposed to end up all sophisticated and modern and completely entangled in the politics of your opponents. At this point the endgame kicks in. Everyone undergoes a revolution in which there's a total power reversal and the most oppressed citizens rise to the top.

It looks like Bre's winning, which means there's a good chance she'll lose in the end. It's a tough line to walk. Nate says he loves the underdog effect and tries to play it up as much as possible. Luis, pretty much legally blind without his glasses, must've gotten screwed because he's already out of the game. He sinks into the couch, trying to solve one of those brass puzzles where you have to get the loops off the chain-links or whatever.

"I'm telling you it doesn't work like that," Bre is almost screaming now. "You don't have to teach language; humans will learn it just by being around it."

"Right, but this is what I'm saying," says Jonas, calmly glancing between his cards and Bre's chin. "There are mathematical fundamentals to which the same principles apply. Think about spatial awareness. Think about counting."

"Numbers have to be taught."

"Okay but you can count without numbers. You don't need numbers to count."

"Counting isn't math."

"An infant knows the difference between a pile of cookies and one cookie."

This is not the only argument alive in the room. Flynn McCord, who wears a baby blue t-shirt one size too small with gold glitter letters that say *World's Best Boy*, and Olivia Stang, whose face is half obscured by a jungle of red bangs, meander around a common GSB topic: the presence of Californians in the State. Olivia says, "At least Californians sometimes try to adapt to a country way of life," and Flynn replies, "Usually it's your typical spoiled asshole local country boy whose rich white daddy sits on a pile of money derived from generations of exploiting stolen land—these assholes want to live the illusion of having balls without putting in the work." Most of the gang agree. It's the name of the game around here. GSB: the *Grow Some Balls* club. They refer to themselves as rustic revolutionaries in a fight against wasteful technology. For example: speedboats. GSB hates speedboats. "Grow some balls, learn to sail," they say, and not only do they say it, they make stickers that say it and they slap those stickers on speedboats all around the state. Hunting's another big issue. GSB isn't anti-hunting but they consider anyone who shoots a non-aggressive animal with a gun to be the lowest form of pansy. "Grow some balls, hunt with a bow." Same with fishing: "Grow some balls, crimp your barb." The point is you don't belong here because of who your parents were, you belong here (or don't) because of how you engage with the land. These guys are on a mission to humiliate people who couldn't give a fuck about the land or about developing the courage and character required to manage it. The FBI website lists GSB under "terrorist activity." Mostly for property damage. Lots and lots of property damage.

Nate throws a corn chip at Derwin. "Where've you been?"

"Went to see the bear."

"You took *her*?" Her meaning me.

Bre laughs. "It's still there?"

"Yep," says Derwin.

"Can't believe no one's shot at it yet."

"Fucking hunters."

"Fucking guns. GSB."

"Hunt with a fucking knife and a hard-on if you think you're so badass."

"Pansy-ass wolf trapper bitches," Nate says. "Big man with a gun. Get in there with your teeth and see what happens."

"We should go back up. Take some pictures."

"It's almost Uprising," says Bre.

"The game's not going anywhere."

"The bear's not going anywhere."

Clayton told me Bre single-handedly blew up a stretch Hummer last year using explosives she could have gotten from Richey Buchan. Left behind her calling card written in Sharpie all over the wreckage. "Grow some balls, ride a horse."

That was officially the moment when GSB became a thing. I've heard they've filled coal trucks with jello. Put popcorn in exhaust pipes.

Luis keeps messing with the puzzle. Sometimes he just says random shit. Right now it's, "Everyone you meet knows something you don't."

"Dude, it's 9:37 already," says Jonas.

"I was just thinking it's *only* 9:37," says Bre.

Bre grew up on the Rez until her dad moved them into town because he wanted to throw her into a multi-cultural high school. Spends half her time with GSB and the other half working with an indigenous Canadian activist movement called *Gravel's End*, whose mission is to stand up for native rights and save the planet in the process. They've put together documentaries, ended fracking operations, organized the removal of small abandoned dams, set up railroad and highway blockades to prevent the building of pipelines—all using peaceful and more or less legal methods. GSB is her dark side.

"Minnesota lakes hit record temperatures this year," Luis says. "And the fish? They're eating each other."

"What the hell is that thing?" Jonas asks.

Luis holds up the puzzle. Nobody cares. "Whoever invented this is a person I hate."

Luis' frizzy red hair doesn't quite match his patchy red beard, perpetually struggling to grow out. Likes to wear blue hoodies and a pair of Keds.. "Did you guys know that the poorest half of the country only owns something like less than 3 percent of the wealth?" he says.

"Was I not just talking about that five minutes ago?" Nate says. He's usually wearing this small grey fedora that he picked up in Italy. Since I got here the hat has been on a couple heads. Bre drops it back on Nate and says, "Suits your face."

"Yeah but it goes with your hair," Jonas says. "Put it back on for a sec."

"Pretty hot." Nate smiles at her as she adjusts the brim. "Very '30s. You could be black and white."

Luis says, "Hey Nate, you want to go ride bikes later?"

Nate goes cross-eyed. "What am I doing tomorrow? No. I'm fucking busy. I'm picking up paint."

"Who says, 'ride bikes'?" Bre laughs.

"We could ride down and get some paint."

"I like it on Jonas," says Derwin. "Makes him look like a spy."

"He's totally a spy."

"You want us to carry nine gallons of paint on bikes?"

"You're never any fun."

Nate looks genuinely hurt. "I'm fun."

"Put it on the new kid."

Derwin snatches the hat off Bre's head and drops it on mine.

It's way too big for me, covers my eyes. I don't move. They all chuckle, but it doesn't mean anything. I'm nothing to them. Not that I'm desperate to become one of them or anything, not that everyone in the school isn't banging down my door to be friends with me. Obviously.

Jonas turns over a card. "Endgame, bitches."

"About fucking time," says Nate. "Break out the seeds!" The tradition is during Endgame all snacks and booze go away and the only thing anyone can eat or drink is sunflower seeds and water.

Derwin goes to the pantry. "Where are they?"

"Up top."

"Nothing here."

"There were six bags yesterday."

"Empty."

"Bullshit."

Jonas checks, then Nate. Someone looks in the fridge, under the couch.

"You have $10k in gin, but not one bag of seeds."

"We can't play like this."

"I could tough it out a round or two."

Jonas grabs his chest, falls off his chair and curls up fetal by the table leg. "The peasants are starving," he groans.

"Someone just go get some."

"GSB," Nate says, and everyone mutters it after him like some kind of litany, but no one moves.

Derwin nudges me. I see him flick a little nod toward the kitchen, and I look, but can't figure out what he's trying to say.

"It's like everyone in this town is on edge," Nate goes on. "Expects the world to end any day now. Mr. Treig puts his pennies aside to save the environment from global warning. Mi

111

psycho madre won't shut up about Galactic Alignment. Age of Aquariums, Age of Asparagums."

"Where's the seeds?" Jonas cries out to the ceiling.

"Bird flu and walrus flu floating around us! Millennialists and Zionists and Survivalists." Nate hops up and starts pacing. He talks like a preacher, waves his hands in the air. "We're all suckers for zombie this and zombie that, disaster flicks, conspiracies. See the headlines that the LHC is gonna turn space-time inside out and make it so the universe never existed at all. You read that shit?"

"My dad predicts the collapse of America within 70 years."

Derwin nudges me again. His eyes go wide over a crafty smile. "Silverware drawer," he whispers. I look again. I see one drawer that's slightly open.

"That one?" I whisper back. Derwin nods.

Nate's still pacing. "Did you hear in Africa they're considering a law where corporations will have to legally own their employees? That way they'll take a more vested interest and be encouraged to treat them better and take better care of them."

"Fucked up," Jonas says.

"True story," Nate says. "The worst part is it's kind of not a half-bad idea. Practically speaking. Like the sad thing is it might actually work."

Third nudge from Derwin. Okay, geeze! I guess I get up and walk to the kitchen. Making any sort of sound or movement is the last thing I want to do, but no one pays me any attention. I pull on the drawer and see a pile of forks and butter knives. I shrug back and Derwin flaps his fingers at me. I open the drawer farther, reach in and feel something like a plastic beanbag.

"Corporations are the problem," Luis says.

"Networks are the solution," Jonas says. "This whole polyamory thing. Thruples. It's a good idea."

"Poly's just legislated cheating," says Luis.

"That doesn't even make sense."

"World's too entangled anymore. Time to complicate the romantic calculus a bit."

"Imagine it," says Bre. "A network of complex self-correcting entanglements, an overlapping diagram of lovers. You could find someone who's your very favorite, but you might not be her favorite. The thing is, everyone will be someone's favorite, and they all hang out and do stuff together, coalescing as long as every party desires, to whatever degree initiated, with the goal of the greatest possible amount of love bestowed upon everyone involved. And way more potential for sex to be spontaneous and natural—like it should be."

This idea of a matrix of romance makes me stop, my hand still jammed in the drawer, resting on what I already know is a package of sunflower seeds. I picture a community of triads: two girls and a guy, two guys and a girl, all of them interlinked each night by whoever is not sharing the main bed. The odd-ones-out connect with each other like sexual clockwork that generates a rhythmic mandala energized by its own geometry and the free flow of distributed passion. I can see it unfolding in beautiful patterns when I close my eyes.

"I'm too alone to settle for just one soulmate," Nate says, "or to expect anyone I care about to settle for just me."

Bre slaps her hands together, commanding attention. "Monogamy is two people saying, hey I love you so much let's make a pact to never let each other experience this wonderful feeling ever again."

I'm standing at the edge of the table between Nate and

Derwin. I've got the sunflower seeds in both hands, holding the package up to my chest. Should I slam it down on the table or give it to someone or what? I don't know. Derwin's head wobbles. Everyone's laughing at what Bre said, just starting to subside. It's Luis who notices me first. "Hey, the new kid's got seeds."

"Seeds!"

"New kid. Did you just happen to have those with you?"

"Do you like always carry seeds wherever you go?"

I set them on the table. Nate picks up the bag and examines it in the light. Derwin pushes his fingers into my hair and scratches my head like a puppy. "See, she's cool," he says. Nate rips open the bag with his teeth, takes a mouthful and passes the rest down the table.

"Check this out, new kid," he says. "This is Uprising. This is Endgame."

8

TODAY I LEARNED NOTHING, TALKED to no one, and after school I wandered to work in such loops and swirls that from a distance the people of earth probably thought I was a wind-up toy. I barely touched the sidewalk. I hunted for grass, hopped up on rocks with both feet, and only ever stopped to examine cracks in the concrete or tie my shoes. I squeezed myself into old jeans, torn and patched, re-torn and re-patched. The plaid curtains of a mini-skirt over top, swishing my thighs. I didn't think a single romantic thought about Mirielle and I don't even care. By the end of the night they were calling me "seeds girl" instead of "new kid." It's filled me up, and I've got Derwin to thank. Now I just want to repay him, get him the woman he loves. He can have her. I don't want her. I don't. Why should I be hung up on someone who doesn't want me back? I feel electric, liberated, confident, more comfortable with the ground than ever before. What a thing to touch. To stoop down and run your fingers over the skin of the planet.

I'm a part of this. Everything I do and think and feel is a part of this. If the vision is real, it's a part of this; and if I'm insane, then that is a part of this too.

When I try to put it in words, this thing—if I stare myself

down in the mirror or whatever and say: "My purpose on this earth is to make sure my best friend's older brother knocks up the girl of my dreams so that their child can come into the world to either kick enough ass or come up with some brilliant idea to save us all from self-destruction"—when I think this in actual words I can only laugh. It's ridiculous, okay? I get it. But when I'm not thinking about it, when I'm distracted writing music or trying to come up with a real GSB zinger to like, impress the gang, that's when the emotion of it all starts to swell again, and sometimes I'm so consumed I can't function. I know have to do it even though it's absurd. Maybe because it's absurd. Go forth and do the stupid thing, Lexie. Feel the rushing wind. To whatever end.

Today the old prunes of Chestnut Homes squeeze into their foldy chairs and lean over their dinner trays like Generals analyzing plans of war. Brooks sits beside me, ripping open one of those weird "New Deli" Masala Lunchable things. He stacks all the bits and pieces on the back of a cafeteria tray, assembling squat sandwiches of naan, tofu, and paneer. Gives each one a dab of radium green mint chutney from a squeeze tube. Across from us, Darla wedges in between Terrance and Oliver, where they slurp spoonfuls of mashed potatoes and stab forks into tiny cubes of roast beef. Only their arms and jaws move. Torsos frozen in a like 20-degree tilt. They can't be bothered wasting the energy to lean back until all the food is gone. Ancients at the trough, their methods have been honed to perfection after a lifetime of practice. They chew deliberately, clear their throats, reach to slurp their milk or juice through straws from sparkly purple plastic cups with orange flower print patterns.

Terrance offers me a dinner roll. "You're not eating," he says.

"Not hungry," I say.

"Are you one of those anorexics? A binge-and-purger? Kids these days are stupid. In the '30s people would kill for a little meat on their bones."

"You weren't alive in the '30s," I say.

"This from a girl who thinks 1962 is ancient history."

"What'd you say?"

"Ancient history?"

"No, you said a year."

"1962."

"Why that year?"

"I don't know," Terrance says. "I just picked a year."

Other than this delightful topic, the cafeteria is free from conversation. I'm surrounded by six or seven dozen mouths committed to a single purpose. Hundreds of teeth—real, fabricated, or somewhere between—all in rows like the rows their owners sit in, all chewing in broken rhythms. Chewing, slurping, swallowing. Sporadic coughing and throat clearing and face scratching. From the confines of each isolated prison chair. Everyone but Pasha, who is more of a mural than usual, the lone man standing, flush against his chosen wall. Today he has with him a little potted plant, wedged into the crook of the elbow of the same arm whose fingers dangle a milk-dripping spoon's belly above a cereal bowl—this flat on the palm of his other hand in perfect suspense four or five inches beneath his parted lips. Gaze fixed on the plant's leaves. Pilea peperomioides, a Chinese money plant he usually keeps on a windowsill in his room.

I poke Brooks in the shoulder and ask him if he's nervous. Meaning about his VNS operation.

Brooks shrugs. "It's a simple surgery."

"But what about after. Do you think you'll change?"

He shakes his head. I can tell he's scared though. It's an

outpatient procedure, but I've never not been creeped out in a hospital. All I can hope is it does more good than harm. I want to hug him, but I know it would just make him feel nervous. Brooks quickly changes the subject and starts talking about how Derwin has been down at Hidden Needle all day hanging his photos for the Art Walk. Barren, bleak pictures of Midwestern landscapes, Arizona mesas, old abandoned grain silos and other ghost-town remains from the high line, empty train tracks, swamps, houses broken to shit by the wrath of god. He shows me a couple black and white prints, this one shot from below so in the foreground the dusty road leads to a kind of tin structure —maybe an old factory. Whatever was painted on the sign has faded to a skeleton of letters. An X, a C. The door padlocked and chained shut. Each tiny window boarded up. White clouds flare in a grey sky. Sloppy white paint on the siding that has become the canvas for anonymous messages: *T for Texas, T for Tennessee.*

"This is what he's been doing the last three years?"

"America is a wasteland waiting to happen," Brooks says. "That's what he thinks."

Derwin's obsession with America started when his mom ordered one of those '70s coffee table books about New Mexico. One image in particular: a man sitting in Acoma Pueblo, staring over the edge of the mesa, only the corner of one deep-set eye visible. Derwin would have come to America on his own if he'd had to. His real name is Dominik, after his father, but he changed it to Derwin because he likes the twang. Brooks always Brooks, and I'm not exactly sure why. When I asked him he didn't seem to understand the question.

"Did he show you the bear?" Brooks says.

"Yeah. You?"

He nods.

"Cool, huh?"

"No," he says. "It's not good."

"What do you mean?"

"You need to come over for dinner tonight. It's important."

Even for Brooks, he's acting really weird.

"What's she making?"

"Hungarian goulash. The good stuff."

"You're a traitor to your people."

"Not my fault Czech food is boring."

Brooks' mom is a savage cook. But it's the inevitable little kid pictures of Derwin that keep me coming back. Their younger brother, Gabe, who's like four, is another reason. I don't like to admit it but cuteness still has a lot of power over me. And then there's their nuts-as-balls grandma, this tiny 80-year-old lady who only speaks like six words in English that never make any sense. Eva managed to move her over a few years ago with the help of Life Swap production funds. They got her a visa and slapped together a special welcome-to-America episode.

When I lean my head on Brooks' shoulder, he stiffens a little, but lets me get away with it. "I want to," I say. "But I have homework. How about when school's done?"

He savors a pause. "Mirielle's gonna be there."

"Where?"

"At dinner."

I sit up straight. "What the actual fuck?"

"Mom loves her," Brooks says.

"Did you make this happen?"

"I suggested a call."

"And she said yes?"

"Derwin doesn't know," he says.

"Holy shit."

"Who's awesome?"

"What about Matthew Craig?"

"He won't be there."

"But okay, wait. She's really? Like, you mean—*her*?"

What is this feeling? Is it getting them in the same room together? Or is it getting her in the same room as me?

"It's kind of obnoxious the way you don't say her name," Brooks says.

I take a careful breath. "Mirielle." My voice is pleasant. Then I say it three more times.

I don't want her, I remind myself. *I don't want her.*

"I won't be able to focus at work now."

"Like you ever do any actual work."

My arms fall on the table and then my head falls on my arms. Will I really be eating actual dinner with Mirielle this time tomorrow? It doesn't seem possible. I can't even start to imagine what it might be like. I try to picture her and Derwin across from me, the two of them stammering, awkward and confused, but falling back in love. Caught in our spell.

I don't want her.

Brooks abandons his food for a minute. He digs out his camera and starts fiddling with it.

"Did you get new film?" I say.

He aims at the floor. The gears groan. He takes the milky print and leans halfway out of his chair, holding it toward the space by Pasha's feet.

"What do you see?" I ask.

"Just one," Brooks says. "Trying to tie Pasha's shoelaces together."

Pasha pokes at his plant with the nipple tip of his spoon's silver handle, folding a leaf forward so he can get a better look at some iridescent insect that's crawling there. I've read in Pasha's journals how sometimes he imagines what it's like to be that small, how at any particular moment something huge could come along at a high speed and squash you without either you or the thing that killed you even realizing it. He writes about how terrifying it would feel to always live with that possibility. Or what if the insect was hunting for food and it happened to crawl up on someone's shoe, and what if that someone happened to get up and hop into his car and drive even a mile away, which would be like a thousand miles to an insect, and then the little critter would have to live the rest of its days in a strange habitat far away?

Pasha doesn't really think this will happen to him if he steps away from the walls, but it's one of the stories he tells himself to make sense of why he can't take those steps. This is a guy who has to plan trips to the bathroom hours in advance.

He wasn't always like this, though. There was actually a time when Pasha was kind of a spectacle around town. Back when he lived in a shed out behind his daughter's house. Kept out of sight during the day, but at night he'd drag himself downtown to get liquored up at the Elephant's Den, which is like the diviest of dive bars, and what happened then became legendary.

Whenever Pasha Luski drank the right amount of liquor, in just the right combination, he turned into a woman. And what a woman!

The lineup had to be perfect. Whiskey alone wouldn't do the trick—he'd pass out too fast. Tequila put him in a grouchy mood. Too much beer and he'd just sit there laughing. If Pasha didn't kick off according to the right specifications there'd be no reason to stick around. But if he started with one shot each of Vodka, Apple Pucker, and Jagermeister, word would spread and kids would gather outside the bar below the little alley-side window waiting to watch the magic happen.

If it started at all it would start early in the evening, a few minutes before sunset. Pasha'd be sitting alone in his usual corner table. After the initial formula he'd move on to a glass of red wine, and here if you paid real close attention you could see the first changes—mostly in attitude. He'd sit up straighter and his eyes would go from a dead stare to an active curiosity about his surroundings. Sometimes he'd feel his shoulders and arms, maybe touch his face. In the dying daylight Pasha's profile would loom over scarred and swollen hands, cradling the chalice. Greasy matted grey hair hung down like frayed ropes. His skin always made me think of worn-out corkboard, pockmarked with scars and sores. Gaping nostrils. Eyes like broken clouds. Before the wine Pasha was only a pile of rags, but the minute he slid the second empty glass to the edge of the table his lips had plumped out into two bright red balloons. Here he'd raise his head and glance out the window—he did this every time like he was checking out his reflection. We all knew to duck down and count to fifty before popping back up. A shot of Old Granddad next, then a gin and tonic with for some reason a straw and frilly umbrella. With each sip Pasha's ragged beard would slurp back up into the pores of his face, and his hair would sprout out in long, nested curls whose shade became more and more blonde with each shot of peach schnapps. Three dark beers, then a Whiskquilameister and a Redheaded Slut. By the time he'd taken the last gulp of Guinness, crusty old Pasha would be a full-bodied bombshell.

Then she'd slip out of her coat and stuff it under the table. She always wore some or other sexy number underneath, strapless and buxom. She'd cap off the night with a martini and walk (and on this point most kids swear to god) walk without the slightest stumble toward the dance floor.

Brooks was with me the first time I ever saw it happen, and actually it's kind of how we became friends. Since we were among the smallest and youngest we usually got crowded out of decent window time. I'd occasionally catch a glimpse of the initial transformation, but as soon as Pasha was all-out morphing the bigger kids would form an impenetrable wall and I'd have to get the play-by-play second hand. This time Brooks and I ended up sitting beside each other, leaning against the bricks while the others stretched and shoved. The sun started to sink and shadows fell over his starchy grey corduroys. In that moment where the natural light outside dims just enough that the artificial light inside becomes visible, the pale yellow glow from the bar cut a scar down the side of Brooks' face, crossing his blue eye. His hair looked like a pile of sawdust. "I got you," Brooks said in that calm quiet voice I have never doubted since. He grabbed my hand and lifted me up on his toes, then somehow managed to hoist me onto his shoulders. My face mashed against the window just as Pasha's right hand brushed back a lock of honeywine hair. Her face turned toward the window and everyone ducked in the usual way, but being on shoulders I couldn't get low enough. The lower I ducked the higher Brooks would lift me. My head hovered there like a jack-o-lantern. Pasha looked me in the eye and smiled. Then she vanished through the back door into the dark caverns of debauchery I was just old enough to start fantasizing about, her ass swaying like a pendulum.

There were always rumors flying around about what happened to Miss Pasha on her nights of transformation. Stories ranged from the promiscuous to the slutty. I heard she liked to line them up in the bathroom, that she'd walk out with six or seven different guys, one at a time over the course of an evening. Now that I've gotten to know Pasha a little bit I think all she ever must've done was dance with the ladies and sip on a single martini until closing time, then drift off alone to change back to plain old Pasha at dawn. If I was a weird old dude who could turn into a bangin' fox at sunset I sure as hell wouldn't be out fucking a bunch of stupid frat boys.

"Dinner, huh?" I say.

"Yep."

The more I think about it the more I think I might be starting to panic. It almost seems too good to be true. What if it works? My heart hammers savagely against my ribs like my worst mistake beating its head against the wall.

I don't want her.

I feel my good mood slipping away.

Brooks hands me the photograph, all done. There's a weird white line on the otherwise bumpy grey image.

"It's a weird white line," I say.

"We're getting closer."

Now out of nowhere this whole thing with Derwin and Mirielle starts to feel like a huge mistake again. Two minutes ago it was everything perfect and real, the purpose and call surging through me like something essential to my survival. Both feelings I have literally felt on the tips of my fingers at various times. Feelings are the now of the body, and they solidify and dissolve with the lighting. What I feel or don't feel for Mirielle, and what I'm beginning to feel for Derwin and GSB—it's all messy, all overlapping. When a feeling leaves me I can't be sure it's gone for good and I sure as hell can't gauge when it might come back. Like how she's with Matthew Craig right now, but even that could be over in a second. Where will she sit at the dinner table?

Across from me? Beside me? Will I fill her water glass and wait for her smile? *I don't want her.* The words seem less and less genuine every time I think them. The memory of how it felt to want her swells up inside me. I miss it and resent its fading. Wasn't enough that I fell in love with a girl I will like never have the slightest chance with, but at least I still had the feeling. At least I still had the intention.

Yep. My good mood is definitely gone. I thought I had a handle on this. Like, seconds ago. Just pretending I had my shit together, I guess. Using the happy GSB feelings to overshadow all my hard questions. But my odds of getting in with those guys are about as good as Mirielle falling in love with me. I feel all of this. But I still don't feel like I have a choice. I don't. I want her. I don't. I do.

Poor Pasha slurps his cereal and I can hear it from all the way across the room. He's barely keeping it together: spoon, bowl, plant, and wall. How does a man who was once a town legend become such a shadow? The decades that must've chipped away at him, imperceptible nick and scratch after imperceptible nick and scratch until you're sliding along the walls without even enough volition to raise your voice. Things were easier when I was an idiot teenager in love, smoldering in bed and writing bad poetry. I want my heart back is what I want. I want to be Matthew Craig with the power to call up Mirielle anytime, to hold her hand, to breathe her in. I can see no path from here to there.

"Let's go," I say.

Brooks takes a snack tower, dips it in the masala sauce, bites down on it within an inch of my face. "Go where?"

"Wherever. Rec room?"

"Now?"

"Why not?"

"I have this… this city of food under construction."

"Fine," I say.

"You're a real grump today."

"I'm not."

Really, I'm not.

It's just a long time until tomorrow.

9

THE RICHTERS LIVE IN A double-wide by the river. I don't know exactly where their money comes from. Eva's garden shop job is only part time. I guess they still get stipend checks from Life Swap, but Brooks says they're smaller every year. Somehow Eva takes care her mom and Brooks and his little brother Gabe, and dreams of a day when maybe she'll have grandchildren. Back when Derwin was chasing Mirielle, Eva used to be totally nuts over her and she still wishes that things would have worked out between them. She's an ally here, is what I'm saying.

Brooks and I are the first to arrive. Derwin's probably still hanging pictures. It hasn't fully sunk in that in a few minutes Mirielle is going to be here, in the same room, maybe sitting right beside me. As soon as I step in the house a heavy feeling plunges from my ribs to my stomach. It'll be the first time they've been together in any significant way since he left, so this shouldn't be awkward or anything. But it's safe to say I have a mild addiction to drama, so I guess I'm looking forward to it.

The dinner table is solid oak. This and the fancy dishes are the only things of value in the house. I guess they brought all this family heirloom stuff over from the Czech Republic, and not much else. Eva keeps plants hanging all over the ceiling, lining the walls and covering the windows. Derwin called to say start without him but that's the last thing his mom will ever do, even with Brooks sulking around the living room moaning about starvation and child abuse. She marches us to the table and drops a plate of bread and butter between us. Little Gabe sits in a highchair coloring in a book of Aladdin cartoons. His hair's such a light shade of red that blends in with his scalp so well he almost looks bald. We gobble up the bread. Brooks shoves a piece in his little brother's mouth and Gabe bites and chews without a break in his coloring. Grandma stares at us all, one by one, not exactly smiling. Her glasses make boulders out of her eyes. Every time she looks at me I feel like she's trying to remember if we've met before.

Eva walks to the window and peeks between the drapes. The sun's nearly down. "Don't fill up on bread," she says.

"Let's just eat," Brooks says. He gets no reply, so he butters another one up for himself and one for Grandma. She touches it to her nose and sniffs before setting it down on the tablecloth. "Lepší doma krajíc chleba než v cizině kráva celá," she says to Brooks, pinching at the air in front of her like at his cheeks.

"It has come to my attention," says Brooks, "that my very life is at the mercy of an experimental mother who is being paid off by the government to report and analyze my response to hunger."

"Spearmental spearmint!" Gabe screams, looking up for the first time. His grin is a sailboat that slowly sinks over the horizon as his eyes wiggle beneath invisible eyebrows like a goofy pair of rising moons. His face takes on a kind of sudden serenity I've never seen on any other four-year-old, or anyone really.

Gabe's father is some douche from Minnesota who married Eva for almost two years and then left her with the kid. Eva gets some sort of child support but almost all of it goes to Gabe's tuition at a private pre-school for Buddhists. No one in the family is a Buddhist, and even Brooks can't explain Eva's obsession with giving her youngest son some religion. Gabe's father is the furthest thing from a Buddhist, but Brooks is convinced that he had something to do with it. I think it's because of everything that Derwin's been through. She's trying to fix problems before they start. I refer to Gabe as my little Bodhisattva and mess with him by insisting that the material world is all there is. When I do this he will either throw a fit, or, in more enlightened moods, shake his head and call me a child.

"Mom," Gabe says, loudly and distinctly.

"Yes, miláček," she answers from the kitchen.

"Is this being looking out through my eyes my ego self or my higher self?"

Brooks spews milk from his nose.

Eva comes in with a bowl of olives and gives us a hopeless look. Brooks wipes his face and regains something like composure. "What do you think, Gabe?" Brooks forms a spider out of his fingers and makes it dance on his brother's blush of hair.

Gabe ponders for a quick sec. "I think it's my higher self."

"Sounds good to me," says Brooks.

I sneeze without warning.

"Zdraví! That was a mighty one. Are you okay?"

"Yeah, no I'm just randomly allergic to things."

"She's allergic to enlightenment," Brooks says.

"Everyone is 'lightened at all times forever," Gabe screams triumphantly, flinging a rainbow of crayons into the air.

Eva sets the olives on the table. Slimy green olives that look like those cocoon pods from the movie Alien.

There is a wooden knock that sends a chill up my legs.

"One moment," Eva sings, moving across the brown shag carpet to open the door.

"Hi, Ms. Richter."

Her voice. The only instrument I would ever need. My skin feels like snow on a volcano. Okay, I was wrong. I understand now. Of course I still want her. She's all I want. Take me, enslave me, put me in a box. My abdomen aches; my throat clenches up. If I could just spend my life standing beside her, invisible, present, lost in her footsteps. She is too close and not close enough. I can see only the top of her head past Eva's shoulder. She's here for me.

Eva steps aside and Mirielle enters the room. She's wearing loose jeans and a blue t-shirt with a fake brown leather jacket and shin-high boots. Eva reaches up to untangle the swaying legs of a spider plant that have snagged in her hair. All of us are watching. Even Gabe has taken on the countenance of silent observance. Somebody's going to have to say something. I could do it. I could say something.

"Oh, my dear, it's been so long," Eva says with a mellifluous lilt that is a little too enthusiastic to be convincing. "How beautiful you are. So grown up. Welcome to our home. Please sit down. Dinner is almost ready, and Derwin should be here any minute." She leads Mirielle to the seat directly across from me. I consider offering her some bread.

Eva makes introductions to Grandma in Czech, and Mirielle blushes. Grandma doesn't speak or even attempt to smile. Gabe is back to his purplization of Princess Jasmine's face with the single crayon remaining on his tray, and Mirielle comments on how big he's gotten. "And you know Brooks and Lexie," Eva says. She knows me. She knows me.

The thunder of his bike rattles the windows. Eva rushes back and opens the door for her eldest son, who comes in without looking around. He hangs his leather jacket on the back of the door, and then reaches down to pick a crayon up off the carpet. It's at this point I think he finally gets a sense for how quiet the room really is, and I start waiting for the sparks to fly. When he looks up and sees her I can't decipher his eyes' peculiar gleam. There is one empty seat beside her, and one at the head of the table.

"No one told me there'd be a party," he says.

Mirielle doesn't look up.

Derwin kisses Grandma on both cheeks, leans over to draw something in crayon on the coloring book until Gabe acknowledges him. Keeps turning his head toward but not directly at Mirielle.

"You are not vegetarian, are you?" Eva says.

"No. Thanks for asking." When Mirielle speaks her eyes dart around the room like she's absorbing the scene one random atom at a time. When she falls silent she picks a safe place to settle her gaze. Right now she's staring at my hands. She thinks my hands are safe. Eva comes out of the kitchen with a crock pot of steaming goulash, sets it in the center of the table and tells us to dig in. Our bowls are already full of dumplings and covered with cloth towels to keep the heat in. Eva beckons me to serve myself. Brooks goes next. Derwin dishes up for everyone else. When he gets to her he slows down. They look at each other for the first time.

"I am so happy all my family is together again," Eva says. "And you girls are family here, too. Eat, eat!"

"It smells delicious." Mirielle takes small bites using only the tip of her fork.

Eva brings Derwin a pilsner in a skinny green glass. Derwin eats fast, Brooks eats slow. Derwin is a Leo. A lot of people forget that because he doesn't really get in your face or muscle for the limelight. I don't believe in astrology, for the record, but well maybe I do a little.

"So, Mirielle," Eva says, "this is your last year of school?"

"Yes."

"Are you moving away for college?"

"I don't know," she says, her voice reserved. "I might take a year off."

"That can be a wise decision."

"I don't really know what I want to do yet."

Grandma stops eating. She puts her spoon on the table and the dark red juice seeps into the cloth. She leans forward and points at me. "Little," she says. "Fat." What the fuck, Grandma?

"You have time," Eva says. "I believe you will figure it out."

Mirielle's faint smile is the delicate undergrowth in her forest of dark mascara and nervous eyes. I think tonight she might be using makeup to hide how pretty she is. She seems cagey, cautious. I try not to stare. I feel a draft and wonder if they left the door open, but when I look there's no door at all. Just an open arch with darkness beyond. I think I sneeze again but no one seems to notice. I shouldn't be here. Everything is going to change soon. I can feel it.

"Who are you?" Gabe asks.

"That's our friend Mirielle, my little guru," Derwin says. "Enlighten us, Gabe."

Gabe says, "Okay," and keeps eating.

"I bet you're happy to have your son back," Mirielle says. Suddenly there's intention in her voice.

"Yes."

"Your English has gotten good."

Eva blushes. "Thank you. I still have a hard time finding the right words."

"We've been covering the Cold War in civics class. What was that like, growing up? If you don't mind my asking."

Derwin laughs. He shoves a forkful of dumplings in his face. "Everyone asks."

"It is important," Eva says. "A good question. This was a hard time. My father owned a farm outside Kutna Hora, but the government took it away. My husband drove a truck. We only tried to make our children happy."

"I had a great time," Derwin says. "They let us stay in a little house on the farm. The army used the land and some old buildings for storage. Still lots of places for me to run around. Climbing on those green trucks all the time. And soldiers. One time there was a tank."

"Then you moved here?"

"After the revolution my husband became the mayor of a district in Prague," Eva says. "We left. The life was not for me."

"I remember thinking America was all cowboys and gangsters and drugs," Derwin says.

An awkward silence follows, but I'm not exactly paying attention anymore. Something's changing in me and around me. I'd never even like considered sitting around having a normal conversation with her. It creates a dissonance in my mind that tries to drive her away, back to her mythical status, and it's pushing everyone away with her. I still hear them talking, I still hear voices, but more voices than I should be hearing. The lights seem to dim. Grandma picks up her bowl and puts it back down.

"Derwin has always seemed so American," Mirielle says.

133

"I am proud of all of my children," Eva says. "They are not like everyone else. This is good."

"Especially Brooksy," Derwin says. "Remember that time when he was Gabe's age?"

"Oh god," Brooks mutters.

"Okay so listen to this!" Derwin parks his fork in his bowl and turns to Mirielle in full-on storyteller mode. Even as guarded as she is right now, they seem comfortable together. Like they could melt into one another. "You know the trick parents use with their kids when they're out in public and the kid won't come along because he's just into his own thing, and the mom always says something like: 'I'm going now, Brooks. I'm leaving. Goodbye,' and usually the kid panics and runs to his mother, right? Not my little brother. Brooks just says: 'Ok, bye,' and takes it as a sign to wander closer to whatever he was into. I don't even remember what."

The voices in my head are growing louder, making it harder to concentrate on Derwin's story. I look through the darkness of the doorway. Small blue lights sparkle in the corners of my eyes, and I sneeze. I don't realize it until a second after it happens. I hear Grandma chanting some soft Slovakian rhyme, but when I look her mouth is closed and she is staring at her reflection in a spoon.

"And Mom just stands there, right?" Derwin is across from me but his voice seems to come from behind. "Too stunned to do anything. She looks at me and I know what she's thinking. So I let her walk away while I stay back. 'Goodbye, Brooks,' she keeps saying, but he doesn't care."

"All my sons have found early independence," says Eva with pride. I find it strange but not unnerving that the door has vanished off its hinges. My periphery goes black, conforming to a space of intense focus until I can no longer see anything. But I know my eyes are open; I can feel myself blink.

"He's wearing this big blue coat and a little wool hat with earflaps, and he's waddling over to this table—we were at a market or something. He was a chubby kid."

"Fat," says Grandma.

"Fat," repeats Gabe, a voice from the far end of a tunnel.

"I was not," Brooks says, like a whisper or a thought in my own head.

And then I'm no longer in the room. Suddenly it's like I'm wandering through narrow streets in some crowded medieval town. That's my experience, fading in like a screen over the dining room, like a filter or a projection. Brooks and family get lost in the horde of hundreds of scrambling, terrified villagers trying to prepare for whatever's coming. They're all saying, *It's coming*. Women grab their children by the wrists, hoisting them onto shoulders or clasping them tight against their breasts. Skinny men cluster by the walls, trembling in armor that doesn't fit. I don't share the sense of urgency. I consider the faint memory of having recently been sitting at a dinner table. This is nothing like imagining. I walk slowly as the crowd surges around me. I hear music up ahead, drifting down a narrow alley. A drumbeat of raindrops and here comes the song of what must be some long-necked gourd with a hundred strings. Then a clarinet. I turn.

"I wanted to see what he would do," a woman says.

"He was pulling on the man's tablecloth. He was a little troublemaker."

I barely hear their voices. Then the trill of a bird in a tree becomes Eva's fond giggle.

"I don't remember any of this," Brooks says. "For the record."

The people are packed too tightly here, struggling to get through the alley. But for some reason I can slip between them all without any problem. Someone screams, a little girl in a pink skirt and Hello Kitty scarf—a scream of delight, I realize now, seeing her face. She's dropped her ice cream and instead of crying she thinks it's hilarious. Her mother is hysterical and babbling. In English. These people are tourists.

Derwin's disembodied voice drifts by: "He would have wandered off on his own forever. That's when I knew he had mental problems."

"Dominik," Eva scolds.

"He knows I'm joking."

"He takes everything you say seriously."

"Mental problems," Gabe nearly yodels. I'm still hearing all this like from around the far bend of the stone corridor.

"You're the one who jumps onto subway tracks." The voice belongs to Brooks, but it comes from the mouth of a soldier at the wall.

I can imagine Eva's eyes admonishing her oldest son. Brooks is her baby. "You need to grow up," she says. It's like a threat. My head wobbles and I can feel the wood of my chair in my hands. I wonder if, back in the dining room, I'll fall.

"Fat," Grandma says.

"Just because you left home does not make you grown up," his mother says.

"What happened?" Mirielle's voice breaks through the fog. "Did you have to stop him?"

"He found me. I thought I was hiding real good. But he just looked over his shoulder and saw me and walked up to me and he says, he says—" Derwin stops to laugh. We all wait. A storm is coming. I can no longer distinguish faces in the crowd.

"Domi, he says to me... *you better go with Mom*, he says. He actually says this."

I know Brooks won't be smiling because he hardly ever smiles, but I'll bet he's happy. This is a story of respect. Eva refills everyone's glasses. I follow the effervescence, walking further along the cobbled stones until I reach the source of the music. Here a trio of men with short beards play their instruments in a small plaza of flagstone and orange trees under a red archway. Playing a song about the Tongue. For all those who fear it, there are just as many who welcome the inevitable: the sustenance and the oblivion it brings. The crowd's pressure builds against the narrow alley walls and in a rush they flood the square. The drummer leaves the strings to a solo while he gets up to dig out an extension cord from a hole in the cathedral wall. He connects it to an electric keyboard and I see red lights flash. There is a boom like a battering ram striking the gate. *It's coming*, someone says. I see soldiers on the walls. An old man pushes past me, carrying palm fronds. Splinters of wood and fragments of stone soar overhead. The soldiers don't move; what can they do? In the alley two dark-haired young women sway their hips. Their hands clutch heaps of hair. Someone asks me for change, shaking a crumpled paper cup in my face. The distant sounds of screams oscillating between panic and ecstasy, the rumble and grind and splash of crumbling walls. This mix is fucked. Bass is essential but show some versatility, people. An old woman grabs my shoulder and spins me around. She is sickly and yellow, all rags and glasses. There is dirt in her hair. Dried saliva cements the cracks of her lips. "To the sea," she says.

The woman takes my hand and drags me down an empty street. Looking back I see the courtyard has exploded into an all-out dance party. Two girls grind in slow motion, one of their backs to a tree. Ghostly and androgynous forms distend from the branches to smell her hair. In the foreground several small children tie a man to a rock with an anchor's rusted chain. A girl shoves a t-shirt into his mouth to stop his screaming. Brooks throws a dumpling at Derwin. They laugh like brothers. Eva allows herself the shadow of a smile. Mirielle's hand falls close to Derwin's like a dove landing on the edge of a basin. Less than an inch and they'll be touching. The courtyard is gone. I'm sitting here blinking and realizing the shape of this room and the people around me and there's a voice in my head assuring me that I've been here the whole time.

Derwin leans over and whispers something to Mirielle, who for all the defensive congeniality she's trying to give off can't help a genuine smile that's exactly like someone flicking a cigarette lighter in a dark room, and this is the only clue I need to know they've been in touch for months, even while he was gone and not contacting Brooks at all. Maybe they even met up somewhere—I'm thinking Memphis over Spring Break, where they stayed together in a shitty hotel room for a couple days and made out in a hallway at Sun Studios where Rock and Roll was born. He brushes something off her shoulder. She hooks her pinky finger around his, then thinks better of it and lets go.

But that touch is enough. I picture myself pushing Derwin casually off the side of a bridge. My image of him doesn't react, just falls like a man asleep. She's mine.

Mine.

"So. Oklahoma?" I say.

I've never felt so in control of a room in my life.

The walls continue to wobble. I see stone, brick, stars. No one knows how to respond to me, but Mirielle narrows her eyes at Derwin, which I think yes this was probably my intention.

"It's just I heard you're moving again." I'm saying these things.

Derwin considers his response. "I was thinking about it," he says cautiously. He smiles at his mom. "You know me, no real plans."

"Is Bre going with you?" I ask.

In the quiet portion of my mind a little voice tells me this is not what I want to be doing right now, but I can't stop. She belongs to me, see, is the thing. My question goes unanswered. Brooks kicks me under the table. Derwin reaches for his beer. I look to Grandma for some kind of escape, but strangely she's already watching me, staring into my eyes before they even find her face.

Mirielle's body stiffens. "Bre Running-Crane?" Her gaze furrows first into the table and then into the side of Derwin's head.

I see them laughing, stumbling through a doorway near the Elvis exhibit. He's moving backwards, pulling her by the hands. Their foreheads are touching and she's unbuttoning his shirt. He spins her around and pushes her gently against a wall. I can't stop this.

"You're fucking *her*?" Mirielle's voice cracks.

Three of Eva's fingertips dart to her lips.

All Mirielle needs is a single second of Derwin not saying no.

"I knew something was—" she says. "That you could even —" Her chair topples as she stands, the wood sinking into the carpet. Her resolve crumbles. Her shoulders go limp. I pinpoint the slight extrusion of the brace through her jeans, an outline I could identify in the dark. A rapid and nearly inaudible stream of words accompanies her rush toward the door. She turns to walk out, stops, faces Derwin. I've never seen hatred like this.

"You're an asshole," she hisses. "I can't believe I ever felt the slightest bit of anything for you."

"Mir," Derwin pleads, scrambling to his feet. His knee hits the table and goulash splashes over the edge of my bowl.

"Fuck you," Mirielle says.

"This is our home!" Eva's trying to remain calm. She loves everyone, but everyone hates each other. I can see her heart breaking over whose side to choose, and how thoroughly to choose it.

But her words do the trick. Mirielle's eyes widen and soften. There's fear. She can't even choke out an apology. She stutters, turns, and runs out the door. I hear heels striking the sidewalk. Derwin runs after her, slamming the door behind him. On the way out his shoulder hits the hanging plant that had just been creeping Mirielle's hair. Swaying on nylon cords. The back-and-forth motion gives me something to watch, a safe place to direct my attention.

Eva tries to smile it all away. The maternal instinct for damage control. "Who wants coffee?" She starts filling our cups whether we say yes or no. Brooks stares at me like I'm crazy. We hear shouting from outside. Mirielle's voice thin and fierce and distant: "Get the hell away from me!" Grandma finally starts eating her food. Eva can't stop moving around the room: clearing plates, shuffling containers of leftovers, scrubbing the counter. We are just waiting. There's nothing to say. I'm alone with the memory of city walls and the smell of the sea that throttles an archway of torch-teased shadows. I can feel the old woman behind me, Grandma's hunting eyes. The silence amplifies the smack of her lips over warm goulash.

I hear Gabe's small voice, "Now that I've burned down my house I can better see the sky."

✳

When Derwin comes back his head hangs low. He isn't angry with me, just confused. He goes for another beer. His mother follows him, touching the back of his head. They talk without words by the open refrigerator. Grandma's hands flat-fisted, knuckles on the table's edge. She's downright peering into me now, eyes in slits, brow wrinklier than ever. I wonder if Eva will move her to Chestnut Homes. She leans forward with a gradual body stutter like she's starting to fall asleep, but her eyes are burning, telling me to go. Her head sinks lower and lower toward her plate. Her lips twitching and murmuring, lapping like little waves. "Fat," she whispers. She's telling me to go after her, chase the object of my desire. There is no life for me until I do.

Vines grope at me as I walk outside. The darkness beyond the porch could be anything. I hear Brooks call my name. Out here the city walls give way to soft earth and quilts of grass. The trees cluster to the north, and to my left I see the Tongue. Truly as wide as a river, flowing across the hills from where it bisected the village, sloping peacefully now down into the street and between orange rocks to this grassy cliff overlooking the sea, where it suddenly plunges underground near the crumbling remains of an old courtyard mosaic in the tall grass. We are illuminated only by a gibbous white moon. I cannot see the dark water except as an extension of the night sky swooping down into an undercurrent that crashes against the shore far below the cliff's edge. The cathedral on the hill has been crumbling for centuries. The apiary has rotted and burst and the bees no longer swarm the meadow. I pass between towering corpses of stone, a buttresses from some long-toppled wall like jagged shards in a broken window frame, and on the ground: a million colored stones, illustrating a single tree from end to end. Branches of purple and brown. Instead of fruit, animals sprout from the budding twigs. Grotesque sea creatures on the lower branches; sleepy beasts in the middle; birds, griffins, basilisks and other winged nightmares at the heights. The branches expand horizontally from the canopy in absurd lengths that circumscribe the outer sphere of the mosaic until they wrap back around where dragon tails and worms tangle up in the tree's roots. I know I've seen something like this in Pasha's notebooks. A woman stands alone beside a dead tree. Her hair is drenched with honey. But when I try to touch her, all I feel is water dripping down her face, bubbling up out of her head. It's only a stone statue—a fountain in a neighbor's yard. I put my fingers to my lips. The far end of the ruin, where the Tongue vanishes, is overgrown with thorns.

Something stirs in the grass, a wall of fur.

Mirielle slumps in her white hatchback, forehead on the steering wheel, hair hanging down. She's sobbing. The streetlamp I mistook for the moon cuts halfway across her face. I step into the road and she lifts her face. Our eyes meet. The look I get is impossible to read. She starts up the engine, and the sound is like waves breaking over rock. A fan belt squeals with a seagull cry and I watch her tail lights shrink far down the empty road until they burn like torchlight. Something is on fire. The bear moves from the corner of my eye to the back of my head. I turn and turn but all I see are little trailer homes trapped behind sagging fences. The orange light keeps flickering. I spin circles and it stays just out of reach. I'm lost in the mosaic, crawling through the grooves of a turtle's shell. The black clouds are poisoned. The lights draw near. Two torches held in gloved hands.

I'm shaking. At first I think it's just the cold, but then I realize I'm doing this to myself, forcing my deltoids and trapezius muscles to contract violently. My shoulders shudder. My head vibrates. I bring the lights in and out of focus and my imagination follows. It's all bullshit. This is not a seizure, this is not a vision. It never has been. It's me forcing myself into the symptoms that I've always read come along with prophecies and face-to-face hookups with gods. Like trying to get a scar by wearing bandages. I keep telling myself this even as the tremors take on a life of their own, feeding back, seizing control, and suddenly I couldn't stop if I wanted to. The foundation of this fraudulence forms a reality I would otherwise never experience. I lie at the foot of an old man's deathbed. Nurses bring him a newborn. At the moment of his passing he will concentrate intently on what it must feel like to be that infant, and when his heart stops his soul will launch into the child instead of the void. He wants to show me how it's done, but I can't understand. My vibrations are all wrong, he says. He tells me that the secret to life lies in sharing the madness of God. A nurse hands me a hot orange coal, and though it burns me I can't let go. We enter an age of comets and calderas, neutron bombs, a war between super viruses. My flexors and abductors constrict impossibly into the heat until the coal fuses to my fingers. I'm covered in ants. My body thrashes around my spine like I'm trying to throw off my skin. My mind fills with the melting coal's pale glow—a ring around a hole I'm burning into my memory. It only vaguely sinks in that anything is happening at all.

Muscular and visual tremors escalate with violence until chaos resonates into unity, like the dissonant peak before sound coalesces into harmony, and suddenly I phase into a feeling so calm and pure and so little like a dream I can only be more awake than I've ever been. I'm in the same place, still on the cliff, but now I inhabit the body of an old man. Standing in the dark grass, aware of every spider nest and snake hole and dazed rodent's eye. I know that I've come on a long journey, following the Tongue across mountains and forests and deserts. I've abandoned my friends and my home. I've been wandering for years, and my quest has taken so long that it has redefined itself. I decide maybe it would be okay to die here on the edge of this cliff. It's a decision I've had to make every day, where it would be okay to die. By enemy hands, or the slow jaws of hunger, or by the sting of some poisonous thing, or lost in the fatal euphoria of the Tongue. I might die in the next ten minutes. I might make it down the cliff only to slip and kill myself accidentally at the last ten feet. I might die lost and forgotten in a sandstorm. I might make one small error that leads to an inescapable and foolish death. I need to be aware of this, and be okay with it, and every day I've made the new decision that I am. Okay with it. So I can press on.

My finger burns and itches. The bear sits on a stump, staring at his paws. I look out over the bay and see a white city floating on the waves, hovering in a narrow muted space of mist or mirage. The city's skyline juts up toward the moon like the profile of a key, and the sky accepts its complementary shape. I see the world thrown off its axis, where a double helix coils around the world tree, choking off the water supply. When the old gods die we still have our jobs to do.

Then I see her. She stands in the middle of the Tongue, directly on top of its slathered surface but impervious to its allure. She has Mirielle's eyes and Derwin's nose. All the failed leaders of the planet surround her—they're trapped, snared in the Tongue's sticky saliva. She must be eight or nine here, but everyone looks to her for guidance as civilization collapses around them. She kneels down to trace words on the Tongue with one finger. She has something special, a secret plan. Something so brand new no one has ever come close to thinking of it before. Something so ancient they all feel they should have known all along. Carving letters into the Tongue with her fingernail. The people around her seem to understand, and one by one they start to get up off the Tongue and walk away. She's changing the whole goddamn fate of the planet right there in front of the corner of my eyes. I know who she is. I know who her parents are.

10

THEN I'M LYING FLAT ON the clean tucked sheets of an orange gurney. My mother brisk beside me, holding my hand as EMTs with rolled-sleeves and blue gloves wheel me toward the flashing hazards of the ambulance. I feel empty. They've removed all of my inner organs. A firetruck nearby for moral support. I'm wheeled through slats of darkness on a carousel of streetlights. My mother signs something on a clip board and Derwin shakes the driver's hand. All engines revving. I turn my head, looking for a last glimpse of the Tongue before I'm swallowed in through the yellow-and-black stripes of the ambulance's back doors, and suddenly I recall the very first memory of my life. A bee sting. I'm three or four years old, standing on a little lawn of some house I don't even know where, looking at some flowers that I think were probably actually weeds—feeling like they were some distant part of myself. The bee landed on my right digitus secondus. I remember the surprise of the sting and the sudden awareness of my finger. I must have touched it without thinking, and that's when it stung me.

Later I'm running in circles, squealing. I can't recall if it's terror or delight. Now it's naptime and I'm in a dark room and we're all lying on mats in this like starburst formation. Heads in the middle. I'm paralyzed. When everyone wakes up and goes out to play I stay curled up like a fetus, embarrassed because I pissed myself. Several moments of complete panic where not even my mother can comfort me. I'm screaming and all the sounds and colors and smells of the world rush into me. I'm absorbing too much at one time. Random words haunt me and I repeat them over and over, sometimes for hours.

These reflections occur to me sequentially as I drift in and out of consciousness. The ambulance shifts into gear and starts to roll. I'm chambered in soft polygons of white light. Out the window I see Derwin's hand fall on Brooks' shoulder, while his other takes his mother's. Neighbors watch from porch steps thinking, *One day they'll come for me too.* My head tilts back. My fingers uncurl. I'm missing the whole chunk of time between collapsing in the street outside of Brooks' house and the arrival of the ambulance and of my mother who helped me onto the gurney even as the paramedics kept trying to hold her back. This has all happened before.

When I'm five years old I get something in my eye and my mother pretends she's cutting a window in my eyelid so the thing can come out. "Palpebra," she says. She makes me say it back three times.

She moves us up to Santa Cruz where we live in a tiny apartment close to the water. I still can't swim very well so I never go in. Me and the ocean, we only look at each other across the sand. I start to pretend that the beach is another world, my own made up place. There's a cave beneath a cliff where my mother takes me by the hand and leads me over the seaweed-skinned rocks and we hunt through tide pools for starfish and I poke around sea anemones until their sticky green tentacles gobble up my fingers. But I never go in the cave.

My mother steps out in front of a car and fractures a hip. They take her in for psychiatric evaluation and I stay with a friend of the family for the weekend, but I don't go to a foster home because my mother swears on a bible that it wasn't a suicide attempt. The first time I see her in the hospital she won't look me in the eye. She wears a yellow gown. A two-inch strip of milk-white tape fixes the needle to her hand. This becomes the image that pops into my head whenever I hear the word *fragility*. We keep moving north.

The heads of grown-ups occasionally block out the overhead lights. I'm lying on my back, staring up at the roof as the ambulance roars and turns. I feel no pain. They're running tests, checking my temperature, my blood pressure, my oxygen levels. I only vaguely understand their questions. They listen to my chest through a stethoscope and tell me to breathe.

The most scared I've ever been was when I was about six and I tried to comprehend infinity for the first time. I'd won a gold star in school for counting. The game was we had these long scrolls of paper and we were supposed to write as many numbers as we could, one on each line. A beautiful rising sequence. I can't think of any reason they had us do this except to keep us busy. I wrote the most numbers. I don't remember how many. Thousands. Every other kid got sick of it and stopped. They have to take the scroll away from me because I just keep going. That night in bed I continue counting. I can't fall asleep. Sometime before dawn I wander into my mother's room. I'm hysterical. "It never ends," I say.

When my mother quizzes me about anatomy her fingertips fall on various targets on my body and I'm supposed to respond with muscle, bone, and nerve cluster. Sometimes I give the wrong answer on purpose, but she can tell whenever I do this and she ignores me and moves onto the next spot.

I am 100 trillion cells, 100 billion of which are neurons. I am 800 muscles. I am 78 organs. I am 206 bones. A community of 100 trillion bacteria live in my guts. Trillions of microbes establish colonies on my skin. I am innumerable thoughts and fleeting feelings. What is atomic and enduring from one heartbeat to the next is a name, a fingerprint, a Social Security number, a recognizable shape, a DNA signature. I am decomposing and reconstructing simultaneously at all times. I am legion. I am whole.

They recommend an overnight stay for observation. Just precautionary, they assure my mother, in case of head trauma when I hit the ground. She asks what's wrong with me. This bald old EMT who smells like vaseline says he wants to get me in for a psych eval in the morning. I overhear another doctor tell my mother there's nothing physically wrong with me. They tell her the best thing to do is feed me drugs and make me sleep. My mother demands that they take us home. Starts screaming at the driver, ordering him to turn around, turn around right now and drop us off.

When I'm about seven or eight we drive through the Nevada desert. My mother takes me to a place without visible elevation on any side. The flattest land I've ever seen. We stop the car and watch the horizon for over an hour. I wonder if I'm actually breathing during the times I'm not thinking about breathing.

I dress like a boy, put my hair in braids, get in a fight in third grade and break a girl's tooth. They suggest putting me on meds but my mother won't let them. My cousin Max in Ashland gives me his old CDs: Throbbing Gristle, Whitehouse, Velvet Underground, SPX, Interpol. I listen to them on my mother's laptop every night through shitty headphones. Max tells me about sex. He says the best sex he ever had was with this girl and neither of them got off. They just did it until they couldn't move anymore and lay there shuddering and he fell asleep inside her. I find it all disgusting and fascinating. I finally know every inch of my body and the Latin names that comprise it.

We keep moving north.

Somehow she talks them into it, or drives them crazy enough, and the ambulance swings back and pulls up next to Brooks' house. He and Derwin are still on the porch, not talking, just floating around with their eyes. The paramedics me up and now I can walk okay, but I'm still shaking. They inform my mother for the millionth time that it'd be better to go to the hospital. She ignores them and helps me down onto the street and leads me to her car. Looking out the window I see Brooks waving at me, but I can't remember out how to wave back.

I feel clueless about the world. I read everything I can get my hands on. There was this phase where I worshipped Tesla as a god, but then I found out about how when he was old a pigeon visited him at his window every day and he said she was his soulmate. Somehow this made him accessible, and that was the last time I ever fell in love with a man.

I listen to Depeche Mode's *Violator* over and over on a long road trip after visiting my grandparents out East. I put one song on repeat and I just keep letting it play and watch the plains drift by and the mountains rise out of the fields until twilight turns to night, and somewhere between the reflection in the window and the world outside I see a crack of pure white light opening a door into another world. I think about reasons why no one ever remembers falling asleep.

One day I become fascinated with the texture of a door

frame and when my mother opens it I get my little finger caught in the hinge, slicing off a bit of flesh. She rushes me to the ER so they can sew it back on. "Digitus minimus tertius," my mother says, and she makes me mimic her as the lidocaine surges through the extensor sheath. First pain, then no pain.

She meets this bald guy with a mole on his neck and we all move to a farm in southern Oregon to join a cult. They don't call themselves a cult, but I think fifty people praying to a basket of flowers three times a day probably counts. They're okay I guess. Mostly entirely self-sustaining. They generate their own electricity. Pomegranate trees and veggie gardens and compost piles and goats for milking and bee boxes and the windmill I'm not supposed to play around but do anyway. I get along with the kids okay. The oldest girl is Charlie, who always talks shit about the cult even though it's her folks who run it—or maybe that's why she does. She secretly sneaks in tracks from the San Francisco electronic music scene and we share headphones to listen.

During the ride home I start to scream and cry. I insist that I'm in love. I'm in love and she has to let me go back to Charlie. She has to let me go to Mirielle. I have to stop Derwin from stealing her away from me. I have to sleep. She throws me in the bath, won't stop taking my temperature. I come to, submerged in lukewarm water. I'm drowning in briny waves, tangled in seaweed. So exhausted that I can't control my own muscles. What I can do is I can make my jaw tense up and go slack again, and I can blink. Burning and shivering at the same time. Crying, drifting in and out of a dream that I'm only a silly high school kid with fleeting passions and delusions and no use to anyone.

Nothing especially creepy goes on with the cult while we're there, at least not that I can tell. Maybe there's a lot of sex I don't hear about, but everyone's pretty nice and they don't really seem to want anything in particular to happen. Except Charlie, who I can tell is looking for a fight. She keeps me close, and after I show her the Tongue she starts to tell me her story.

Charlie and I spend a lot of time together, but not as much as I want to because I'm not exactly her focus. She talks a lot about her plans to leave the commune and move to Greece, and at some point the grown-ups basically accuse her of trying to branch off her own cult within the cult, so they start keeping a closer eye on her. But anyway it's around this time is when my mother decides to get out. She's sick of it, I guess. Breaks up with her guy. She sells our car and buys two bus tickets north, and when she tells me we're leaving, I flip out, knock over a table, won't let her touch me, won't look her in the eye. Her tone of voice changes then and it never fully changes back. I feel her emotionally withdraw. It takes time for her to get angry. She says she'll have the deacons tie me up and force me onto the bus.

Charlie and I talk about running away. We get as far as the edge of the farm that night. We sit by the fence. It's the first time I see her cry. She changes her mind. She won't leave. Says I should go. Then the last thing she says is that the best thing to do would be forget each other and move on. "Seven billion people in the world, sugar," she says. "You and me, we're just two of the many shapes the sunlight takes." I don't understand what she's talking about. I'm not really listening anymore. I leave her in the field and don't sleep for three days.

My mother wraps me in a blanket and holds me on the couch. She says stupid shit like things will get better and I'll understand when I'm older. She thinks I'm hysterical. She touches parts of my body and I give her the latin and this calms me down a little. Each word becomes a mantra. I repeat them all three times. My voice drones on, my eyelids narrow.

Charlie texts me twice while we're on the road. I don't call her, don't send an email. She sends me five, but I don't respond, and then that's it. No real goodbye. It just stops.

It's shortly after this we end up in a trashy diner in Oregon where I sit facing a wall with this huge white sign of the number 62. I start to remember all the times I saw that number while we lived on the farm. It had been everywhere. On the water pump, in the library; it was our house number, it was on license plates. I'd flipped randomly to page 62 in so many of the library's books. It's clear the number has been following me.

My mother and I spend a few months in a little town five miles south of Seattle and I start to notice 62 everywhere, hundreds of times a month sometimes. It haunts me every day. Clocks always showing 26 minutes past the hour or else 12:06 or 6:02. Speedometers hovering around 62mph. Mile markers on the side of the road always seem to be 26 or 62. I see it in gas prices and on billboards. In my math homework and all over the Internet. One night when a truck drives by with the number 62 painted on the driver's side door it occurs to me maybe for the first time that I'm growing older every second, and even between the seconds. Getting older never stops or takes a nap. Even when I sleep. And I'm aware that someday I'll be old like my grandmother and then I'll be dead like my grandfather.

I become aware that there's such a thing as a first memory, and I spend a lot of time going over details of the bee sting. I'm fascinated by the notion that all of my conscious life has developed out of that moment. I can't remember the pain itself, just the existence of the pain. I understand the pain more than I remember it. The memory is of the awareness of the feeling, not the feeling itself. There's no actual pain in memory. There's the word for pain. I remember that the bee fell to the grass and disappeared. The more I think about it the more I think I probably never actually saw the bee, even though I have a picture of a bee in my memory. But it's so obviously a fake cartoony image of a bee compared to the realism of the memory of myself and the environment. The bee is too big and bright and yellow, too artificial and exaggerated. The real parts—the parts I know and trust—are less vivid, while remaining clear, if that makes sense. They never change, but my mind can make the bee do whatever I want it to. I can still close my eyes and see the grass under my sandals, the blue floral print of my dress, the small violet flowers by my feet.

My mother and I fall asleep together on the couch. I don't wake up until morning and I have only one dream. The next day she calls in sick for me, takes off work, and fawns over me like I'm seven years old again. I watch movies and eat ice cream. My memories keep coming in flashes throughout the night, but I can't tell the difference between dreaming and remembering and imagining.

I know there was a time when I imagined myself in a man's bed with the voice of my children coming from the other room. There was a time when all I wanted was to do good things and take care of other people and be just like my mother. She played rock-and-roll for me in the womb and later in my crib. There was never a moment without music in our house. For me, music was never the revolution. Silence was the revolution. The breath before the song, the gap between beats, the null zone where the reverb shudders and burns and disintegrates.

I think about Charlie and I swear I will never fall in love again. My mother says something cruel and I swear I will never forgive her. Time incinerates these promises, along with the memory of why they were made.

We keep moving.

11

I'VE LOST A DAY OF useless classes to fever, sleep and soup. We sit in the back yard at Chestnut Homes, on a stone bench under a sky of insignificant clouds. I'm holding one of Pasha's notebooks unopened. I can see him through the screen door where he clings to a wall in the empty back room where nurses and residents trade their shoes for slippers before going outside. His grandson is with him today, holding up Pasha's little potted plant in one hand and watering it from a Dixie cup in the other. Matthew Craig has been trying to encourage his grandfather to go outside for the last half hour. As always, Pasha refuses. There's something about the outdoors he doesn't trust.

Brooks and I haven't talked at all about the other night yet. I keep waiting for him to bring it up, but I should know he won't ask. I can't tell if he doesn't want to or if he's already forgotten. Also, okay probably the real reason I haven't said anything is I still feel like an idiot for the whole Oklahoma thing. Ask me why, Brooks. Ask me what the hell I was thinking. Then please tell me.

"I haven't given up," I say.

"I know," Brooks says.

"Was she at the show?"

"Nope."

Derwin's art show, which I missed on account of my trip to the hospital and all that.

"You should go see it, though," he says. "The black-and-whites are amazing. There's this one with a tractor."

I squeeze my forehead. "I really fucked up."

"Yeah. You did."

"I just—I want her, you know? I can't help it."

"It's your choice," he says. He doesn't know he's being preachy.

"She was really pissed," I say.

"Well, yeah."

"Way more than I thought she'd be."

"They hate each other," Brooks says. "Mirielle and Bre. Or at least Mirielle hates Bre. Hates her."

Obviously.

"It's not just Derwin," he says.

"What do you mean?"

"I mean Jason."

And when he says the name I know exactly where this is going. Jason: Mirielle's brother, who killed himself three years ago with a .38 caliber pistol. His face is as clear in my mind as Brooks is in my line of sight. This is not a memory.

"They were living together in a rental garage," Brooks continues. "She was that girl."

Everyone in town knows the story. Jason was seeing someone, some mystery girl, right before he vanished off the map for almost nine days. They found him at dawn on a Monday. In a park. He did it while sitting at the base of a tree. No one gave the new girl a chance to explain. No one would talk to her after the funeral. Jason was popular, maybe one of the most popular kids in school. That's what mystifies people about the suicide. But I don't know—I can fathom it. Popularity has nothing to do with happiness, and even less to do with contentment. Not that I've ever been popular, but I've had it good enough to realize how meaningless even the really good stuff can seem when you feel like shit and don't know why.

So that was Bre.

People have called her a witch. They say things like she seduced him and tricked him into killing himself. More rational people call her an "enabler," that somehow she helped him do it, or at least helped him feel it was okay. She didn't try to stop him anyway, that's for sure, and she didn't tell anyone what he was planning. Yeah, I've heard all about her, but I never even knew her name. Of course Mirielle hates her guts. Could Derwin be going out with her out of some sort of payback?

The first time I ever saw Mirielle and Derwin together was right after the suicide. Three years ago. Just a couple of days before Derwin left town. More rumors flying around than I've ever heard before or since. I remember people saying Mirielle was fucking Richie Buchan (which is not even remotely possible in any universe) and that the school was threatening Derwin with expulsion and deportation and execution for reasons ranging from too many skipped classes to foreign espionage. I remember seeing them through the window of a coffee shop, sitting across from each other, not talking. He was staring at his hands. She was looking at the floor through a pair of sunglasses.

"So anyway," I say.

This and the subsequent pause, that most people would pick up as a like social cue, goes right over Brooks' head. I open the notebook of Pasha's that I swiped earlier and start flipping through pages. Of course the first place I land is page 62, which here he's just drawn a bunch of tree diagrams: the close-up of a dissected leaf, the cross-section of a tree trunk, a root system. All of it annotated and labeled.

"So anyway, they tried to take me in for observation," I say.

"Yeah?"

"Mom wouldn't let them."

"Psych eval?"

"Maybe I need it."

"Naw," Brooks says.

"This was weirder than the first time."

"Another vision?"

"Stronger this time. More detail, more in and out of my body. I left the room."

"I know. You went outside."

"Right, but before that even. Like I was in two places at once. Then when I actually went outside it got worse. I guess it was like a seizure, maybe?" Saying this in particular feels stupid and arrogant. Like I could even compare the other night to the hell Brooks goes through. He doesn't respond. I flip the page. "I'm not saying I've got your thing—not even close. And really, okay, not at all because the weird part is I think I was faking it, actually."

"Faking it?" Brooks says.

"I mean, okay, so here's the thing. At first I was faking it. Then it took over. Then it became real."

"Why were you faking it?"

I don't know. I wanted whatever I was experiencing to fully consume me? For it to be as non-intelectual as possible? To find out if it was just as in my body as it was in my head? To prove it was real.

"I feel like a jerk."

"Sometimes it's like that," Brooks says.

"Like what?"

"Like you're trying to pretend to be in control so you can make sense of it. It's when you can't tell the cause from the effect that it really crackles."

"Do you ever see things?" I said. "Go places?"

Brooks shakes his head. "When did it start? Is that why you said all that stuff about?"

I shrug and flip the page. No, when I said that stuff about Bre and Oklahoma I was definitely in my right mind. In Pasha's notebook is a perfect circle surrounding the sketch of an old ruined city and a wall of unreadable words.

"I saw the Tongue," I say.

"The Tongue? You mean like the little globe the Tongue or the big huge tongue-in-Charlie's-story the Tongue?"

Is my brain just somehow trying to make her story play out in my life because I miss her and I'll never see her again, is what he's asking.

"I saw it, Brooks! Like I was connected to someone else's eyes. Seeing what they saw. Someone with all of these memories of things that haven't happened yet. I saw a bear."

Maybe it is all psychological stuff vomiting up to the surface, but it's the annexation of my senses that makes it so I can't not feel like this has to be some signal or something reaching toward me from the outside. A really low frequency signal because obviously the occurrence of things like the number 62 could be like way more overt, except that okay maybe whoever is sending the signal (and yes I've considered it might not be a signal specifically to me, but just someone throwing it out there to whoever is crazy enough to pay attention), maybe they have enemies and so they're trying to fly under the radar, and they can

161

only get away with signals just barely more random than seems normal and barely less random than you would expect. Something easily mistaken for confirmation bias. Just enough to catch my attention but not enough to give away the game.

"You're not crazy," Brooks says.

"I don't know."

"I mean it."

Brooks' determination is a force to be reckoned with. He's more convinced than I am, I think. For every argument I raise he's there to tell me why I need to trust my gut. Not that I even know where to begin. Let's just say for a minute, for the sake of argument, let's just say I'm dead sure about all this and here we go. Here we go where? How is a kid like me going to talk two people who hate each other into getting it on, and while we're at it she really needs to be ovulating at the time if it's not too much trouble.

"What am I supposed to do?"

Goddammit, Lexie, get your head out of your ass, that's what! My father's voice echoes through my skull as unimpeded by inattention or interruption as if he were really here. So what the hell—I open my bag, pull out a yellow notepad and a pen, and hand them to Brooks. "Okay. Fine. Ideas. One. Forge love notes."

"Really?"

"Just write it."

Brooks points to the door. "You know Matthew Craig is right over there."

"Write!"

He writes "#1" on the notepad, then my idea.

"What about flowers?" he says.

"Who sends flowers anymore?"

"Better than a stupid note."

"Like you'd know."

"We need danger," he says. "Can we make a plan where we put her in a deadly situation and he has to save her?"

"What is this the middle ages? Why can't she save him?"

"Okay let me think." He presses the pen to his lips. His face takes on the look of focus I've seen so often before.

I stand up and pace around the garden. Over at the Home I see Pasha's face creeping behind the screen door. I walk up the concrete steps and he jerks away as I open the door and go inside. Then I get beside him, pressing my butt and hands to the rough texture of the wallpaper, and start to slide alongside him, synchronizing my movement with his, which I think this freaks him out a little. "What's up?" I ask. He replies with a moan and won't look at me. Pasha's personality is as fluid and mousy as his world of notebooks is mechanistic and monstrous. Sometimes it's comforting to be around someone crazier than you. I want to cradle his head. He looks at me for a long time, examining my face, and then, in a rare moment not even remotely familiar to his usual freaked-out expression, Pasha's tongue lolls out of his head and he crosses his eyes. I hear Matthew Craig's little nervous laugh as he throws out an "Oh, Grandpa." But Pasha stays locked on me. Eye contact unbroken. Is this some kind of message?

It's sweet the way Matthew Craig tries to relate. I can tell from his smile of approval that he wants me to know we're on the same team. Poor guy. I'm gonna take your girl, mess with your life, charcoal your heart.

Tongue still extended, Pasha reaches out toward his grandson's arms, where the little potted money plant nestles. Matthew Craig's bottom lip flops forward because he cannot believe what happens next. Pasha pinches one of the little leaves and plucks it off of its stem. He holds the leaf between his boney fingers for one cunning moment, then proceeds to stick the leaf on his tongue, roll the tongue back into his mouth and slowly chew.

Part of Charlie's Tongue story had to do with these characters called Mechempath, who are part of a scientific monastic order that live near the Tongue, studying it but resisting its seductive powers. They've figured out that all the plants and trees and streams sprouting up near the Tongue are actually made up of zillions of the remaining nano-tech-like machines that splintered off the supercomputer after it crashed. From Pasha's notebooks it's clear that he also believes that a lot of real plants are actually machines— he's even identified several suspects around town. "Invisible polymer-silicate clockwork powered by photonic circulatory systems 90 to 900 atoms across," is how Charlie described the nano-machines, and if he knew the words they might be exactly how Pasha would describe the building blocks that make up the old elm in front of Chestnut Homes. He's drawn plenty of diagrams anyway. Sometimes I get the impression that he thinks communicating with plants isn't something anyone's figured out yet, and other times it reads like a few special folks are out there and just don't know it. Or that they know it too well, communicating all the time with trees to the point where they don't realize it's even a thing.

The Mechempath in the Tongue story believe that someday a hero will be born who has the capacity to communicate intuitively with the nano-machines, reconnect with the missing computer god, and return unity to the world. The story really picks up when these guys get a hunch about one of their own, an elder Mechempath who for years was a bumbling nobody until someone noticed the machines would organize around him and kind of give him whatever he wanted—so the high council decides to send him off to follow the Tongue all the way to its bitter end. He leaves the order and starts a years-long journey in which, after countless little adventures, he finally reaches the cave, and there he discovers the brain of the Mabingestialbogoblin, who it turns out has been experimenting with various forms of being by assembling new hybrids from bits and pieces of whatever creatures the Tongue has dragged into the earth. The computer momentarily fuses its consciousness into each incarnation—trying on the experience, hoping to learn what it means to feel what other beings feel.

Sometimes my visions occur to me like weird memories I never had. A memory in isolation, without any memory of remembering the memory before. Memories that don't belong to me, even though I'm right there inside them. More like someone else's memory of me, or someone else having the memory through me. Like watching myself over my own shoulder. Maybe they're kind of leftover thoughts from my ancestors, is something I've considered, or at least the kind of thoughts they might have had. Or maybe my future self somehow figured out how to send thoughts back to me now. If memory is just your past self talking to your present self, isn't that like some weird form of communication? So why couldn't the conversation go both ways? Whether they come from some omniscient cosmic agency, or a time-displaced parallel me, or random hormone surges that my brain has packaged into some sort of bare-minimum intelligibility, or just a really annoying and autonomous colony of my imagination—whatever they are—they're in me now, no matter where they were before. It's all in my bloodstream and I can't just shut it off.

Really what it comes down to is there's no way to know if

I've imagined myself into this or not. By now I'm already working with memories of the memories of remembering what I think I saw. I doubt yesterday's doubts as inauthentic, and the voice in my head analyzing the meaning, truth and origin of my vision sounds as legitimate as the one analyzing the value of the act of analyzing meaning. I'm left with the suspicion that my own brain is tricking me into weird ways of trying to get what I want and can't have, or at least another way to want it. I cling desperately to any memory of certainty. Replaying over and over the thoughts connected to the overpowering physical feeling that struck me in the lunchroom. Her unborn child's heartbeat ramming into my mind's eardrum, vibrating along some inner psychic skin. I try to recall the image of her on the Tongue outside Brooks' house. Such serenity and confidence, details I can already feel slipping away down an array of black cinematic hexagons behind my eyes.

I feel so weak and vague, nothing like the people we read about in stories, the ones compelled to step up and be a fulcrum, who hear voices and follow their visions into places no one else can understand. Into fire and water. Noah built a boat, Mirabai danced in a frenzy. I have to hook up a couple kids. But the doubt is where it all falls apart. You read about prophets like Merlin or Rasputin or those Greek Oracle chicks and it seems like they totally had their shit together. Right? Like their mental life was a perfectly engineered conduit. But who talks about what Agrippa was like when he was fifteen, or whether Joan of Arc ever spent years agonizing over whether or not she was crazy? They had to have started out as clueless as the rest of us. Then maybe they figured a few things out, but mostly I think the only trick is figuring out how to fake it. Shut off the doubt, take the chaos of the brain and turn it into pictures. Then risk everything.

Risk is essential, risk is the key. You throw yourself into the volcano and hope the gods find you amusing. Telling the future is just a story like any other, and if that story comes true you're suddenly a big deal, and if it doesn't they kill you and time forgets you ever existed.

But I don't think the doubt ever goes away. Even if you're right—even if you're lucky enough to watch it all play out in the real world just the same way as you saw it—say you imagine a thing and it comes to pass and you save the day. When the world all of a sudden doesn't end, do you get some huge comfort out of it? Or do you live out the rest of your life wondering if maybe you still messed up somewhere and the real doom is right around the corner? Did Joan of Arc face the stake driven mad by that little voice telling her she'd wasted her life on an illusion? I imagine Eyes of Fire growing old and sick with variations on the end of all life in the universe playing out over and over in her dying thoughts. She did the best she could. But the reel rolls on until the bulb blisters the film.

"I've got it," Brooks says, waving my notepad in my face. I didn't even notice him come in. Pasha and Matthew Craig have slipped away down the hall, on their way back to the rec room, grandson holding the plant away from the wall in case Pasha decides to eat any more of it.

"Got what?"

"Read."

Brooks points to a series of words and diagrams,

"I don't get it."

"Disguise Derwin as Matthew Craig," he says. "Send him over in the dark."

"You're an idiot."

"No. I'm awesome."

The first time I ever saw Mirielle and Derwin together was one of those days where the number 62 kept coming up everywhere, in stray things people would say on the street and in the choice of songs on the radio and on cars that drove by. I felt it buzzing under my skin, threads interconnecting from an invisible backstage where things that tend to tangle out here have more space to breathe. Everything was shuffling that day. It's like some migratory wind swept through our town at 62 degrees southeast. That was the day I started to associate the number with my death. Would I die at 62 or would that be the age of the person who kills me? Or would the number just be there somewhere in the room: on a sign, a screen, a painting, a coffee cup? Because all this was coming down on the tail of what happened with Jason, who'd only killed himself four days before. What a long, weird week it was. Pasha, Derwin, Jason… Feels like there must be some connection even though I guess shit just goes down and sometimes it clusters and sometimes it doesn't, but it all sure seemed to be stacking up then, pointing in one direction. Everything whispered death. Like someone was trying to warn me or prepare me for something. I had no rational reason whatsoever to believe this but I sat there and got on the phone and called Charlie for the first time in years. I got her voice mail, spilled my guts. Until Brooks, Charlie was the only person I'd ever told about all the weird things my brain does. I pictured her holding my hand and telling me I was cute when I was crazy and that everything would be fucking a-okay. She never called me back.

"Why does it have to be this huge ordeal?" Brooks says. "Let's spray her perfume on his sheets. Or bring up songs and movies he was into three years ago. Drag him over by where they met."

"That ugly-ass moose sculpture?" I say.

"What? They met at a book club."

"No they didn't," I say.

"Um. Yeah. They did."

"Whatever. This whole thing is stupid."

"I thought you were serious about this," Brooks says.

How the hell does he manage to control his emotions the way he does?

"I want some ice cream," I say. "Do you want ice cream?"

"Don't be a baby."

"I am a baby. I'm a fucking baby."

I called Charlie that day because when I first saw Derwin and Mirielle together was probably as close as I can figure to the time I started to transition from one love to the other. I didn't really expect an answer. Just hearing her on the machine was enough. *Aw, I missed your call*, was the crooning voicemail greeting, then the beep. My message was a rambling mess. Derwin left less than a week later. Back in those days I would lay awake in my bed retelling myself Charlie's story about the Tongue, trying to mimic the little phrases she used, trying to make sure I never forgot her voice.

"I'll change my mind tomorrow," I say.

"No more dinners," Brooks says.

"I know."

"Things are pretty screwed up now."

"God, I know. Shut up!"

He does. He always does when I tell him to and I always feel bad. "It'll be okay," I say. "You don't get that angry if you don't love someone."

I think of Charlie as the one who first brought these things out in me. There was this one day, we were sitting on the gate of an empty corral, and she read me a story in a magazine about a guy who collected pigeons on his roof. Lulling them, feeding them, gathering more and more for like five years, building new cages every month. Spent hundreds on bird food. Then he locked them all up for seventeen days and wouldn't let them out. On the last day he pulled a lever. All the cage doors opened at once. Nine hundred pigeons launching into the sky. When asked why he did it—Charlie stopped reading and looked at me. "What'd he say?"

"About what?" I said.

"About why he did it," she said. "What was his answer?"

"How would I know?"

"Guess," she said.

"Just tell me."

"Guess. Close your eyes."

When she smiled that way I'd do anything she wanted. Now days, if I'm trying really hard to listen to something, I close my eyes. Sometimes I'll call people "sugar" just because it makes me feel like her. This is how I keep her with me. Wrapped up in phrases and mannerisms, in small inflections and body language. My personality is a collaboration frankensteined from tiny scraps of everyone I've ever loved.

I waited in the darkness until she touched my hand.

"Well?" she said.

"Just to see," I said.

"Look," she said. "Look at the words."

12

DERWIN PICKS US UP IN the old red Chevy. Brooks makes me ride in the middle, and I can't look Derwin in the eye until he forces me to play three games of one-handed RPS, which he lets me win two out of three, laughs, calls me a natural, and refuses to drive until I bump knuckles with him. I wish I could feel as forgiven as he wants me to. We head across town and pull up at Nate Pavelich's place. "You guys come in," he says. "I gotta pack some gear."

Bre's on the couch using a safety pin to poke air holes in an unlit cigarette. Tonight she's all bangs and eyelashes, covered in silk from neck to ankles. Red silk sports bra, black silk boxers, and a black silk bathrobe barely covering it all. The robe slips off of one leg, its hem cutting between her knee and a leather thigh holster packed with a can of Diet Coke. Each of her toenails is a different color.

Nate's on the floor in the middle of the room, sitting across from Jonas, a chess board between them. It's Jonas' move. "She did the eyebrow thing," he says. "That's a pretty clear signal."

"If you can describe the exact signal she was giving off, it wasn't a signal," Bre says.

Nate yells into the kitchen: "Time?"

"Nine," Jonas says without looking away from his pieces.

"Exactly?"

He checks his phone. "Five till."

"Five till nine," Nate yells. "Tank's full?"

Luis pulls his head out of the fridge. "Huh?"

I slink to the floor in the corner closest to the door, where no one can really see me unless they're looking. Brooks hops up in the broken vinyl recliner that if you push it back too far the whole thing springs out flat. His hands vanish down between the plush armrests.

Nate scratches his ear with a blue cattle marker, then wags it vigorously in the air. "The car," he says. "Gas."

"It's full," Luis says.

Nate looks at Bre. "Pretty sure I can tell when a girl wants me."

"You can't even tell what you want," Bre says.

"What's that supposed to mean?" He shouts into the kitchen again, "No more beer, Luis!"

"We're out of beer?"

"It's nine o'clock. Stop drinking."

"I've still got five minutes," Luis says.

"You're missing the point," Nate responds. "And it's more like four."

"I can down a beer in four minutes."

"Ever heard of a thing called spirit of the law?"

"I'm totally sober."

Bre stops stabbing the cigarette. She wraps her lips around the filter and starts looking around for a lighter, flicking at the air with her thumb.

"Everyone ready?" she says.

Luis wanders back into the living room with an open beer. "You really not coming with us?" he asks.

"How will you ever manage without me?" Bre winks at him. She takes Derwin by the hand and they go off into the hall to talk. Luis waves Brooks out of the chair, sits in his place and starts flipping through a comic book. Brooks drops his ass on the floor next to me and lets his fingers comb through the sheared carpet.

Nate throws a peanut at me. "What up, Seed Girl?"

When Derwin comes back, he makes Brooks scoot over. He spreads a three-foot by three-foot tarp out on the ground between us, smooths a bandana in the center. On the bandana goes a box of waterproof matches, a flint, a small Leatherman, fishing line, two bundles of thin nylon rope, and a compass.

"Whoa whoa whoa!" Nate shouts.

Luis looks up. "What?"

Nate points at Jonas. "You cheating bastard."

"Me?"

"Yes, you. Luis, did you see that?"

"I didn't see anything, Nate."

Nate rips the comic out of Luis' hands. "Look at the board."

"I missed it," Luis says.

"Look at the fucking board."

Jonas shakes his head in slow, incredulous waves. "Where did I cheat, you crazy ass?"

"How can you deny it? Is that a knight right there where there once was no knight, or have I been drinking bottles of dextromethorphan this whole time?"

"I didn't cheat."

"Bags, people," Bre growls from the hall. "Are they ready?"

Derwin folds the bandana up into a pouch and ties it off. "Four pounds," he says to me. "The essentials. I never go out with more than fifteen, and that includes the weight of the bag. I like a small backpack I can fit under my raincoat."

"We're going to starve to death," Brooks grumbles.

"Derwin's the king of the forest," Nate says. "No glamping for this bitch. Not even at a car camp event. Balls for miles." Nate points at the board again. "Well? That a knight or not?"

"This is stupid," says Jonas.

"Yes or no?"

"That's a knight, Nate," Luis gurgles through the lips of his beer bottle.

"So what?"

"So I obliterated that knight two moves ago. And now suddenly he's back on the board?"

"You're insane." Both of Jonas' fists are clenched. This is the only place on his body where he lets his emotion show. Nothing in his face, or in his eyes, or in his voice.

"If there's a confession somewhere in what you just said, I completely missed it." Nate leans back, all conciliatory. "Look, the balls you displayed just now are staggering yet huge, but you have to 'fess up. If I had a video camera I would instant-replay a close-up of your mighty stones before a live studio audience. I would personally take out an ad in tomorrow's paper proclaiming the exact measurements of your impossibly swollen testicles, which the priest fondled as you confessed your ruthless attempt to cheat me out of hard-earned money."

"We aren't playing for money," Jonas says.

Nate is out again with his pointing finger. "I'll pay you cash right now. Ten bucks if you say it."

Jonas breaks into a laugh. "You're fucking nuts!"

Luis says, "Do you guys want to hear a joke?"

"Is this funny? Let's go down to the courthouse. I will wrap a lie detector machine around your cock and you can press one to tell me in English or two for Spanish, the entire epic novel about how you didn't cheat."

"I don't cheat!"

"So there's these three guys right?" Luis says. "A black guy, a Mexican, and a kike—"

"I fucking saw you. Eye witness testimony. Ask Seed Girl. Did you see it, Seed Girl?" He doesn't look at me. I say nothing and he forgets he asked.

"—and they're all on a spaceship to Mars, okay? They're in, like, suspended animation, you know? And when they get into orbit, they all wake up, except for the kike, he keeps on sleeping —"

Nate redirects his javelin finger toward Luis. "Jew."

"What?"

"The Jew keeps on sleeping. I'd appreciate it if you didn't use the term 'kike'."

"Sorry, Nate."

"No one even says kike anymore. Where are you from?"

"Sorry, Nate."

Bre steps between them, looking Nate up and down. "Is that what you're wearing?"

Nate lowers his chin to self-examine. Pleated pants: brown. Button-up shirt: light cotton with faded burgundy checks. Top button missing, not that he'd use it. "So?"

"You look scary, man," Derwin says. "And not in the cool way."

"What do you mean?"

Derwin rolls the tarp up around the bundle.

"Not in the way that would frighten off predators."

Nate says, "You know what I like about you, D? You still think wilderness is a real thing."

Derwin laughs. "From a guy who's never been camping longer than three days."

"Wilderness is a construct," Nate says.

Derwin shoves the tarp into his small black backpack. "Whenever I have to wrestle with the idea of not coming back, wherever I'm forced to face my mortality—that's wilderness."

"There was no wilderness until the white man came along is something that's been said."

Derwin zips up. "Anywhere uncomfortable," he says. "Anywhere I can't help thinking, I could die right here right now."

"Wilderness is the last Disneyland of the American dream," Nate says.

Bre spits in the sink. "That's the stupidest thing I've ever heard you say."

Nate ignores her, tosses a peanut at Derwin, who catches it and pops it in his mouth, shell and all.

"You ever get any camera crews following you out on the road?" Nate asks.

"Why do you think I left town?" Derwin laughs.

"Hell, I actually kind of miss those guys," Nate says.

Bre's face thaws into a nostalgic smile. "I forgot about the Life Swap thing."

"I guess they stopped by to check on us last year. Right Brooksy?"

Brooks nods absently. He's discovered a broken Rubik's cube and is repairing it.

"They're too busy with the latest and greatest to give a shit," Derwin says. "Maybe we'll get a 15-year anniversary mention."

***

"Can you picture an LA camera crew thirty miles deep in the Hob?" Nate says, and everyone laughs.

As easy as it is for me to stay in the shadows, to avoid the kinds of movements or words that would make other people consider noticing me, it seems just as easy for other people to do the opposite. They say hello so naturally. They shake hands, have a drink, flirt, fuck, and as far as I can tell they find something together that they were missing alone. I meet no one. I have nothing to say. Some people think I'm stuck up, but I'm just not good enough at being a person. I don't have whatever it takes to impress or entice. I sit against walls, I lurk in shadows, I make my own company. What's it going to take for me to stick my neck out, to force these people to see me? If I can't think of something it's going to be a lonely three more high school years as a nobody.

Derwin checks the side pockets of his bag for easily-retrievable necessities: knife, flashlight, water bottle, matches.

"You guys hear about the killer deer in Canada?" Nate says.

I have! I have heard about those deer. This is where I'm supposed to like blurt out some interesting detail. To get involved. I resist an impulse to raise my hand.

"They get habituated," Nate says. "Aggressive."

Derwin gets to his feet. "Bambi the man-slayer."

"They take over people's lawns, eat their plants, won't let people walk into their own homes. It's a territorial thing. They chase people away from their own doors."

I want to say something, but what? Everything I can think to say gets caught in my filters. How stupid will it sound? Is it something everyone already knows? Will it seem like I'm just trying to look like I know what I'm talking about? No words can get through these hoops in time to keep up with the conversation.

Bre grabs keys off the table, tosses them to Luis who just barely manages to react and catch. She squats next to Nate. "Is your bag ready?"

Luis finds a lag in the room's sonic space. He says, "So anyway the, um, the colored guy he's trying to wake the Jew up but the Jew just keeps snoring no matter what the guy does—"

Bre touches the top of Nate's head. "Hey!"

Mostly I think to have a pretext to keep ignoring Bre, Nate leans back and changes the music. Buzzsaw bass and an anxious beat. "Get juiced up," he shouts into the room.

"The black guy, he's tried everything, buckets of water, tickling, poking, fire. But nothing's working."

"Na-ate…" Bre sings the word, touching his shoulder.

"Okay so anyway, to deal with the deer problem they've got all these trained border collies."

Bre holds her phone in front of Nate's face, forcing him to look at the digits. But she can't force him to see.

Luis says: "Then the Mexican gets this idea, right? He's like, I know what will wake this kike up. And he says—Ah… what's it called? How, like, all Jews are, like, what is it? When they cut your dick skin off? It's like a rite of passage. What is it?"

Nate explains that the border collies haze the deer. They create a sense of predatoriness without being a danger to humans. Derwin snorts. And here is where I finally open my mouth. Like the levee bursting under my desperation. My volume is too high and the pitch is all wrong. "Grow some balls, right?" is what I say, and I say it right at the exact moment where no one else is saying anything. I can hear my words echo through the room and then fall flat on the floor. Or maybe it's just my mind repeating them over and over, and each time they sound stupider and stupider. Everyone looks at me at once, most of them like they didn't even know I was there.

This lasts for approximately ever until Bre starts tapping Nate on the forehead. "I've got to go. Are you guys going to be okay? Is your bag ready?"

Nate pushes her hand out of his face. Luis picks up his comic book, flips page to page, not reading but thinking, trying to find the word. Hunting through the caverns of his mind. He knows it's in there somewhere.

I'm sweating like crazy: my palms, my axilla, down my back and into my gluteal cleft. No one's looking at me anymore. I don't remember when they stopped. I'm invisible again, and it's a little bit better this way.

"You gotta get one of those camera crews to come out with us on a raid some night," Nate says to Derwin.

Bre points to the hall, her eyes matriarchal, her voice rising. "Go!"

There's another lull, just wide enough to leave space for Derwin, bundle packed and secure, inching toward the door, waiting for Bre. "Camping time!" She gives up on Nate and scratches Jonas on the head. "Take care of them, okay?" Jonas gives a mock salute and Bre nuzzles up inside Derwin's jacket. He kisses the top of her head. Then he tosses me his keys.

"You drive," he says, and like hell he really means it, but what matters is people see this. Nate and Jonas and Luis: eyes locked on the jagged metal sticking out between my fingers. And on my way up the stairs Nate keeps blinking at the spot on the floor where I'd been sitting, like he can't quite put it together that I was just there a minute ago and now I'm running off to drive the town's most notorious son up to a party in the woods. This has to give me points.

13

THEY'RE LIGHTING THE FIRE WHEN we arrive, kindling the dry bark by pushing a torch through a narrow space between two small logs on a stepped pyramid of gathered wood. Others have already begun to surround the outer ring of stones. Kids wear everything from designer tees to second-hand jeans. Lots of loose hoods among those already dancing. A few still wear shorts and sunglasses even with the mountain air brisking up and the sun all but down twenty minutes ago. There's some mystery behind the people who organize this event, but the ones in the know are the ones closest to the music. They wear earth tones, homemade and patchy with muted colors and vivid integrations like jagged blue zippers or neon-pink seams. They huddle and whisper, they laugh out loud, they pat backs and rub shoulders. Three stacks of butterfly cab speakers triangulate the scene, patched into a nearby DJ booth with buried cables. I'd kill to play something like this.

Derwin and Bre put up the tents. Brooks avoids the fire for a while. He goes down to check out the creek and see if maybe anyone has any food. Across the water there's a muddy basin where you can stomp through the brush to get to some fishing holes and where a mamma and baby moose sometimes hang out.

All around the perimeter tiny aspen saplings sprout up like something straight out of Middle Earth.

It took almost an hour to get here, deep in the canyon, way past Sheldon's land. There's good odds Mirielle will end up here tonight with her new snack Matthew Craig, but no one mentioned it on the drive. A mob just about smothered Derwin the minute we got out of the truck, like everyone had been waiting on him before getting things started. His old friends swarm on him like some ancient legend, like a symbol of rebellion and release from the quote system, from the day-to-day and the stupid rules and the unreasonable authority figures and the bullshit classes and every other scapegoat for the secret things that really oppress us like our self-loathing and the terror of reputation, our contradicting lusts and desires, and every other tyrant of our own design.

"Tonight's a good night," Derwin told his brother before releasing us to do our own thing. "Don't drink too much."

"I don't drink," Brooks said.

"Still?" And I saw him look at his brother with a smile teetering between pride and amusement. I couldn't tell if he was just happy to be home, or happy to introduce Brooks to this world, or really and truly happy. For one small second he shared that look with me. I blushed all over, dammit.

June is coming. The time of year when everyone starts spending their weekends in the hills. Older kids with cars drag their freshminions along to have someone to torment and do their bidding. There's always lots of beer and plenty of girls. This festival is no different, and though there seem to be deeper intentions here—from what I've heard, some local old hippies or pagans make this space available—everyone is welcome from frat boys to rednecks. Brooks is just walking back from the creek where a little foot bridge leads to trailheads that go in 40 or 50 miles deep, places that serious wilderness junkies will tackle as late summer melts the snow and the alpine lakes and mountain peaks become a reason to suffer through long hikes with heavy gear. The fire illuminates only the boundary to this hidden world. We're all summoned, but this is as far as most of us ever let ourselves go. Tonight the campground becomes a parking lot. Tents litter the grass, but no one will sleep until morning. The fire matures as the sunlight fades. The music starts down-tempo and ambient, gradually building to a gentle beat that anyone can sway or dance to without looking stupid. The circle tightens, the blaze peaks and narrows. The pyramid of logs hollows out at the base where a carpet of white ash forms.

Someone slaps me on the back and before I know it I'm holding a can of beer. Now what? Am I observing or participating? Is this an experiment or an experience? The real question is, how can I not drink it when it's been handed to me? Like, okay, this isn't a matter of peer pressure. I thought I was invisible, but someone saw to include me. Instead of saying *what is that little nerd doing here*, they said *join us*. One won't kill me. Just to see how it feels to open the can.

It's easily the most disgusting thing I've ever tasted in my life. "People drink this shit?"

"Tell me about it," Brooks says.

"This is worse than Brussels sprouts."

"Not mathematically possible."

"Show me the numbers," I insist.

"I've got a pie graph."

"Mmm… Brussels pie."

"Don't talk to me about food," Brooks says. "I'm starving to literal death and there's nothing here but liquor and mushrooms."

He looks around the fire and the things I see—people starting to come together and open up and share themselves—go right over his head. He's bored and hungry. I've never known anyone so hungry as this kid. He wishes me good luck with my beer and takes off, probably to go count stars or something. I should go with him but I'm magnetized to this spot. There are so many beautiful people surrounding the fire. Two girls in belly-dancing outfits, one made out of gold medallions, the other a sheer red fabric, start to drag people out of the crowd and encourage movement. I can't tell who's on drugs and who isn't. Before I know it my beer is gone. I find myself shyly hunting for more.

After the original pyramid of logs collapses I hear a voice behind me say, "Thank you for keeping the fire going." Someone ushers me out of the way and that's when I see the grizzled old man move past me to drop a new log onto the flames. He doesn't wear gloves. His left arm is shorter than his right. The backs of his hands are covered in a fine silt of singed black hair. The almond-shaped hollows of his eye sockets are shadowed in ash. Lips slack. There's something strange about his movements. He practically tumbles down the slope toward a waiting pile of wood. Then he bends down, flinging out an arm in one grotesque motion, elbow locked so the arm swings loosely like from a dislocated shoulder. As he drags himself back through the crowd his left knee doesn't quite bend. He holds the log but distributes most of its weight behind him until he throws it into the fire. His breathing labored. As the log leaves his hand his shoulders slump for a weary moment and I fear he'll fall in after it. But he picks himself up, loose-necked, and like some sort of zombie he stumbles back to the wood pile for more.

Rae Stryker dances up beside me. She's got six inches on me and her tiny eyes vanish when she smiles, leaving only one gleaming tear from her torn duct. Her smile makes my chest tingle. She says hi and shakes my hand and asks me what my name is, and I'm just going with the motions here because no girl since Charlie has walked up and given me the vibes like that. Is she into chicks? We dance together, or near each other anyway, for a few minutes. I start to move my hips, not that I know anything about dancing. Her scent is drowning out the fire. I'm desperate to make conversation happen. I'm like, "Crazy about doulas, huh?" and she says, "What's a doula?" and tries to soften her look of confusion with a smile. She hands me another beer and we cheers and she keeps checking in with smiles and the occasional pointless question, to which I try to answer just yes or no, or clearly I will babble like an idiot. When I open the beer and take a sip she gets down by my ear and points over my shoulder and says, "Look who decided to come out." I see the white full moon slipping away from behind a whale-blue cloud.

Everyone's dancing now. The beat rattles underfoot, the sparks of the fire cross paths with the sparks from the warm electronic tones that skip across melting bass lines. The shifting smoke and variable heat keeps us all consistently fluctuating—all except a small few who get closer than seems reasonable or even possible. I only notice them when a girl in a wool skirt lifts her shirt to warm a pair of the most delicious breasts I have ever seen. Strawberry nipples and no shred of shyness to her movements. Her hair is dirty blonde, shoulder length, framing a face far superior to any this town has ever produced. Her features are exquisitely plain, the symmetry broken only by a silver ring on the left side of her nose. Her dance is slow. Every movement flows from her hips. Two men stand on either side of her, watching the fire. One wears a leopard-print robe. His head is shaved. A single trail of ink the same width and color as his sculpted facial hair drains down the bridge of his nose from the apex of an upside-down triangle tattoo locked between his eyes. Darkness cowls the angles of his body. The other guy is lighter, rounder, softer, but just as beautiful. His robe is simple, thick hooded around his hair and ears. These three, the woman and her two lovers, they're more than human. I've seen pleanty of kids at school play dress-up, but this is the first time I've ever seen anyone I would really call magic. Their gestures seduce the flame. Her hands press together in a salutation and her shoulders are serpents cradled by the leopard-robed man. Her thigh nuzzles his hip. He makes an arch of her spine, draping her backward over his hands. Her hair cascades through the dust, her throat revealed to the stars and he cups the tip of her chin that surrenders to the ripeness of his lips.

The old man brings more logs, two at once this time. His head flops to one side and sways. His eyes dead as he walks past me, gazing into the immeasurable distance of the night. Tosses one log, then the other. Dust clouds his ankles. His boots are dirty, tied but flared at the tongue. Suddenly it all comes together. I've figured it out. The beautiful sorcerous ménage-à-trois has enslaved him. This thought expands until it occurs to me in an instant that all across the world sinister young wizards are enslaving old hippies with new drugs to work their festivals. The priestess drifts around the fire ring toward the ham-fisted old troll who sways there, panting through lead lungs. She places a finger to the hinge of his jaw, pries his teeth apart and reaches between his trembling lips to put the poison on his tongue. She kisses his forehead and he gets back to work.

Rae dances up to me again. "He's like a fire elemental," she says. I can no longer control my panic. I feel like I've seen something I shouldn't, discovered a secret not meant for me to know. I'm simultaneously freaked out and intoxicated by all the tall and sexy ladies dancing circles around me. I can't stay here. I look for Derwin or Brooks. I have to leave the fire before they turn me into one of them.

I stumble into the darkness toward the glowing dome lights and flashlights. My eyes adjust to the moonlight that gathers on the low grass like water flowing downhill, moistening the outlining black wings of the trees. I hear something in the bushes and my first thought is that it's the bear. He's rising, he's awake. He's looking at his paws. He's looking for me. Bre sits on the tailgate of Derwin's truck, leaning back and staring at the sky. When she sees me she sits up and hands me another beer.

"First party in the woods?" I say.

"Not even close. How about you?"

"Yeah, I guess," I say. "It's a little intense around the fire."

"Good music, though," she says.

I try to sound grown up. She probably finds it cute. "Yeah, pretty standard stuff. I wish there was a decent DJ in this town."

"All I need is something with a beat," she says.

"Also there's this weird guy."

She looks around. "Is someone messing with you?"

"No. The old guy putting the wood in the fire. He seems, I don't know, fucked up."

"Probably," Bre laughs. "Oh, you mean William? He's a sweetheart. Comes out to all the festivals and takes care of the fires."

"He was walking funny."

"He's an artist," she says, "It's part of his thing."

I don't know what that means. I open the can, feeling less like a newb.

Bre says, "So I heard you told Mirielle about me and Derwin."

Shit.

"It just kind of came out."

"She'd have found out somehow. But not from Derwin. He's got balls up to here except when it comes to her."

I know the feeling.

We don't speak for a while and drinking becomes my substitute for talking. The whole thing seems kind of ridiculous. I don't know if it's the beer kicking in or what but I suddenly just want to get to the point. "You want to know what I think?"

"Of course," Bre says. "Tell me anything."

"I think you must have loved Jason very much."

This isn't what she's expecting. Maybe no one has ever said anything like that to her before.

"I did," she says. "For a while I thought I didn't, but I'm sure of it now."

"People say a lot of stupid shit."

"I've heard it all," she says.

"They want someone to blame."

"I guess."

"Did you think people would love you for it?"

"No. I knew everyone would hate me, but that's not what I told Jason. He worried about me. I told him everyone would be grateful for someone who could give them insight into what he was feeling. But no one asked. Even Derwin hasn't asked. The police asked."

I straighten my back. The funny feeling gets funnier. Her face is round and perfect. "You know what I've heard people say? People say *why her*, like he should've picked someone else. First they talk about how shitty it was of you to even be in that position, that you didn't tell anyone, and then the next minute they're like *why her*—like they would have been a better choice or something. People just feel things and their words don't make sense. We need a separate language for feeling than the one we use for thinking."

I don't blab on like this to anyone but Brooks. And barely even to Brooks. Must be the beer. This magical ass-flavored elixir really does work. Also, I feel amazing. I scrounge around the bed of the pickup for more cans. Bre opens two and hands me one and we say cheers and all that.

"So I figure it's a combination of envy and confusion," I go on, "and obviously rage and powerlessness. The people who really loved him have no one to hate, because they can't hate Jason, right? So you get the job, but they're jealous too and that's just more hate on top of the original hate. And it's worse for Mirielle because of the brother-sister thing. They were really close. Only a couple years apart, right?"

"I met Jason at a tennis match. My boyfriend at the time was playing." Her voice has grown quieter, slower. She looks straight at me when she talks, but when I'm talking she looks at the ground.

"Jason played tennis?"

"His girlfriend did," she says.

"Oh."

"I can't tell who hates me more, her or Mirielle."

"There's a lot of hate to go around," I say.

"I saw him standing behind the bleachers. He wasn't doing

anything. Not even trying to look cool. That's what I noticed first. He seemed to have this super ability not to have to be doing stuff. Like he could just go on pause and be happy. We ended up having a lot in common. And I figured out pretty fast how sad he really was."

"Pretty fucking sad, I guess," I say.

She gets this little smile that's like the offspring of fond memories. "Actually… okay, actually that day—the day before it happened—that day he was happier than he'd ever been. And really all week his mood was growing brighter and brighter. It was like the happier he got the firmer his decision became."

"That makes no sense. How many beers are up here do you think?"

"Why don't you slow down a little?"

"I'm young and resilient. I need my first hangover. You can be my enabler."

This is supposed to make her laugh, but she gets quiet, folds up her hands in the crooks of her elbows and closes her eyes.

"Sorry," I say.

"I don't have any doubts that I did what was best for him. But I have to live with the guilt anyway. My certainty doesn't change that. It makes it worse a little."

"Why was he so happy?"

"He was on an upswing," Bre says, "and he said he never wanted to go through his depressive phase again. Jason was bipolar."

"Really? They said he didn't have a history of anything like that. His mom said—"

"I know what everyone said. But whatever, words are words. Maybe he wasn't. Maybe there's no such thing as bipolar. I don't know. We tend to over-generalize disease, I think.

Pharmaceutical corporations profit off that shit. He told me about his dark times. It was bad, kid. I can't even describe the kind of things he talked about. There was a tone to his voice. But for most of that week, he was up. He had all these realizations. Every little thing was like magic to him."

I scan the dark road and see a Brooks-shaped shadow drawing lines in the dirt with a stick. Concentric circles, rake stems with spiral tails, letters from a language he's trying to invent.

"But you told him—like, you actually said, hey it's okay if you do this?"

Bre nods. "Only when I was sure it's what he really wanted. At first I tried to talk him out of it. For three days I begged him to get help. And then there was the day it all turned around. I was the one telling him it was okay and holding him while he sobbed and told me how scared he was. The day after that life got really weird."

"I have this image of you two sitting in the dark."

"The emotion was intense," she says. "He was rolling through every mood, testing me to see if I'd leave him. I gave him the freedom to do or say anything. I don't think a single thought went unsaid. I didn't go in there with any intention. I just wanted to stay with him. I was determined to know him. But I fucked up I guess. I don't know. It seemed so magical and important back then, and I guess I never thought he'd really... but people have a right to die, even though I wish he'd wanted to live more than anything. I know I'm a horrible person."

"You know what you are?" She looks at me, afraid of what I'll say. "Same thing as me. Same thing as all of us. You're a little bit of sunlight that found a way to slow itself down so it can experience time."

An engine guns behind me, tires scraping in the dirt. Bre squints against the flood of headlights. A caravan of three or four cars joining the party. I want to drink more. I feel something desperate and sinister crawling around inside me, a formless and radiant song whose tonic I have chased all my life, that I've never felt so close to attaining before. I have to find out just exactly how awesome I can feel before it's all over. My attention drifts. I look at the stars, I look for cans, I want to smoke, I want to kiss. I want to run into the dark of the woods where my eyes can adjust gradually to a world of blue outlines and heavy shadows. I hear a car door slam, summoning a lull in the general madness. Then a can cracks and fizzes, followed by a shriek, like some girl just got it in the face.

I lean into Bre and whisper, "The two of you are cute together, you know."

She gets a blush I can see in the dark. "He still believes in the open road. It's gorgeous."

"Derwin's a catch," I say.

"He's just so present, anytime, all the time. A stranger could ask him for directions and he'd sit down and make sure they understood perfectly. The first time I met him I wanted to lick his face."

"You're just hot for foreign boys, sugar," I say.

Bre bites her lip. "Sometimes his accent comes out and it's the sexiest thing ever. Do you want to dance?"

The bearded old troll has hauled the last log to the fire. He leans across the flames and balances it on the tip of another. "See?" Bre says. "An artist. A fire artist." Definitely less like a zombie now. Not at all, actually. Bre rubs my arm and smiles. She hugs me out of the blue and tells me everything's okay. Then the beautiful priestess girl walks up to the old fire guy and wraps her arms around his neck and whispers something in his ear and they laugh and talk like normal people. Everything seems different than before. I can't even guess where those dark thoughts had come from. The spell is broken. Bre calls out, "Hey William!" and he walks over. Not even a trace of a limp or fucked-up joints or mind control.

"Dance with me," Bre says. Our hands clutch and she pulls me into the music. I'm feeling more like a girl than I have my whole life. Her momentum becomes my own, radiating from the space between us, constructing a pillar of the breathless swarm to which we pin all our bullshit. She's talking but I can't understand a thing; I just listen to the sound of her voice. We move in so many circles. Derwin shows up and breaks out the fist and the palm and trounces everyone. Brooks looks up from his formula, staring down the road at approaching headlights. Freshmen grip each other in Greek wrestling poses, struggling for the honor of their senior overlords. I feel my skin expand away from my body, reaching out to touch the branches, the leaves, the sky. I fall in love with whatever I see.

We dance closer to the center of energy where conversations overlap, finding airspace enough for everyone. I drink another beer and keep one in my pocket. Derwin tosses me a third and I let it drop at my feet. College kids start to arrive. One new voice takes my attention, a guy from up north. He's with his wife and the presence of marriage in the mayhem generates a strange center of social gravity. He talks about hunting deer in Wisconsin, about his eighty-year-old grandfather climbing trees to cut down diseased limbs. He has the voice of a radio DJ, but it's the deftness of the way he and his wife co-handle the storytelling that draws me in. They operate like a sailing team, him on the mast and her at the rudder. His constant flow of anecdote after anecdote meekly interrupted at moments where his concentration falters and he starts to derail—here she tosses out a word or phrase, lobbing them into the path of his voice. He catches each one and slides back on track, every now and then acknowledging her assist with a "thank you, babe" or a pat on the ass or an arm squeeze or just a self-conscious "right" followed by an amendment based on her interjection. His stories are boring, but the juggling act between lovers hooks me. I find myself longing for that sort of partnership, something smooth and polished to the point where it seems natural. Is this what drunk is? My eyes start to cross. I have to stop myself from laughing at sad stories.

I can still hear the husband's voice in my head when I realize he's no longer talking. Matthew Craig has arrived and he's jumped on the guy's back and is slapping his belly from behind. I didn't even notice them drive up. He takes the husband down to his knees in like a tickle fight. I start looking for Mirielle. Nothing is visible outside the immediate circle of the fire. When she walks into the light, she does so right where I'm already looking. At first I think she's coming to me, but then she hits the arc of her path and I can see her eyes strike out past the fire. She sways up to Derwin like a metronome. Her hair is wild and she wears a red broomstick skirt. Orange firelight reflects off the top row of her teeth, and for a minute I think things might be okay until I realize how wasted she is. She nearly collapses into him, throws her arms around his neck and starts trying to dance. I've never seen him so uncomfortable. She's whispering in his ear and he's trying to get away. The moon is high, running through a maze of cloud breaks. Mirielle turns her head, looking for Bre. When she sees her she only speaks in a whisper, but it's the clearest voice I hear. "There's the bad girl bitch who killed my brother."

✳

Derwin wiggles out of Mirielle's grip. Bre steps between them like a wall. Mirielle smirks. She shoves Bre with both hands, forcing her to take a step back to keep her balance.

"That's it?" Mirielle slurs. "Just gonna take it? I thought you had some big balls club or something."

Bre says nothing so Mirielle walks around her, lunges again at Derwin who's trying to take steps backward. Wraps both arms around his neck, saying things that might be words. Derwin pushes her off him again, and this time she falls on her ass in the gravel. Her legs flat out in front of her. Her face hidden behind her hair. I can't tell if she's laughing or crying.

"Whoa, whoa, whoa!" Here comes Matthew Craig, climbing out of the puddle of testosterone. Derwin throws his hands up in abdication. He's so calm I can't stand it.

"You asshole," Mirielle says. It's a voice that sounds like it comes from a seven-year-old.

"Dude," says Matthew Craig, and he says it again. He likes Derwin is maybe the reason fists aren't flying right now.

"*Dude*?" Mirielle screams. "That's what you're going to say?"

The look Matthew Craig gives is precious, stepping up on Derwin. His right fist cocks back like a shrug. Derwin shakes his head.

"Not cool," Matthew Craig says. Derwin drops his hands. He braces by relaxing.

Matthew Craig swings without enthusiasm. Sort of slap-slugs Derwin somewhere behind his right eye. He stumbles back, but doesn't fall. They stare at each other. Matthew Craig's whole body is apologetic. Derwin's merely still.

Matthew Craig hopes it's enough and looks back at Mirielle for like affirmation. "You're an animal," she hisses, though I'm not sure who to.

Bre huddles into Derwin's side and he puts his arm around her. "Let's go," he says.

"That's right. Run away, you prick," Mirielle screams. Her palms are flat on the ground like she's drawing energy from the earth.

I feel Brooks next to me. "Information," is all he says.

"Run away," Mirielle taunts. "It's the only thing you're good at." The crowd forms an instinctual hemisphere around her, drawn to the simmering violence. Waiting for it to explode.

"Dude."

Bre and Derwin have left the light of the fire. She's trying to touch his face, and he keeps pulling back. Mirielle still screaming. She is an unstoppable winter storm. "When I needed you. After that bitch murdered him." Bre stops, turns around and comes back alone. She gets within a foot of Mirielle, crouches down so they're face to face. "I'm sorry you're hurting," she says.

"Thanks a fucking lot, Dr. Kevorkian," Mirielle says. "Is that what you told my brother?"

Their eye contact holds. Mirielle scoops up handfuls of dirt, lets them fall into tiny mushroom clouds of dust. Derwin comes up behind Bre and puts his hands on her shoulders.

"You and your stupid goddamn jacket," Mirielle says.

I see the moment. The night of the funeral, the night he left. She's begging him to stay, clutching his arms. He's pulling away. She's not letting go. Him feeling that he either had to stay forever or slip out of his jacket and never look back. Leaving her holding onto the inside-out sleeves, sobbing into the cracked leather.

"Information wants to decay," Brooks says.

"What are you talking about?"

"Nature is the decryption of the cypher of death."

Matthew Craig crouches down to comfort Mirielle. "Hey, are you okay?" he says. She thrashes around, hitting him in the arms and chest. She shoves him back from where she sits. "Get away from me." Each of these words is smaller than the last.

So when did he get the jacket back?

Derwin and Bre return to the car and he opens the door for her. He glances around, looking for us. I want to tell him to just go. Or maybe we should run to the truck. Brooks doesn't move. I imagine his mother's voice: *I'm leaving, Brooksy. I'm going.* Feels like the music has grown louder. Derwin gestures at me. I shake my head no. We've got a tent here. He's reluctant but Bre leans out the window and they talk. Then he smiles and waves to us, and they drive away. This is the best thing that could have happened.

"We are a high frequency transmission," Brooks says. I turn to face him. He's shivering, looking past me. The kid only brought a sweater.

Mirielle's still on the ground. I want to swoop her up. Fuck this ego-laden visionary shit. It isn't fair. "I want her, Brooks." My hands are in fists and I don't remember how they got that way. "I want her so bad."

Not shivering—Brooks is shaking. He's in another aura is what I suddenly realize is happening. His eyes go glossy, pupils dilate past the white edge of awareness. Not looking anywhere.

"Oh my god."

"I'm fine," he says. "Go to her."

I've learned to trust him in times like this. He knows something, like he's connected to some invisible transcendent space. There's nothing we can do here anyway. If a seizure hits, it hits, and we'll hold on until it passes. So I obey. Everyone else is

197

sort of milling around, trying to decide when it will be cool to start having fun again. Matthew Craig doesn't know what the fuck to do. I stand facing Mirielle. She can see my shoes. Her hands huddle under the canopy of her hair. She's trying desperately to light a cigarette. The flash comes and goes. The crack of a shit lighter. The smell of scorching hair. I wait for her to notice me. She drops her cigarette on the ground. "I don't even smoke," she says. All her rage precipitates into sorrow, brokenness. Her face may as well be spattered in rain, teardrops smearing to speed up their decay.

"I'm not a raving bitch," she says.

"I'm drunk," I say.

I reach for her. I know she can't see me but her hand finds mine and I try to help her up. She's so wasted and I am too a little and I just end up falling down next to her. She grabs the cigarette from the ground and crushes it. Fragments of dry tobacco slip between her fingers. I should be trembling, desperate for her hands again, but I feel nothing electric when I touch her skin. She seems like a child to me right now, like someone I need to be close to for her own safety. I am on watch tonight. Her head sways between her knees. We don't speak. The music ushers indifferent gods to pore over the flames. The minutes sweep everything into shadow as conversations spark around us like little exploding charcoal mines. I am warmed only by the realization that tonight is just one of billions of campfire nights that this planet has seen or will see, enmeshed in music and cheap intoxicants while burning plants make the rounds between those who can afford to provide and those who have to accept what is given, with whatever spectrum of pretty girls and dudes—cool and shy, reckless and broken—hangs beneath the occlusion of smoke, with their recurrence of idiotic conversation

✸

masking the surgical arrows of unnaturally enhanced feelings that will linger on into dull days and weeks of images reshaped, from the awkward to the legendary to the eternally unreclaimable memory of this brief and neverending night.

14

IN THE MORNING I HAVE eyes of wood and fingers of glass. My mouth is sticky with signal noise. My hair is an orchard in winter. My lips are sun-dried tomatoes, my teeth are at war, my belly button hates everyone. I run my fingers violently through my hair. Is this my first hangover? All the awesome I felt last night has inverted itself into one tiny searing needlepoint stitching dura matter to the calcified ledge of my cranium. The sun already high above the ridge. I can't remember falling asleep or even lying down. Apparently I never made it to my tent, but someone was nice enough to cover me in a scratchy wool blanket.

The only thing that revives me are the ambient sound coming from the speakers. I've heard about morning sets but this is my first experience with them. I always figured it would be annoying, but it's beautiful and comforting. Music that seems to rise up from the ground and settle as low as mist, like if I stood up my ears would be too high above the sound to hear it.

Brooks isn't in the tent, but his sleeping bag is unrolled and unzipped and crumpled up like someone used it. I check down by the fire pit where a few kids hunch over in meditative poses or poke sticks into the lingering coals. I find Brooks on the little wooden bridge over the creek. He's dropping stones and watching the ripples. He doesn't look at me.

"I couldn't get you to the tent," he says.

"It's okay."

"Like trying to roll a boulder uphill."

"I feel like shit."

"You threw up."

"I did?"

"There were these couple minutes where I thought you were dead."

"Is your brother coming to get us?"

He shrugs. "She's still here," he says.

I'm starving, which means Brooks probably can't even think straight. I guess I'll tear the tent down. I'm supposed to be at the Home at two for work.

As I try to cram the rain fly into a bag that was barely big enough for tent poles, Derwin's truck pulls up. He's alone, leaning out through the passenger window. "You guys ready?" He's got a nice little shiner from last night, and one hell of a guilty look to go with it. I want to let him off the hook somehow so I point up the road to where I last saw Brooks, but Brooks isn't there anymore. It's Mirielle now, disheveled, facing away and looking into the treetops. Derwin pulls forward and parks, gets out and goes to her.

"Where's what's-her-name?" Mirielle says. She puts a fist on Derwin's ribs and won't look at him. Drops her head onto his chest. They walk farther up the road to a little windfall and sit down on the bleached corpse of an old tree.

"Matthew took off," she says.

"I heard," Derwin says.

"Do you love her?"

"Yeah, maybe."

"Do you ever think about me?"

The car door slams and when I look it's Brooks sitting in the driver's seat, knuckles studded on the steering wheel until Derwin pushes him over. We all drive out of the mountains together. Mirielle doesn't say a word the whole trip, just keeps her eyes latched onto the crawling road. Halfway down the mountain she leans over and puts a finger under Derwin's chin, tilting it toward her. She examines his eye, touches the purple bruise. There's no emotion in her face. Brooks talks about last night, how he went walking through camps and getting people to give him hot dogs to roast, about whittling a stick with their dad's old pocket knife, about watching little demon cities disintegrate in the coals. He doesn't mention me at all, though he must've seen me do some stupid shit. We stop in front of Mirielle's house. She doesn't say goodbye. She gets him by the eyes and they stay there for a while before we let her out. Brooks doesn't even notice. He's trying to show me the pocket knife, but I'm watching her, waiting to see if she'll say something to me. Does she even remember?

After she's gone my heart sinks. I'll never love again. "Don't tell Mom I left you alone," Derwin says. "She'll skin me. You guys had fun, right? Feel like a couple grown-ups?"

"We're cool," Brooks says.

At home I dig around the pile of clothes between my closet and my bed, then fall in and lie there for a minute. Something like sleep happens until my mother bangs on the door.

She drives me to work without asking anything more about last night than if I had fun. She doesn't want to know, I figure. But she can tell I'm out of it. She nags me about cramps until I pretended I can't hear her. My four-hour shift is most likely going to feel like it lasts the rest of my fleeting childhood. This time dilation is not just a result of the extreme boredom I've come to expect from putting up with old people. It's mostly my head. I've been sort of stopping now and then to zone out, and this makes me feel a little better. I take two Advil and drink some water. Don't have the guts to take my temperature, but my face feels hot and the word *fever* keeps flashing in my mind. If I have the flu I should definitely not be hanging out around old people. So that's how this girl's logic works: Since I am hanging around old people, therefore I must not have the flu. Then there's the mindfuck of everything that has gone on inside and outside of my head over the last few days. All of this together makes the clocks take their sweet time. But there's nowhere like Chestnut Homes to make feeling completely batshit crazy a community project, so at least I'm in good company.

I hover conspiratorially over Darla's shoulders, pretending to cut her hair. She asked for it and I was bored, but there's no way I'm actually going to cut her hair, so at most I shave off millimeters at a time. She won't notice the difference anyway. I snip the scissors harmlessly in the air and hope the sound comforts her. Occasionally I get into a rhythm of snipping that lulls her to sleep. Her head droops for a second and then snaps back. If I was actually cutting her hair, I probably would've impaled her nuchal region four or five times by now. We face the cream soda wall to the left of the doorway, and I find myself in a stare-down with this old painting of a fire extinguisher that apparently has been hanging there for ages but that I'm only just now noticing. More orange than red, ambiguous background, overly dramatic lighting, hose mysteriously animated to oppose gravity, nozzle aimed threateningly at the real world beyond the canvas, suggesting clownish plumes of magical baking soda coming at me. I want to build a fire and throw the painting on top and scream *where's your god now!* Snip snip. Behind us at the computers Terrance attempts to hack Mirielle's email for me. If I plan on getting her and Derwin to hook up I'm going to need all the help I can get.

Terrance bitches about usernames. "*Mir19*?" Terrance scoffs. "How does it feel to be the 19th Mir, I wonder? You'll never find my real name out there."

"What's your email?" I ask.

"I've got hundreds of 'em. An empire of usernames and personas spread out from Facepalm to 4chan. Some are automated to randomly update blogs and status messages based on statistical modeling of current events and historic reactions to weather, politics, holidays, etc."

The extent of Terrance's psychosis is becoming clear. I start to drift, glancing up at the ceiling where the shadow of a black spider dances across the divots and dried globs of paint texture. Does he realize he's upside down? He stops and slaps his butt on the ceiling a few times until he's nailed a wad of thread down, then glides as if along an invisible fire pole toward the top of Oliver's head. I can't watch.

Terrance is saying, "…that order personalized gifts to be shipped to friends on their birthdays. Automated scripts to update message boards, send congratulatory emails, post book reviews. All based on different aspects of myself. Multiple handles, multiple users. Pieces of my identity who will live on after I die, dispersed across time and space."

I have no words to express my respect for this man. Still, it's been a half hour and no password progress. "How long's this gonna take?" I ask.

"Depends on how stupid her password is."

One console down, Oliver picks away at Google's video search. Every few seconds he grunts in time with the obnoxious looping Nintendo-ish music coming from a hidden window he can't figure out how to close. The spider changed his mind about Oliver's head and is trickling back up the thread to the ceiling where he moves down a few inches before doing it all over again. This time his descent brings him to the mousepad. Oliver's jittery fingers wobble above him. I wonder how many yards of thread dangle unnoticed from one wall to the other.

"Not too much, dear," Darla says for like the zillionth time. She scratches her nose. In lieu of a barber's chair, Darla sits within the bracket of her high-class walker that looks like an inverted starship console. There was a time when Darla used to work as one of those ladies who made recordings for companies like Audichron and Bell and AT&T in the '60s or whatever. Terrance says she and someone named Jane Barbe shared some boyfriends and things got pretty nasty for a while. He found this clip on the internet of Jane saying, "I'm sorry all circuits are overloaded now," and he swears this was recorded the morning after some serious drama and that there's a twinge of rage in her voice. I don't hear it at all. Terrance makes Darla say things like, "Your call was not completed as dialed, please check the number and dial again," and she always does it, flattered that anyone remembers her.

What I love about cutting my own hair is the freedom of movement. I can do it in front of a mirror or lying on my bed. I can do it in stages and stop when I get bored. I can live dangerously and do it while I'm dancing. A pair of scissors in my hand will never hurt me, and the more reckless I am the more tenderly they care for me. But it freaks me out when someone else does it. My mother for instance. Static and statuesque I am vulnerable. I fear the intention of scissors disengaged from my own personal movement. Some forgotten childhood misbehavior lurking around in her psyche subconsciously moving her hand a quarter inch too far and there'd go my ear. Sometimes she insists. I can come quietly, she says, or pack my suitcase and my aesthetic sensibilities and move into Chestnut Homes.

Oliver has spotted the spider. He's fixated by its presence. The spider stops a fraction shy of the mousepad's dead center. Seems to perform squats on all eight knees. Oliver's fist rises like a hammer. A murderous look in his eye.

"It's bad luck to kill a spider in your own home," Terrance says.

"I didn't take you for the superstitious type," says Oliver, wavering.

"It's pure logic. You wouldn't understand."

"Why does it keep saying *rejected*?" I ask.

Terrance slaps his mouse up and down on the pineapple mouse pad. "Rome wasn't built in an hour," he shouts. "It's these damn GUIs. They slow me down!"

Oliver's fist still raised, his eyes firm on the table. I think he's forgotten what he was intending to do.

"She won't be able to tell, right?" I say. "Like, she can't realize we've tampered here."

"What are you saying, honey?" Darla croons. I tell her to shush and stop moving. I keep snipping.

"You just worry about your end of the bargain," says Terrance. "Remember, extra-peppered. None of that teriyaki shit." I've promised a box of Slim Jims upon successful access. "A whole box," he reminds me. "My own son won't send any more. Says they're bad for me."

207

"They *are* bad for you."

"I'm 75. Breathing is bad for me."

I give the mirror to Darla and let her admire the transformation. I bust out the Tongue and roll it from hand to hand. What a shitty mood hangovers make. I don't think it's worth it. Haven't felt this low since winter. My brain goes around in circles until I want to scream. Everything I was fired up about last night drowns in doubt today. I wish Brooks would show up. He promised me a maybe.

"You guys think people can see the future?" I ask the room. No one hears me.

Pasha slides back and forth between an electric outlet and the painting of the fire extinguisher. Seriously, who the hell thought anyone would want to look at something like that in their twilight days? I walk over and wave the Tongue in front of Pasha's face. I want him to admit it. Admit he knows that I know. There it is, right out of your notebooks. The flashy movement entices his reptilian brain, and he takes it, his face a slack drooling procession crawling through the mouth of Castle Tonguesworth. Don't stop believing, buddy. I ask him what he thinks about prophecy. He gets a cute little smile and nods with enthusiasm.

"Yeah? Like Nostradamus and Merlin and shit?"

He nods again.

"I don't know," I say. "I think it's stupid."

He points to his chest.

"Don't fuck with me." Once the words are out I realize that I've just mimicked my father's tone. Pasha scowls at me, slides back around the corner, and vanishes into the hall, taking the Tongue with him. I guess that was mean, but I couldn't care less. I'm in a cruel mood. Everything hurts. And the part of me that doesn't believe it, that can't believe it, is what's captaining the ship today, pissing all over the part that wants to believe everything that's been happening to me is legitimately a part of the first real, qualifying quote unquote visions of my life. Like, with real objects and voices—seen, tasted, smelled. I was transported in the lunchroom and in the street. How can I explain? I can't, and because I can't, it can't be real. This rebellion in me will not be suppressed.

"A little more off the sides, dear," Darla says. This is going to be the longest haircut in history.

It's a thing of wonder to see a woman in her eighties admiring her own face. That little smile. What does she see? I'm a ghost creeping in the background. Can't go five minutes here without thinking about the spirits of little kids running around. Wish I could see them. Charlie never believed in ghosts. Blamed it on infrasound and other subtle twitches of nature. She did believe in other worlds, though. Had some weird ideas about a multiverse. I remember one time she reached for me, but didn't touch me. Stopped centimeters from my skin. "Do you feel that?" she said, and I did. "Close counts," she said. "There's millions of universes where I *am* touching you, and they're all rubbing up against each other. The composite. You can feel it. It's your multifaceted neural network. And now…" Then she looked at her hand and my eyes followed her lead and she was touching me. But I didn't feel the difference until I saw it.

I take back the mirror and re-arm myself with the scissors. I snip innocently above Darla's ears. "So I hear this place is haunted?"

Oliver grunts. "Screaming kids running around the halls. Every damn day."

"They're adorable," Darla says.

Back in the Chestnut Hotel days, all the property out behind the grounds belonged to the city. In the early 1900s they had a park back there, and a little wood at the boundary looking out over the river. No one was ever murdered or anything like that as far as we could figure, but it was a place kids grew up.

Of course, Terrance will argue against anything supernatural. "Not a shred of empirical proof for paranormal phenomena," he says.

"Except I hear them every damn day," Oliver says. "That proof enough for you?"

"Proves your brain is in the late stages of atrophy." Terrance slams his mouse again and growls. "This was an art form once. Now it's all trial and error. In the old days I'd overflow a buffer, creep in through the stack and swipe the hash file."

Maybe after they died, wherever they were, the ghosts of neighborhood children wanted to come back to a place they knew it was cool to hang out and worry about absolutely nothing. This whole idea of ghosts lingering right where they died seems dumb to me. If I was a ghost I'd use all my spooky powers to get me the heck somewhere fun.

"How about telepathy," I say. "Possible?"

"Pah!"

"Oh, yes," Darla says. "I went out with a psychic once. He used to anticipate the weather, knew who was calling when the phone rang. He could definitely read my mind."

"In the sack," Terrance says.

"Can you remember a time?" I say. "Like a time when he knew something would happen and then it did?"

Darla thinks for a minute. A long minute. I start to wonder if she didn't hear me or if she's forgotten the question. Terrance taps on the keyboard. I'm going to be pissed if he can't pull this off. Pasha slinks back into the room, still with the Tongue in his right hand, but now he's got like this red duffle bag in his left. Looks heavy. He rests the Tongue on the top of the bag and fumbles around for the zipper.

"He knew I miscarried," says Darla. "Knew it before I knew it."

The rec room door slams open with signature force. Only one resident has the spare energy to waste on grand entrances. Donald Victoria Estringi has wheeled his way downstairs for the first time in weeks.

"Blow up the world, you rotten ragheads," he shouts, "so I can die already!"

He wheels himself by Pasha, saying, "Heya, Chuck, you old Bolshy Wallflower," then diagonally through the center of the room. He hits the brakes behind Oliver. "Spoonbowl. Report!"

Oliver's fist slams into the table, though the spider is long gone. I can hear his false teeth grinding. Darla swoons and Terrance laughs. Generally everyone's pleased as heck to see my old dad. But there's just so much celebrating people their age can do, and the smiles and handshakes only keep his interest for so long. By the time my father goes blazing back toward Pasha, Terrance announces that he's in. "I seduced the pants off the mysql daemon. This query application granted me show access to the user table. See?"

"Not a clue."

"Well, there it is anyway."

I hear the slow crawl of Pasha's duffle bag zipper.

"That's a pretty intense password."

"It's still encrypted. Now I crack it."

Donald's wheels stop an inch from Pasha's toes. He says, "What's that abomination you've got there, Chuck? Report!"

I've shown my father the Tongue a hundred times and he never remembers, which is exactly what I tell him now. He snatches it from Pasha's hand, holds it close to his eye. Turns it and turns it, checking out every angle. "Never seen this before in my life. Don't fuck with me."

"Whatever," I say.

"That a tongue?"

"Yeah."

"Reminds me of Berlin."

Everything reminds him of Berlin. He spins in his wheel chair, pushes himself toward me in jolts, saying, "We raided this old Nazi lab. Shelves and shelves of tongues just like this in jars of formaldehyde. Each one labeled with a mysterious Babylonian symbol."

"Gross."

"You look like hell," he says. No chance I'm going to tell him about my hangover.

Darla watches Donald like a hawk, and Oliver watches her watch him, and neither are even remotely subtle about it. It's both sweet and disgusting the way I can see lust dripping out of their pleated eyes. When Oliver looks at Darla he seems ten years younger. I can picture slow hairs sprouting up through the shiny white top of his scalp.

"But those tongues were nothing compared to that hole we found," Donald says. "And you wanna know how we found it? We'd covered that area a hundred times. Dogs, choppers, radar, satellite imaging. You get right down to it this land was not our land. Bohemian country. In Doubleya Doubleya Two Hitler had a Jewish psychic. We brought in locals. Told us that the same patch of land, if you walk to it by a different path, will become a very different place. It's not the location, it's the map you use to get there. Changes the whole outcome. Exact same GPS coordinates, exact same environment. But take a new route to the same destination and you end up somewhere else entirely. First it's all roots and rocks and concrete slabs. Next time it's a bottomless pit to hell and back."

He turns his attention back on Pasha, rolls up real close so he can nudge his legs with the wheels. Pasha slips further down the wall. He's still unzipping the bag, a few teeth at a time. "How deep was it, you ask? No one knows. We tried to measure it. The Marine Corps of Engineers of the greatest nation on earth could not plumb its depths. Where did it come from, you ask? We never figured that out either, but maybe you know, eh Chuck ol' pal?" His pursuit of Pasha prods him until he's forced to retreat again, but the poor guy is running out of wall. "Come on, Gingerheart, let go, take the plunge. What would your comrades think?"

"Oh, leave him alone," Oliver says. "He's got the right to stand wherever he wants."

"But he's taking the whole thing for himself. Maybe there's other people who want a piece." Donald wags a finger at Pasha. "Got his own two legs and won't even stretch 'em out. It's an insult to the infirm. Come on, Chuck, have a heart!"

Pasha continues to flee. He's got the bag open now, red flap flopped over like a tongue. Maybe I should see what he's up to. Visions of school shootings juxtapose with the absurd image of Pasha's skinny arms trying to lift any kind of weapon. Is this it? Pasha's moment of glory? Will he gun us all down as the recoil pushes him into the sheetrock, fusing him at last with his wall? His moans increase in intensity as Donald backs him into the corner. Dealing with this kind of thing is supposed to be my job, I guess. "Come on, Donald," I say, "let's play chess." Maybe I should wheel him back upstairs. I put the scissors in my pocket and make a move toward my father. But he senses my approach, momentarily dropping his torment of Pasha to slip my grasp, then zooms over to the other side of the room where an old lady named Ane Lopez Lopez has drifted into a nap over the span of the last ten seconds. Donald thrusts his Dionysian nose up to her slumping head. "Woman," he cries. "Defend your honor!" Ane's eyelids nearly launch off her face. She squeezes her sagging boobs, groping for her heart.

"There's fifty ways I could have killed or otherwise defiled you just now," my father scolds her, wheeling himself in slow circles. "Sleep with one eye open. Don't you know life's a fragile thread that could be snapped at any moment?"

"Oh, I don't care," Ane mutters.

Donald is on his way back to Pasha. When we cross paths I give him a warning glance. He returns an impish grin, wheels by, and starts up again. "Chuuuuuuuck!"

Darla pulls the towel off her neck and examines her blouse for bits of hair. I shoot a quick text to Brooks saying we really have to talk and I wish he'd get over here pronto. I pick the mirror up and glance at Terrance's console. "I may not be a big, tough hacker like you," I say, "but I know what 'access denied' means."

"Musta fat-fingered something," he mumbles.

"Come on, Chuck," Donald laughs, "hop over here onto daddy's lap. I'll give you a ride. What if I leave the chair? Will you trust me then?"

Oh, balls—really? I turn just in time to see Donald fling himself onto the floor, knees cracking on the ground. I swear I hear a hairline fracture. He teeters there, hamming it up, letting his torso sway. His palms hit the floor. He growls. Pasha trembles, trapped between Donald and the computers. His right hand digs around in his bag.

I don't exactly leap to action. Maybe I should call a nurse. I think I might need one, too. A dizzy spell hits me out of nowhere. I look for something to stabilize myself and I find Darla's shoulder.

"Are you okay?" Darla says. For a second I think she's talking to me. Three fingertips shelter the lavish concern of her mouth. Her eyes are latched onto the prostrate and maniacal form of Donald Victoria Estringi.

"Come on, Chuck, crawl on down here with me. Climb on my back. I'll take you over the rainbow bridge." He reaches for Pasha's ankles. Pasha manages to dodge, wild moans rising in pitch, filling the room, ramming into my headache. He kicks at Donald's hands, but his kick is more like a harmless wiggling of the toe. Donald toys with him, slapping the bottoms of his slippers. Darla hoists herself off of her walker to intervene. As far as I can tell she has no clue what a jackass my father is being, only that he's fallen and he can't get up.

I get a text from Brooks telling me to stop peeing my pants, that he's working on a plan. He asks if I've seen any ghosts today, but I never see any ghosts. I am not cool enough to see ghosts. All I do is make up visions and pretend that there's magic in the world, but when it all comes down to it I'm obviously just delusional. And not the awesome kind of delusional where you get to talk to people who aren't there. It's the kind of delusional where you lie to yourself with such expertise you think you're something special, and then one hangover is all it takes to reveal the infinite layers of bullshit in your psyche.

I text Brooks no ghosts and not to bother with his plan because I take it all back. *I made it up,* I say.

Donald's got a hand on each of Pasha's ankles. Pasha is no longer fighting back but has slipped into some sort of catatonic defense mechanism. Eyes clenched tight. One hand flat against the wall. He's trying to become the wall. His head cocks to the side until his nose nearly touches the frame of the painting of the fire extinguisher. With my head in my phone I don't notice Darla creeping up behind me. She says, "The poor dear," from like three inches away, right at the exact moment Pasha turns his bag upside down, shaking notebook after notebook out onto the floor until there's like 30 journals splayed open and sliding all over the place. I get the chills and scream, without exactly realizing it's me who screamed, "*Stop it!*"

Donald obeys. He gives me a look like a soldier would give his commander. I just want to crawl under my bed and sleep. Pasha shuts his mouth. Only now that he's stopped moaning do I realize how loud he'd become.

My phone buzzes in the fresh silence. A new text from Brooks. Everyone's looking at me and I look at my phone. *You're just afraid*, it says.

Darla kneels next to Donald. She strokes the backs of his hands. His hands still have a death grip on Pasha's ankles. But he's lost his drive now that he's wrestling with a statue, now that this invasion has come and gone. It wouldn't surprise me if Pasha has jumped so far back in his head he can't even hear the rest of us anymore. Darla pries my father's fingers off of Pasha in the same way I imagine my mother prying the military issue pistol out of his hands mere hours before my conception. One of those random moments in time perpendicular to plan, when we're overcome by the unregulated energies springing up out of the forgotten nooks of our contrived personas to shove habit aside and reveal a thing almost surprising enough to call the true self.

My mother had saved his life and taken him into her body and then he'd followed her all the way here from the other side of the planet. I am a wondrous accident, far more connected with ancient cosmic currents than anything as fashionable as motive, most of which probably only arise after the fact anyway. We are always exploding and recovering, and in our hangover hours we make up stories to connect the disjointed dots of our passions.

Brooks texts again. *Afraid of being wrong. Because you know that if you are you'll only find out after it's too late.*

In other words, grow some balls.

Pasha remains unnoticed, notebooks everywhere. I mimic his pose, flattening myself next to him. My head throbs as it touches the wall. I kind of want to tickle his ribs, but instead I lean my ear against them and feel his shallow breath. Somewhere inside a tiny creature of feminine light hides, aching for release, awaiting her moment of power.

It's already too late, I text back.

"What on earth is going on in here?" Jen, one of the nurses who doesn't completely suck, has arrived on the scene, and is already kneeling down by my father. Short, dirty-blonde hair with a ladybug hairpin over each ear. Bright violet scrubs with a royal purple hem and a yellow sunflower patch stitched above the breast. She never quite smiles, but I like her; maybe that's why I like her.

"My chair has become a hinderance to me," Donald says.

"Lexie, you're supposed to be watching them," Jen says.

"I'm sorry."

With the help of Darla, who's had a lifetime to learn how to love, Jen manages to lift Donald back into his chair. Darla smoothes his hair. Jen sighs, looking around. "Let's get Pasha back to his room, okay? Why don't you follow us, Mr. Estringi?"

Jen takes one of Pasha's arms and I take the other. We slide along the wall with him until he's shuffled to the end of the hall, as Donald wheels himself behind us.

"I've got him, Lexie." Jen is restraining her frustration as best as she can. "Would you gather the journals, please?"

I get everything up off the floor and start shoving notebooks into the duffle bag. I find one I don't recognize. A purple cover, not the standard black that Pasha always uses. These go in the bag, while the new one goes up my shirt.

They're just about to his room when I catch up. Jen asks me what happened.

"I don't know," I shrug.

"Chuck started it," says my father.

"His name is Pasha, Mr. Estringi," Jen says. "Can't you just let him be?"

"You remind me of a woman I used to love," Donald says. "Her name was Eloise."

After we wrap Pasha around the perimeter of his room, following the wall to his headboard, and lay him down under his tortilla flap of blankets, Jen tells him he might need a nap after all the excitement. He keeps trying to sit up and she keeps pushing him back down. I guess I've sort of drifted around the room by now. I drop the duffle bag by his desk. Jen hovers over him, trying not to get too close. Pasha looks across her shoulder toward the ceiling and makes buzzing moans through loose, flapping lips. I tell Jen I need to pee. She seems surprised I'm still there and says to go.

When I walk out Donald winks at me. "You'd have made a good agent," he whispers.

"Thanks," I say. "Chess in fifteen?"

"I'll set up the board."

I find the closest storage closet and slip inside to read, leaning against some old supply shelves. The new book is mostly empty. Just one full page with tiny handwriting and a few sketches. At the top he's written, *Map of the Empire* in gorgeous calligraphy, and below that: *The symbiosis and contrareliance of vegetable and animal respiration.* Then for half a page there's this intricate collaboration of winding lines impossible to decipher. As thick and tangled as a ball of rubber bands. I'd need a magnifying glass to follow any single path. What pen can draw so finely? I picture Pasha dipping a needle in an inkwell, etching his lines for days, stopping only to sharpen the needle with a knife. There are a dozen circular clearings among the—labyrinth, I guess? Intersecting circuits? Each line labeled with a number. A flowing ribbon makes a parameter like Saturn's rings around the outside of the machine. It looks like the Tongue, wrapped in orbit, the snake licking its own ass.

Vegetation deceivest through the illusion and artifice of pleasing shapes and flavors, but all is wholly unnatural. I bring you artifacts from the real world.

Here he's drawn a small black rectangle no wider than a fingernail. On its longer sides several silver spear points spaced equally apart. Like a little square insect with numbers on its back.

...the significant cultural and medicinal employance of ethnobotanicals, specifically the possibility of signal pheromones and other forms of molecular communication...

Another sketch, this time of a bolt and washer, long rusted and brittle, flaking off the top. There's a caption under this one: *A joint of the ancient world, fossil of the gods, flesh of our ancestors. The numeric dynamic behind the construct of the corporeal. Eternal incrimination.*

Then the main text goes on… *Recent experiments with extracted alkaloids from plant matter in a deprotonated amine state reveal molecular structures similar to that of experimental silicon crystals when, at surprisingly high temperatures, a dioxasilirane with an SiO_2-peroxo ring is*—and then something about humans feeding on the fetuses of plants, which is creepy in a way that makes me read the sentence a few times over just for the feeling. After that he starts going off about medicine and drugs and war. There's a drawing of a woman sitting on the ground between two trees. She has something on her tongue. Two wiggly arrows descend from the trees toward her head. Her eyes are closed. Above the drawing, in quotes, Pasha has scribbled: *He is made subordinate to the orderability of cellulose. They shall not always idle.*

Below all this, at the very bottom of the page, are words I read a dozen times over: *In our blindness we are received. Countless spirits surround you now, projecting the images thou dost enjoy. Plump as Cupid, thou art, peeking in from the outside, your face veiled in vines. She is your child, but you are neither father nor mother. How many different worlds will burst open, having drooled to drift, under a candle moon, along the very tips of a coalition of trees, flowing from the heart of the slobbering road down over its waterfall tongue into an ocean of stars. On it's surface she stands, a key to all locks—*

The page ends. I'm huddled forward, knuckles white on either side of the notebook.

Plump as Cupid… Slobbering road…

The closet door opens. Jen stares at me with disapproval. I try to spin up a good excuse but my brain isn't working right. I'm thinking backwards. Effects preceding the cause. "You look pale," she says.

*

...She is your child...

I was expecting an ending. I was sure he'd written an ending. Why else would he take his work out after all this time? Why throw his books on the floor?

...but you are neither father nor mother...

He wrote this page today.

"Lexie?"

He wrote it for me.

"Lexie are you okay?"

Feels like it, anyway.

"Lexie!"

Feels like falling down.

15

I STARE DOWN THE EMPTY hall where two long rows of blue lockers bolt to white brick. This is it. The last day of school. The end of being a dorky freshman. I'm late to class. Not that anyone cares, not today. Voices pop out from behind wooden doors and frosted windows and the atmosphere feels like the launch pad into summer. And last night after they sent me home from work I went straight to bed, but I woke up to a call from Bre on the actual phone where she let me know there's a chance I might be invited on their next raid, tagging GSB slogans all over town and looking for the property of pompous assholes to desecrate. Some sort of initiation may be involved. She said now that I'm technically no longer a freshman they're going to give me a chance. No longer a freshman. This is a theoretical huge deal. Now I have become a real person or whatever. Last day, go away. A few teachers will play a game of trying to enforce the rules until the bitter end, but Mr. Kratz will definitely let us out early. Miss Pushing mentioned something about a party. Mr. Johnson will insist on lecturing about random aspects of colonial history just to torment us, and say things like, *we're here to learn* and *it's not over 'til the bell rings.* A lot of kids I'm sure didn't even show up. Others will leave after lunch. There's not a senior in the building.

A cartoon mural of our school mascot hangs out down on the far wall between two opposing sets of stairs. Reggie the Badger, sporting a maroon sweater and peeking out over these like 80s sunglasses. I stare him down, locking my right eye on his head and closing my left. I hold up a finger to blot him out. Then I close my open eye and open the closed one and my finger magically leaps over to cover his elbow. I go back and forth, faster and faster. Parallax used to be a high-tech navigation technique back in the ancient times; now it's something we do when we're bored. I walk by the trophy cabinet, the announcements marquee, the office. The secretary doesn't even look up. I'm late already, so why rush? I move in a slow deliberate line, the heel of one shoe touching the toe of the other. I stick out an arm and my nails scrape over the blue tin locker doors, snagging the cracks, slapping padlocks that clamor and sway. Music in all of it.

Allegedly, Mirielle hasn't left her house since the party. And she allegedly won't see Matthew Craig or take his calls either. He texts her all the time, reports say. His alleged texts fluctuate between weepy and mental. And Rae Stryker told Gail Langley who told Maggie Andrews who told Clay Driscoll who told Brooks that also that Matthew Craig has been stalking Mirielle on like an hourly schedule, driving past her house and looking in her window. According to unknown witnesses he even walked up and knocked on her door and went inside and had a chat with her parents and spilled his guts and maybe even dropped a few tears, and then he asked her dad for permission to marry her. The teenage network is thick with spies. Information wants to decay. Between texts and drive-bys Matthew Craig has also been allegedly getting wasted and punching alleged faces. Brooks says it's a miracle he's not in jail right now, which is sad because

*

Matthew Craig seemed like a pretty level-headed goofball, and all this raging is quote not in his character, friends report. It's what the Mirielles of the earth do to guys. Not on purpose, but just by existing. With the mere attempt to cohabit with humans the wide-eyed goddess dredges up floods and tsunamis and earthquakes and war.

My finger hits locker 71 and sticks there. I can smell her perfume through the corrugated vents. I'm right between the end of this block and Mr. Fagel's Social Science room, so I stand listening to his incomprehensible voice. Normally he sounds like he's got a bulldog under his tongue, but now I can key in on the rhythm, the pauses between words and the attack of his syllables. He's telling lame jokes. There's a rule against decorating lockers that no one pays attention to and is never enforced. She's painted a big heart with blue fingernail polish so close to the color of the locker itself that you can only see it in the right light. The tip of the heart makes a spiral pointing back to itself.

When my phone buzzes the first thing I think is maybe it's GSB calling me to action. *I'm in*, I think. *I'm in, I'm in, I'm in*! Gonna go bounce around in the dark and wear a bandana and not fuck up. Squeeee! Shush. No squee. Be chill, Lexie. This is not a club for children. Ugh, I can't even look. Phone stays in pocket, which is not easy to do.

Her padlock is long gone. I lift the clasp, let the door swing open. I hang onto the scent, rest my fingers there. It's empty other than some lingering glitter and a blue pen cap, but then I notice something else wedged behind the metal in the back corner. It's the olive green scrunchie that I stole and then left on Matthew Craig's passenger seat for her to find. It's come back to me. Is this a sign? She's mine to have and mine to give up. The problem with nurturing two conflicting desires isn't when they fight; it's when they gang up on me. Sometimes I feel one and sometimes I feel the other, and sometimes they argue over which one is right. Those days I can handle. But it's times like today that wreck me, when they huddle together in the pit of my stomach, side by side, calmly mewing up at me, demanding that somehow I satisfy both at the same time when in reality neither is likely or probably even remotely possible. I yank the scrunchie free from the pinch of metal. There's a list of names written back there too. Some crossed out with angry black lines. Derwin is third on the list, both circled and crossed out. Next to this, in quotes, she's written: "This is the wonder that's keeping the stars apart." I put the scrunchie in my pocket.

My phone goes off again. A call this time. Brooks never calls, so who else could it be? I physically have to stop and control my breathing. I have no idea why I'm torturing myself like this. I'm terrified they'll say something like, "Sorry but you didn't make the cut. Find a different group to annoy."

Closing the locker door and pushing off the wall I take a few more unstable steps in no particular direction, drifting in the silence and emptiness of thirty-foot ceilings that rain down the sickly yellow light of industrial-sized incandescent tubes. A classroom door opens way down under Reggie the Badger's back foot and a dozen kids flood into the hall, shoving each other out of the way in a fierce battle to be the first fucker free. Feet hit the stairs. More doors open. All the doors. The hall starts to swirl and fill with every clique and scene. Thugs, jocks, preps, neo-goths, nerd-core punk drag-queens-in-training, ladyboys, neutards, straight kids who want to be gay, rich kids who dress like the homeless, gamer geeks with self-inflicted tattoos from makeshift styluses assembled out of electric toothbrushes and guitar strings, preppy transplant bitches on the fast track to an

＊

MRS degree, white kids who wish they were ethnic, militant straight-edgers, hyperironic hippie jocksters, acid-head goat-ropers, emo-clown street art political activists, speechie-punk e-tard cowboy scenesters. I recognize none of them. I'm standing in their burning corral. Their torrent of their escape diverges around me as the undertow of some elusive momentum drags them toward the front doors. But there wasn't a bell. How did they synchronize this revolution? I am a rock in the river. I open the palms of my hands, feeling hips and backpacks and jackets brush by. They are running, laughing, screaming. Each face a conformity of communal joy and a unique expectation of the impossibly multifarious possibilities of summer. I see glasses, nose rings, hats, scarves, necklaces, ribbons, chokers, braces, all the lipstick and hair colors of the rainbow, ear gauges, ear buds, lip rings. Half of them hold phones up like above water and update their statuses and snap pictures and dance in place as the coursing tide urges them on. They stick out their tongues; they kiss cheeks; they high five, crack knuckles, slap backs; they grind down on one another's shoulders, grimacing and howling, leaping and slamming into lockers. Their eyes stagger toward the exit and when whoever wins this race for freedom slams the bar latch down, his or her shoulder spearheading the broach of the doors, a rhombus of sunlight sequesters the first lunging tentacle of the horde and its blind victorious roar, and then widens to consume us all. A fanatical swarm, reveling in pure antagonism over the confinement of an entire year—which for us is actually a huge fraction of our lives—seizing the illusion of autonomy with all of the harmony embedded in chaos. They will work and play, spark doomed romances, get out of town for camping trips and city trips and music festivals and summer jobs. Nothing but grins whirling around me now; even the kids who make it a point to never smile like ever cannot help conforming to the total bliss of the moment as they dive headlong into gyrating time, from which some will soberly return an infinite three months from now and others will die in car crashes or other drunken accidents and others will develop exciting new eating disorders or make and blow more cash than they've ever made and blown before while trying to fall in love or fake it as best as they can, or trip over their words and drown in misunderstandings that lead to ruined friendships and abortions and fistfights, or take strange new drugs that will open some eyes to bizarre new ways of looking at the world but cause others to slip into addictions against their will or even understanding, and all shall spark fertile and precarious chains of events that lead to far reaching material and psychological consequences impossible to trace backward against entropy to their elusive origins even if they pay hundreds of dollars to analysts and psychologists, and few if any will remember this frenzied moment flat against the afternoon's seductive embrace, sucked like through the straw of this airlock of enthusiasm which no bell has signaled, which perhaps no single teacher or student has instigated: this irresistible arbitrary moment in time that exploded, spontaneous and unstoppable, at the threshold of a communal flow rising out of the unspoken unanimity of the longing to lunge into a future that is ultimately no different from or more sacred than any other future horizon that tugs us out of every minute of every hour of every day. And, finding it impossible to turn and follow, I embrace the headwind electrified by these diverging filaments, and face the engorged badger who has seen it all before, whose cheesy slanting grin never changes or wavers, who bears the burden of cloaking for a time every last drop of teenage anonymity and energy burning itself out and into space.

＊

The silence left over in the empty hall is far richer than the silence that was here before, encumbered with ghosts and their echoes.

I check Brooks' text. Do I want to see the ocean, he wants to know.

16

I STILL CAN'T BELIEVE MY mother signed off on this. Four days far away from home. I haven't been on the road since we moved here. Careless is the only way to start the summer. I've jammed everything I could possibly fit into my backpack until the zippers become my living nightmare. Clothes, water bottles, pocket knife, Kleenex, pencils, books, notebooks, lotion, clean underwear, a small vial of glitter, scarves, iPod, headphones, and a new fancy pants touch screen portable audio design machine, which for now I am calling my on-the-go laboratory of mad genius. Tampons; fine, mother. Just in case. The olive green scrunchie that I recovered from Miriclle's locker. And snacks. And a water bottle. And that's all.

It's Derwin's trip. He signed up for a tournament that's being held on the last day of the second annual Portland RPS convention and he got us all badges. We don't have to cram into the deathtrap of a Chevy because Derwin's mom let him borrow her car: a little purple four-door sedan with a tape deck. Thank god he has one of those cassettes with the stereo tail that lets you pump digital music over the old bones of antique magnetic swirl. Me and Brooks are in the back. Bre's up front wearing cut-off shorts and sunglasses, looking hot and brooding. It's a warm day on the highway and the windows are down.

Derwin slaps the steering wheel with his radiocarpal joint and sings along to some track from a band he knows back in Czech called *Hog Ranch*. When he sings, his old accent pops out: a weird semi-Slavic rhythm hoisting up the smoothest, coolest tone of everything's-gonna-be-okay-ness. Sometimes Bre reaches over with her fingers to weave around in his hair. This is probably the happiest I've ever seen either of them, and I try not to think about how at some point here I'm going to do everything in my power to fuck that up. Brooks zones out with his own music and watches the world outside. I nag him about his operation. I demand to see the scar. I ask him what frequency he's tuned to and he punches me in the arm.

By the end of the day I have not opened my backpack. I eat two hot dogs, a thing of chicken strips, one Sprite, one orange juice, a bag of corn nuts, a bag of Doritos, and an orange-and-green gummy—what—tarantula maybe? I have had to pee two fewer times than Bre, but to be fair she consumes coffee like it's the air we breathe. We get in way after dark. The city seems bigger, but it looks far more exactly the same as before than I expected. I wake Brooks up so he can see the two Coke-bottle-green glass towers by the river that look like rocket ships ready for launch.

We all share a room on the sixth floor, but we get two beds. The heater is loud, and outside the window I can see a tiny bit of the river bouncing city lights back to the sky. When everyone's asleep I open Derwin's suitcase. I stuff Mirielle's scrunchie in one of the pockets so that just a corner of it sticks out, then return to bed horizontal and anonymous and unable to sleep.

The next morning Derwin and I walk into the general

ridiculousness of the convention floor, which is haunted by a persistent ironclad gravity into whose well only the hardcorest of the hardcore have wagered their entire futures to face. This in hopes of becoming ultimate RPS overlords of the world. These few are easy to spot. They dress without flair, speak to no one, keep a neutral expression, and never practice in public. I guess Portland's one of the smaller scenes. In cities like Toronto or Philly, RPS tournaments can yield grand prizes in the thousands and I've even heard a few of the more consistent champions are starting to pick up endorsement contracts with small, independent brands. I never expected so many marketing spinoffs. Rows of kiosks push the fringes of this underworld, selling merchandise, leading training seminars, writing pamphlets, creating fan art or parody songs, organizing side bets and promoting their hopefuls. Some booths push new tech like RPS training systems and I come across this one app that apparently learns as you play, suggesting moves to you via headset to enhance or randomize your strategy based on a real time analysis of previous rounds.

Derwin's friend Nick sells t-shirts and these like oversized gloves molded into the shape of the three basic weapons as well as the less-used and often-marginalized 'lizard' and 'Spock'. Nick also stocks something called the 'Power Glove' that lights up and makes sounds and mechanically changes its shape when one of five buttons are pressed within the snug interior of the hand chamber. When we're exhausted from walking around Nick lets us chill at his table. I try to be helpful but he isn't really getting enough business to need an assistant. Brooks and Bre decided to spend the day downtown and I kind of regret not going with them, but Brooks tells me he's going to mention the dinner with Mirielle—real casual—because he doesn't think Bre knows she was there. Derwin rests maybe five minutes at a time, then he's back on the floor. I think he must know literally everyone here.

Alone with Nick I get more RPS lore than I'm comfortable hearing. He tells me about how the game goes back to like the Ming Dynasty but that it developed its current form in 19th century Japan, which explains why every fifth person is dressed up like a samurai. Then there's some shit I don't follow about British pulp fiction. He talks strategies and gossips about the big names who are signed up for the main tournament. Tells me something about how lizard mating habits are this evolutionary analog to the fundamental RPS rules. I have no clue. He's one of those endless talkers. I start to zone out. I spot two ladies fighting it out across the hall, one of whom is a seriously banging redhead I would give anything to have the courage to go up and talk to. She has this punk ballerina way about her, like how she always keeps her right knee locked and her foot poised on its toe, and it just drenches me. Her enemy is a sweet-looking younger girl I'd have pegged for a sorority over a nerdfest like this. It's stupid but anytime they tie with scissors I have to laugh.

The variety of stances and throwing styles people have invented blows my mind, whether they're casting attacks into the air or using the more traditional landing platform of the dormant palm. The second hand is the expressive hand. Like for instance rapier-style, raising two fingers behind the head or cocking it on a hip, or sorcery style with the non-dominant hand casting some spell of misdirection, or straight casual with the spare hand in a pocket. There's an occasional cosplay element, and even real serious players will sometimes wear a Zorro mask, or I even saw one guy in this strange wolf-mask, which I guess is supposed to deal with the danger of facial telegraphing. Anything goes, but hiding the eyes like with sunglasses is generally considered cowardly. And ultimately bad strategy, according to Derwin. This is psychological warfare, he says. Your eyes are your best weapons.

After an hour or so he swings back over and invites me down to a little side challenge in one of the panel rooms. Anything to get away from Nick's unending yammering on. As we push through the crowds Derwin keeps looking back to check on me, always with that persistently encouraging smile, just as happy to see me safe and content as he would be to take home the trophy.

"So things are going good with you and Bre?" I ask.

"Yep. Pretty great," he says.

I have no idea what I hope to accomplish here.

We run into someone I've named Mr. Super-Excited-to-See-Us. He's—let's call him portly. Balding. Wears an orange t-shirt way too small for him with this Kabbalah tree of life design that has a different RPSLS gesture (left and right handed) in each of the ten Sephirot. Square glasses frame his pimply little eyes. He bumps fists with Derwin and leans down into my face like I'm a toddler. "This your new girlfriend?" he laughs. Boy does he laugh. "Sorry, hey sorry. Just kidding. I'm Jeffry," and he offers what I think is a sincere hand until I put mine out at which point he goes all scissors and sudden movements and screams "SBP" and makes this cutting off my fingers motion, laughing and assuring me that he's "just teasin'!" He pops back to height and starts blabbing with Derwin as we all three march on. One thing I'll say for Jeffry, he's a champ at bulldozing his way through a crowd.

We end up in a small room with nine dudes and the same two girls I saw duking it out earlier. The sexy redhead leans against the wall while her friend moves around the room writing a number on the back of everyone's hand. She comes to Derwin and they lock eyes while she draws a slow and deliberate I-want-your-cock eleven across his dorsal metacarpal veins.

It's a silent speed match and I have no hope of keeping up. Someone in the cosmos loves me enough to make sure the redhead gets booted first, and she comes over next to me. "You don't play?" she says.

"It's against my religion."

"That's funny." She smiles at me.

"Nice corset," I say. She grabs her boobs and shimmies her shoulders. This is her actual response.

"You here with the cowboy?"

"Mhm."

"He's not bad."

I imagine a world where RPS replaces war. Like just about everything in my brain this gets out of hand fast and I see a planet covered with endless dust storms, whose craters have been terraformed into massive arenas where warriors battle with actual oversized rocks, paper, and scissors—eviscerating, suffocating, and bludgeoning each other for the affections of an acrobatic redheaded princess in a corset.

"So what do you do?" she asks.

"I'm a DJ." Yep, that's what I tell her.

"Cool," she says, turning her body toward me for the first time. Don't let anyone try to convince you lying isn't the best way into a woman's pants. "You play around here?"

Some other poor schmuck has just lost out. Derwin's number is drawn and he steps up.

"No, we're just here for the thing."

"Right on." She's bobbing her head like to an inaudible track I have just spun in her brain.

I see Derwin slam rock, crushing his opponent's scissors. A

risky move, he'd say, throwing rock in a speed round. He gives me a little nod as his next challenger steps up. The thing about a speed round is if you lose one game you're out, but if you win you have to play everyone else until someone beats you, so the better you do the more time the other players have to analyze your technique.

"Wicked parties later," the redhead says. "Any plans?"

"Still feeling up options, you know." Feeling *out* options. Thanks, Freud. I'm pretty sure she doesn't notice, though.

"Totally."

Derwin takes another win, again with rock. There's this technique called the *double run* where you're supposed to watch for two of the same moves in a row. Especially against rookies you can use this maneuver to eliminate one possible attack. A rookie will rarely make the same move three times, so watching for the double run gives you greater odds of a win or draw on the third throw. It's possible Derwin is baiting his opponents, exploiting this technique by stringing together an impossible sequence of rocks. He manages to win two more times with it, then there's a draw, then he mixes things up for a minute before winning again with rock. The stones on that guy.

"He's good," Red says.

But she jinxes him. Derwin throws paper and loses to scissors on the next game. He made it to the top four at least. We sit together and watch the rest play out. Derwin analyzes every move, giving a running commentary without which I like to think I wouldn't be totally lost by now. Jeffry wins it all in the end, which is partially luck of the draw since he wasn't called up until second to last, but Derwin seizes him in a bear hug and treats him like it was a fierce struggle to a grand victory.

"Jeffry's a great player," Derwin tells me later, "but he's got trouble with self-control. He's big into strategy, a double-exclusive most of the time, but he can't seem to relax in the moment. Doesn't handle pressure well."

I spend most of the rest of the afternoon wandering around the convention floor looking for the redhead. I don't exactly intend this. But I'm stuck here and there's nothing much to do after the novelty wears off except go chase something lovely. It helps me get Mirielle off my mind, who—okay but not really, because she keeps coming up even when I'm getting her off my mind. The very fact that she's off my mind reminds me that she is not there on my mind where she once was, making her just as present by her absence. In my mind. So really I'm mostly wandering around pretending I'm not thinking about her, thinking my way around her, looking for the sexy redhead who I will do absolutely nothing about when and if I find her. Just half-heartedly hunting in the hopes that maybe something will surprise me.

I have dozens of imaginary conversations with Derwin. I practice cornering him in the hall. I am a weaver of DNA, and yeah maybe this is all just sublimating or whatever, and maybe I'm analyzing it all to death in a useless drama of coming to grips with the hopeless absurdity of being me, but I really do think they might be perfect for each other. A terrifying perfection. The kind that sometimes ends in violence.

That evening he gives me an opening, while we're standing outside the convention center after they've kicked us all out for the night and we're waiting for Bre and Brooks to pick us up. He brings her up himself. Says he heard I've got a crush.

"Yeah, I guess. She's hot. You know."

"She's hard to miss," he says.

I want to ask if he's still in love with her, but I'm scared he'll say no. But even if he says no it doesn't matter, because I know he is.

"Seniors don't notice freshman," I say.

"You're not a freshman anymore."

That's sweet of him to remind me.

"Oklahoma," I say.

"Yep."

"Sorry about bringing that up at dinner."

He smiles, stares across the road, says nothing.

"I hear the wind comes sweeping through the plains down there."

"You know," he says, "you could tell her. If you wanted."

And if you wanted you could marry her and have a kid. Just saying.

"What for?" I ask.

"For yourself. So you always know you did it."

"Grow some balls?"

"Sure."

"She loves you," I say.

I keep a close watch on his face and if I've caught him off guard he doesn't show it. But he doesn't reply either. Stands there all cool scanning traffic for the car.

"You want pizza tonight?" he says. "I know a good place on Alberta."

That night in the hotel room, the fight comes so out of nowhere and with such venom that I swear we're in an Exorcist sequel and that Derwin and Bre will start throwing themselves at the ceiling at any minute. Brooks and I are on the bed, faces buried in our screens, so I can only guess that she found the scrunchie is what sparked it. The first thing I hear is Bre's voice rising just enough to be uncomfortable. She says, "Wow. You can lie about something, promise me something, fail to keep that promise, get caught in a lie and when I tell you I'm upset, it turns into what you think *I* should be doing differently?" After that I hear so many clichés from the both of them it's like this fight was sponsored by *E!*

We end up getting no sleep. They try to take it into the hall or the lobby and then out to the car, but the proximity is impossible. He chases her back upstairs where me and Brooks watch horrified as she starts packing her suitcase. Where the hell is she going to go? Derwin calms her down for a minute, but then something sets her off again. She's screaming about how he's not even attracted to her and how he doesn't actually want her to come with him to Oklahoma, and when he tries to object every word falls flat because she's shoving her voice so violently into whatever it is he means to get across. Which to be honest I have no clue what that is either. His cool is gone; he's babbling, paralyzed, unable to cope in the face of her anger. She slams the door. Someone across the hall threatens to call the cops. Derwin goes from perplexed to pissed off when it becomes clear this fight is screwing his chances in the tournament tomorrow, and at one point he uses us, pointing to me and Brooks like "think of the children" or whatever. Brooks is already locked inside his headphones without a care in the world. He's playing video games, listening to the sounds of deer antlers scratching on ice or something. But I'm still freaking out, hanging on to every meaningless word. Exhaustion brings her down before anyone in the hotel works up the actual nerve to intervene. She's sobbing on the edge of the bed. He softens, puts an arm around her and she falls into him. This goes on forever and at some point I fall asleep. When I wake up the lights are out and it's maybe 4am and they're under the covers fucking as quietly as they can.

Derwin's up three hours later so he can go down to finalize his registration for the tournament. I don't drag myself out of bed until eleven. By then Brooks and Bre are already up, talking quietly by the door. They shove coffee and doughnuts in my face. We're splitting up again today. Brooks and I are going into the city while Bre checks out the convention. I am completely over RPS at this point. Derwin gave us a twenty in case we get lost and have to catch a cab. We walk the underbelly of the steel bridge and we're lost before we even reach downtown. I don't really need a destination. It's enough for me to walk somewhere where I have no clue what's going to be around the corner. We stumble into this giant bookstore and split up right away. I spend hours flipping through photo books of the Mediterranean, looking for the type of ocean cliffs that might be where the Tongue finally ends. Could be anywhere, really, is the problem. It's not like Charlie's story came with GPS coordinates.

I could read forever, but I get hungry so I text Brooks and find him in sci-fi and drag him out against his will. We get fries and hang out in the park, sitting on the back of a bench with our feet on the seat.

"Did you find out what they were fighting about?" I ask.

"She wouldn't say," Brooks says.

"Was it the scrunchie?"

"She called him a liar."

"He never told her Mirielle was over for dinner," I say.

"Nope. She found out from Rae."

"She's having second thoughts."

On our way back to the bridge we pass a little store with all these stuffed animals in the window, all in this mock-congress layout around a single porcelain figurine of a little girl half my age, but with hair very much like mine, who is wearing a dress and holding her hands behind her back. The way they've set it up is you can't tell if she's lecturing to the animals or standing there for some inspection or judgment. They all look kind of old, like used toys from the early 20th century. There's a lion in the middle, a bear with a top hat, a pelican, rat, moose, cheetah, monkey, parrot, walrus, and on and on—they're falling off the window ledge there's so many. I think about when I was younger and would surround myself with my stuffed animals before going to sleep. We'd have conversations, tell each other stories, work out some hardcore toddler conflict resolution on all the little dramas that flared up between all the personalities of the animal kingdom. Now they live like savages under my bed. I cannot bring myself to box them up. I was a different kind of creature back then, a tiny thing not entirely unlike this porcelain girl. I'd never really thought about my younger self until a few years ago. It's still kind of a new thing for me: remembering myself as someone I used to be. As someone else. How many more selves will I become? Will I remember them sequentially, as a process, as a series of memories stacked on each other—like, this was me when I was really into soccer, or this was me when I got all nostalgic about the soccer-loving me that came before, or this was me trying to reconcile those two earlier selves?

Such a tiny porcelain face. Careful blue brush strokes around her eyes. Someone I was. Someone gone. Who am I now if I leave out all the other Lexies? I can only imagine it for a few seconds at a time, but when I try I start to notice my breath more. I can feel my pulse. I become like a congress of the wild, a hungry thing of the forest.

We make it back just in time for the main tournament. Turns out it's way more intense than I thought it would be. We're in a crowd ready for blood. There's even a ring like at a boxing match. Brooks and I can't find Bre but we get good seats up front thanks to Jeffry, who drags us in from the lobby. He explains meta-strategies, exclusions, gambits and combos. This is a game of skill, intellect and manipulation. Jeffry points out chaos players and the most skilled cloakers. Every contender stands under a hanging microphone so the audience can hear the chatter and the verbal strategies that precede each throw. Derwin likes to let his opponent speak first and these days he's working a technique of affirmation. When his enemy says, "I know you're going to throw scissors," or "You lean rock, I've seen your stats," he gives off a Zen-like calm and replies by letting them know just how right they are.

Derwin's elimination comes quicker than we hoped, but he says he made it further than he expected: to the top 12. Lost to a girl who never threw the same hand twice in a row. Derwin says he noticed too late and could have turned it all around with one more throw.

When it's time for the finalists to face off, it's clear we are watching the physical display of a transcendent mental battle bordering on telepathy. The favorite is a local boy in purple glasses who goes by the name Ingrid Cancer. The other comes from Nebraska. He's dressed up to the nines, for a farm boy, and only offsets his image by biting down on an empty quellazaire. No one seems to have heard of him before. Calls himself Stray. A lot of their work takes place in the prime, each opponent trying to control the rhythm and get the edge on the delivery. One prime goes down so gradually that I expect the judges to stop the round. The approach is almost in slow motion and I can see them cycling through three or more different attacks before the hand touches down. They work the mental space like it's a whole other dimension. Their banter baffles us all. Ingrid recites a short haiku about dragonflies. Stray responds by saying, "The heart is a salad."

"I've never seen anything like it," Jeffry whispers to me. "I can't even track their tactics." There are countless draws and each one seems to heighten the stakes. After a string of about thirteen, Stray wins with paper, but he doesn't seem happy about it. Ingrid breathes what I'm confident is a sigh of relief and Stray gets an anxious twitch like he was counting on a few more draws and now everything is fucked. Somehow the win has thrown off his game and Ingrid takes two more matches, putting him ahead. A comeback seems improbable.

But in less than a minute Stray has won it all. They're announcing his victory and I didn't even see it happen. Ingrid looks like someone just ripped a baby out of him. Stray accepts his trophie with stoic poise. Paper was the winning throw and so this convention will forever go down as a Year of the Book.

Derwin says a million goodbyes and we get out of there, find a fancy place for a fancy meal. Jeffry and Nick join us and when the appetizers are gone everyone is ready to talk about anything other than RPS. After dinner Derwin goes out with the guys to celebrate. Bre decides she's not into it, so the three of us go to a movie and come back to the hotel. Bre keeps quiet. Things between them are pretty obviously fucked. When Derwin comes in at some god-awful hour close to sunrise I expect another fight, but Bre either doesn't wake up or pretends not to. My eyes open wide. Derwin sees me and I wave. He casts a peace sign, scissoring my paper. I might have dreamed it all.

In the morning we pack up and drive to the ocean. I get a chance to glimpse into Derwin's suitcase. The scrunchie is still there where I put it, which means she never found it and this makes me feel strangely relieved for a second, because if she's out of the picture without my having done anything about it—even though okay technically I did do something, but if it never mattered anyway then I'm off the hook, right?—then that's one life I don't have to feel personally responsible for. Being guilt-free makes me happy, which makes me feel guilty about feeling happy for feeling guilt-free.

Not a lot of conversation in the car. Even the music is low. It's an overcast day, and a storm is on the move. We stop at an isolated beach a little ways down the coast, at a small peninsula where a low cliff lunges out over the water. I haven't seen the ocean in years, not since I was one of those littler versions of myself. Her memory clashes with what I'm seeing now, which is a more expansive and devastating version of the coast than what has been in my mind all this time. It is less an epic violent force than a steady restless sleep. But at the same time I know that the ocean I'd built up in my head isn't even close to as profound as the real thing. My imagined sea was taller, but also flatter. Not something I could get lost in. Hardly as deadly as this lulling compound of subtle, jostling stillness. Nothing that could kill me.

We are not under the arch of the sun but its trajectory. A scattered few on the beach: small families, distracted lovers.

I close my eyes and try to crawl back into the vision. I know these things can't be forced, but trying can't be helped. I imagine myself as that old man, standing near the mosaic and the fountain, looking out over the sea. *There's a cave under me, I say, where the Tongue's secret hides.*

I picture the girl, still on top of the Tongue, pointing to the edge of the cliff in my mind where a drapery of green, hoppy vines plunges down toward the small beach. The vines are strong, and I imagine myself climbing meticulously to where a dark cave drills into the mountain. The Tongue unrolling like a red carpet out of the mouth of the cave, licking the surf—a bridge to the sea. I imagine what might live inside: an ancient grizzled skull or a flesh-eating bull; burning eyes, feeble breath. But the first creature to emerge is just a little man, a little man with the head of a boar. His tusks are made of diamond and his eyes burn like coal. He walks with some difficulty because walking on the Tongue is kind of like walking on a waterbed. After him come more half-and-half hybrid type creatures: the head of a fly, the body of a crane; the ears of an elephant, the arms of a lion. Then full on centipedes and chameleons and baby giraffes and hairless monkeys, some dressed in purple hats or bridal gowns or chainmail or straw coats. Everything mixed and matched. I allow my thoughts to go wherever they want with this. Whatever bizarre combination of shapes come to mind, dragged down by the Tongue and transformed by something or someone inside the cave. The monsters of the pageant look content, hardly noticing me, as they follow the Tongue to the surf and into the sea, where the waves swallow them whole.

Occasionally, bees dive past the corner of my eyes like falling stars. I think to myself, *This is my life, the dream of my life*. The last one out of the cave is only a child. A normal looking little kid. Standing all alone, mid-Tongue, a perfect innocent. He reminds me of Gabe. He approaches me and reaches for my hand, unrolls his fingers, and offers me a small red apple. He tells me what's happened to me, what my affliction is, how I've abandoned everyone I claimed to love. But I'm not in a place of condemnation, he says. This is where we go after the hearts we break begin to heal. He says I need to find the mountains and start again. You are no longer a man, he says. Now you have become a little girl.

Derwin drops me off long after midnight. I'm exhausted even though I slept through most of the trip. My mother is up, waiting for me with a sandwich. I tell her about the tournament and about some of what I saw. I haven't been able to talk to her so easily in years. She seems happy for me, and happy to have me home.

Before I go to bed two texts come in. The first is from Bre, letting me know that GSB is ready for me and that tomorrow, Tuesday, is the night, and I need to be there on time and to not fuck around.

The second text is from Brooks. *They broke up,* it says.

I write back, *Sad,* but what I really feel is guilt. I'm not sad. This is how it's supposed to be. Deal with the guilt. But it's not my fault, except it is.

In the morning I wake up to a new text from Brooks. *He's leaving tomorrow,* is all it says.

17

I WISH I COULD SAY we spend the whole day planning, but it's mostly me freaking out for nine hours while Brooks tries to calm me down and somehow not strangle me in the process. I cry a lot. Sometimes I don't even know why. There's these random moments of pure terror, where I feel like what happens now is all that will ever matter. There's grief. I'm so pissed at Derwin for a minute. For going away again. For coming back in the first place. I feel dizzy. I tell myself that somehow this will all make her love me—that I'm doing this for her, and my brain creates this whole other chain of reasoning behind that thought, which seems perfectly logical at the time, but a minute later I can't even describe what it was. Feels like the end of the world, but then that's what I'm trying to prevent. There's no way to tell when one emotion will bleed into another. I indulge the not entirely melodramatic wish that I was dead. Then I announce that I'm going to call Mirielle right this very minute and tell her everything, but Brooks snatches my phone so I wrestle him to the ground where we lie, crumpled and panting, and then I start laughing because I don't even have her number.

We eat some ice cream and I start to feel more in control.

He makes me map out our obstacles. One: Matthew Craig. Oh, Matthew Craig. Latest gossip indicates that he's starting to wear her down. Which means he could transition at any moment from stalking her to getting her in his car. If this happens I don't know what we'll do. Just having him drive by every fifteen minutes is enough of a problem. Two: Derwin. Clearly part of Derwin's heart has moved on from Mirielle. He wants to hop on his bike and head for the sunset, which he already did once. We need some way to convince him that it's time to rekindle the old flame. Three: Mirielle, herself. Definitely seems like she wants to kill him, which could be either good or bad, but I'm counting on that once the other pieces are in place she'll see him there with his swagger and scream at him for a while and maybe hit him a few times, but then she'll melt into his arms. I wonder if she knows he's leaving.

Then there's the matter of GSB and my initiation, which if I'm being honest is probably what really made me cry. Of all the things I have to sacrifice for this insanity, my chance to be part of this group just—argh! Angry. But I calm down. I'm supposed to be at Nate's at sunset. I'll just go early and tell them with words, with honesty. Maybe they will respect it. Maybe they will admire the crazy.

It's about an hour until dark and I still don't have a plan. For any of it. I know step one is to do something about Matthew Craig and the only thing I can think of is to find a way to use Pasha to get his attention, which Brooks actually thinks is a good idea. "You could call him and tell him Pasha's causing a scene," he says. "He'll drive out to the Home and that'll be our window."

"It's too small a window once he gets there and finds out everything's fine," I argue. "Besides, he'll see on his phone I'm not calling from there."

"Then go and make the call from the office. You have those powers, don't you?"

"It's pointless."

"Who knows what'll happen? Maybe he'll get in a wreck on the way down, or get pulled over by the cops. There's a whole universe out there waiting to help you out, but you've got to make the first move."

Brooks' optimism, when it happens, shines so brightly because he so rarely pulls it out of its cage.

"Are you feeling okay?" I ask.

"What?"

"Where is my cynical friend?"

"Do you want to do this or not?"

"I think I figured out what growing up is all about."

"I doubt it," he says.

"It's spending years of your life working for something only to realize you're an asshole."

"Let's go."

We need help, so we text Pender Walsh, who responds with complaints of intestinal issues and a crabby mother. I dial his number and tell him it's urgent, which I think calling instead of just texting should already imply. He wants to know everything. We didn't tell him anything when he helped us shadow Derwin, but now there's rumors everywhere that I'm in love with Mirielle, so he wants to know what's the deal, and I can tell him now or forget about his help.

What the hell. I tell him the whole story.

He laughs before responding, the kind of slow chuckle that betrays some nugget of true delight inside the mockery. This is not the sort of guy who understands convoluted delusions. Pender is a simple boy. Video games and water slides and vacations to the Edmonton Mall. He says, "I'm gonna go ahead and believe you."

The three of us agree to split up for now. Pender will be on the lookout for Mirielle and Matthew Craig. Brooks will find Derwin and try some sentimental heart-to-heart bullshit, which I have absolutely zero faith Brooks is capable of, but what else can we do? I'll head down to the Home and try to make the call.

But first I have to make an idiot of myself in front of the people I most want to impress. They're going to hate me.

Jonas lets me in with a dismissive nod. I take a few steps into the apartment and hesitate. Everyone is quiet, sitting on a couch or the floor, absorbed in their own preparations. Luis packs spray paint, cattle markers, and miniature explosives into a green canvas backpack. Nate, staring at a safety pin, practices single-point meditation according to Bre, who is on a laptop running through a map of town and making notes in a little green spiral notebook. They have a big white sheet up on the wall and are projecting clips from the website of a redneck in the deep South who wears a chicken-head hat and sabotages professional hunting and fishing events.

I'm scared to interrupt. But what I'm really scared of is saying what I need to say. "I can't go." Nobody reacts. It takes my brain a few seconds to realize that I didn't actually say it. I moved my lips. Maybe I whispered it. Bre shuts the laptop and walks over. "You ready?" she says. I'm afraid I'll remind her of Derwin, but she's glad to see me. "If you're nervous you don't have to go," she says. "It's better for us that you don't, if you're not ready."

I nod. Why do I do this? She nods back. It's like a handshake. I'm a dick. Still can't get my mouth to open, so I find a place to sit down until I figure it out. Luis walks by and gives me a quiet little high five. Bre picks up a pile of rope and starts coiling. Nate's crouching in front of me now. He clasps his hands and rests his fingers on his lips, elbows on thighs. He waits for eye contact and when I give it to him he starts. "Everyone hears this story. Ready? It's the story about a group of French guys who in 2006 they break into the Pantheon. You know what the Pantheon is? Really old building in Paris from the 1700's. Started out as a church and then it became a mausoleum during the Revolution. You listening? You paying attention? You've heard of Foucault's Pendulum, yeah? This is where we're talking about. I think it became a church again for a minute, and now it's a secular monument. I can't keep up with France. Point is, it's an important fucking building."

"You gonna hit that?" Luis says. There's an orange glass pipe by Nate's feet.

"Still illegal, right?" Nate says.

Luis nods. Nate acts like that was the deciding factor and lights up. As he sits there holding his breath, he keeps looking me in the eye. His cheeks puff out. It tickles to be stared at for that long. Focusing on the dilation of his pupils keeps me calm, and I manage not to laugh. Alexis Cherry walks by and takes the pipe from him. "Not for long, though. Say bye-bye to the nanny state."

"That which governs least governs best," Luis says.

"That which governs least is a waste of money," says Bre. "If libertarians had any balls they'd be anarchists." She's on the couch, legs spread apart, winding rope around her antebrachium.

Nate exhales, and I get a second of freedom before he finds my eyes again. That probably would have been the best time to say what I came here to say.

"So right there in this public building, in this Pantheon, these guys set up a secret workshop. They break locks, they sneak through shadows. They spend a year on this job. And what do you think they're doing? Trying to steal jewels? Priceless art? Financial documents? Are they there to deface public property? No way. They are in there for one fucking reason and that is to repair an antique clock that's been left to die. One full year these guys are sneaking in and out. Fixed the fucking clock, though. Up there in a little makeshift workshop between the dome and the rest of the building. Call themselves 'cultural guerillas'. Mission statement: to restore the flower of France. Same group of guys built an underground cinema below the Seine. This is real. This is a thing people did. Meanwhile there's plenty of old men in actual power who think the Rapture depends on a war in Israel, so they're trying make it happen. To bring it about. Putting in the political effort to stir shit up. We're blowing up foreign countries so we can excavate fossilized sunlight and power billion-dollar factories to slap fucking plastic logos on hats for assholes. Do you get what I'm saying, kid? Do you understand? Were you listening?"

I nod. I'm lucky I can still nod. It gets worse every minute I wait. Now that he's told me the induction story he might as well have just said there's no going back now. For the next five minutes I fuss around, peeking through windows, opening and closing shoeboxes, tapping rapidly and quietly on soft surfaces.

Nate crawls back to cuddle between Bre's knees. He tilts his head, exhales under her chin. "They're going to catch us," he whispers.

She drops the rope. Her arms fall over his chest. "No they're not."

"Tonight's the night."

"You say that every time."

"This is different," says Nate. "I know it."

"You say *that* every time, too."

She holds his hand, but she won't look at him. There's no warmth in the touch. She gets up and goes into the hall. Nate watches her walk—her slow walk that sort of draws the rest of the room along behind her, a willow-bending breeze.

He catches her outside her bedroom, takes her by the elbow. She stops, refusing to let him turn her around until she realizes he isn't trying to, then rests her chin on her shoulder, facing him with one eye. He pushes her into the wall, drapes around her, gets a hand between her knees and parts her legs. His other hand clings to her ribs. Her lips slacken. She glares at him.

"I'm not coming back," he says.

"Shut up."

He snatches her lower lip between his teeth. She stomps the floor.

"Let me go."

"This is it. They're going to catch me."

"They aren't going to catch you."

He relaxes his hand, but she clenches it with her thighs for one more lingering second. Her lip slips slowly from the needle of his eyetooth.

I realize my eyes have been closed for minutes. When I open them Nate is staring at me from the couch across the room. "Are you sure she's up for this?"

"I'm ready," I say.

What's the point hesitating? I'm either part of this or not. And I'm running out of time.

I take a deep breath. "But I can't. It's not that I don't want to. It's just… Something came up."

"Bre," Nate flips her name into the room like a warning. His eyes narrow.

"I'm sorry," I say. "I know it sounds like I'm being a flake, but this is really important. Probably. Or maybe I'm just crazy. That's more likely. Sorry I let you down."

I try to force myself to wait and talk it out, but before I know it I'm on my feet and rushing out the door. I feel their eyes on me. I hear Nate say, "Told you she was a waste of our time," and then, "Don't come back, bitch."

Outside in the dark, the water on my face isn't tears. A slow rain has begun. I'm shivering, but not from the cold. I wish I could say this is the stupidest I've ever felt. I have all the money I own in the world with me, around 40 bucks. Guess I better catch a cab. Nate's door slams and footsteps come up the stairs. "Hey, what the fuck?" Bre's voice.

"Sorry," I say.

"Don't be sorry. Tell me what's going on."

"It's hard to explain."

She sighs behind me like she's wrestling with her patience. "Did you walk here?"

"Yeah."

"Took balls," she says.

I turn around. "And that's another thing. You know how sexist that phrase is, right?" I bite my tongue, look away. Digging your own grave here, Lexie. But Bre smiles.

"Nate'll get over it," she says.

"What's the deal with you two?"

"I've been with Nate for almost two years. You know Derwin and I were never exclusive, right?" Not even close to what I was expecting to hear. She feels so much like a mom right now. And I feel better, I guess. I just want to forget any of this ever happened and go with them to do their GSB things. Right now.

"You need a ride? It's raining."

"I was hoping you guys would break up," I blurt out. "I'm sorry."

✳

She peers at the side of my head for a while, looking for reasons why I'd even care. We're standing in silence in the rain when the dilapidated old Chevy pulls up in front of us. For a second we both think it's Derwin. But the window rolls down and it's Brooks, all alone in the driver's seat. He's got it jacked all the way forward and there's no way he can hit the pedals with anything but the tips of his toes.

We stand there quiet in the rain for a few minutes. When the dilapidated old Chevy pulls up in front of us, we both think it's Derwin for a second. But the window rolls down and it's Brooks, all alone in the driver's seat. He's got it jacked all the way forward and there's no way he can hit the pedals with anything but the tips of his toes.

"Why are you driving?" I say.

"Why not? Get in."

I have never known Brooks to actively break a single rule in his life; now he's stealing cars and driving without a license. I run around to the passenger side and open the door. Turns out Brooks isn't alone. Gabe is there in a little red and black booster seat, playing with a plastic prayer wheel. "Hey Gabe," I say, as I interrogate Brooks with my eyes.

He shrugs. "Mom has a date."

"You couldn't have left him with Grandma?"

"You're joking."

Before I get in, I shout to Bre over the hood. "Thanks for giving me a shot."

"You still owe me an explanation."

I owe you more than that.

"We're going to bust an old man out of the old folks' home," Brooks says.

We are?

"He doesn't want to die in a cage. He has a right to go out in the open air."

My father's phrase comes to mind. "Only thus can a man hop the tracks of the gods." Bre tilts her head, eyes narrow, contemplating a smile.

"If you guys had any balls you'd help us," Brooks says. He puts it in drive and we chase headlights into the rain.

"What was that all about?" I ask.

"Just felt like saying something dramatic. It'd be a good plan, though, right?"

"Like you could ever get Pasha away from his walls."

Brooks isn't a half-bad driver it turns out. Keeps himself hugged tight to the wheel, straining his neck to see through the windshield as we cruise down empty residential streets. "I totally thought Derwin stole this truck," I say.

"No, it's his. I stole it," Brooks says.

"You stole it."

"I stole it."

"I stole it," Gabe says.

"Did you find him?"

"I've been calling and texting for the last hour," Brooks says.

"Calling where?"

"Mom bought him a phone." Okay so now Derwin has a phone for the first time in his life. I guess their mom decided there's no way in hell her son was going to leave her again without some way to get in touch with him. Not that he apparently pays any attention.

"What's his number?"

Brooks gives it to me and I send the words: *She loves you.* I wonder if Derwin even knows what texting is. From now on I can only do what I do and watch everything fall apart.

Chestnut Homes locks up at eight and I don't have a key. Brooks drops me off and idles in the rain. I stand on the deactivated pressure-activated sliding glass door and stick my face in front of the intercom, standing in a pyramid of yellow light under the narrow overhang where moths bang their heads against a globe filled with spiderwebs and mummified flies. The intercom button is worn from touch. I push it with my nose. There's a little fisheye camera in front of my eye. I try to look casual as Jen's voice comes through. "What are you doing here, Lexie?"

"I think I left my bag. Can I come look?"

"Go around to the service door."

I give Brooks the thumbs up across the parking lot. He texts me that he just got a call from Pender who found out Mirielle has agreed to discuss things with Matthew Craig in a neutral location. They're together now, apparently, but we don't know where. It's a good thing I already started this night without hope. Even if I were to tell Matthew Craig that his grandfather just had a heart attack I doubt he'd leave her now. Jen waits for me at the unmarked grey door and lets me in.

"Is it raining out there?" she says.

"A little."

"That was a nasty fall the other day. Are you all right?"

"Sure, I'm fine," I say.

"The temperature is going to drop tonight. You should be wearing a jacket."

"There's one in my bag."

"Where did you leave it?" she says.

"I don't know. Maybe the rec room, or the break room."

"Well, you go ahead and look around. I need to get back to the desk."

Who knew lying to an adult could be so easy? Once we reach the lobby she'll slip back into her trashy novel and I'll have free run of the Home, including the phone in the back office, which is never locked. The number should come up on Matthew Craig's cell as Chestnut Homes. Fruitless plan going according to fruitless plan.

Then I hear Jen's voice crack: "Oh my god!"

She's seen something in the lobby that takes me a few seconds to make any sense of. The first thing I notice is Ane Lopez Lopez scrawling incantatory symbols on the wall with a red Sharpie. There's a security attendant on each side of her, attempting to stop her without making physical contact. We've had lawsuits before. But even this scene doesn't strike me as all that weird because there's far weirder shit going down on the other side of the room. Oliver Spoonbowl mashes up against Darla Flemming who is mashed up against the glass of the nurse's office under almost theatrically glaring lights. He's got her arms pinned above her head and I think he's sucking on her neck with those bog-person lips of his. I can't tell if her knees are buckling or if she's trying to fight back. One of her eyes is closed —in ecstasy?—but the other distends like a great gaping goblet scanning the sky for meaning or escape. The second night nurse hunches behind Oliver in this sort of linebacker pose, prying and grunting. She's a hulking freckle-faced redhead with tin eyes and this horrible lady crew cut. I never can remember her name. Terrance is here too, inside the nurse's station, banging away at one of the computers, as another young attendant frantically tries to drag him out of the chair. I start looking for Donald Victoria Estringi because obviously no one but my father could be behind all this. I finally spot him by the sliding glass doors of the main entrance, slumped over in a wheelchair—the standard blue push type, not his usual motorized chair. Pasha is with him, looming overhead like some Slavic giant; no longer connected to the walls, no longer connected to anything but the sharp curve of my father's shoulders. The way his thick hands rest there it almost looks like he's finally strangling him, but then I realize how gentle this moment really is. The look on Pasha's face is like a lioness licking her kittens. My father's head flops forward, defeated. I feel my fingernails grow and recede, and in one maddeningly detailed flash of intuition, I understand where all of this started.

18

AT NINE MINUTES TO EIGHT o'clock, around the time I was getting into the truck with Brooks, Donald Victoria Estringi sat in his wheelchair in the dim glow of his Mickey Mouse reading lamp, ordering himself to stand up. Stand up out of that chair and open that door. He talked to his legs. "Legs," he said, "it is time to walk. Remember the way you once walked three miles to gaze upon the crumbling Wall in the wake of our tremendous Western Democratic victory over the forces of evil? Now that was walking." And then Donald Victoria Estringi did in fact push himself up out of that chair. He stood trembling on atrophied feet, and he reached out to open the door.

Around the same time, the usual suspects gathered in the rec room playing a stupid card game: Terrance, Darla, Oliver, and Ane Lopez Lopez. For the last fifteen minutes Oliver had been gathering the nerve to finally tell Darla what a hot piece of ass she is. Terrance was cheating like crazy. Darla kept forgetting the rules. That's when Pasha slipped into the room and, just like he'd done with the journals the other day, he dropped a box of pencils on the floor that spread out and rolled like logs down a bare forest hill. His old fingers fluttered in front of his face, portending signs and wonders. Had he finally finished his manuscript? Were his zillion words all a buildup to some great stirring revolution of the infirm, the ancient, the lingering dead?

Terrance stood up and walked to the doorway, giving Pasha a dirty look. "We're going to see Donald," he said, and then he looked back at the others. They forgot their cards and petty bickering and picked up their canes and walkers and followed him down the hall to the elevator.

At exactly 8:00, Pasha was sliding along the walls behind everyone else, keeping his distance. Oliver had perhaps intended his words to be incendiary, but now Pasha was inspired with a new idea. He decided to follow along and watch. Just wait and see. And maybe, just maybe, finally work up the guts to tell my father off. Maybe if he managed to make it all the way up to the second floor he would feel like there was no turning back, and then he'd let Donald know once and for all what he really thought of him. Revenge would be sweet for the mad prophet of Chestnut Homes.

At 8:02 Oliver & Co. reached the elevator. Pasha watched them pile inside. No one noticed him. The doors closed. Pasha made his way around the little lobby area. He found it difficult to get past one particular end table with the giant rhododendron, but he managed by holding the plant in an awkward and slightly erotic embrace. He had no problem with the elevator. Elevators were just small rooms where you could touch all the walls at once if you wanted to. He got a real kick out of going up. He liked the way the floor pressed on the bottoms of his feet. He continued pondering the best way to tell Donald what was what. He knew he had to do it in as few words as possible. Strike hard and fast. Hit him where it hurts. Something about his legs. *You cripple in your little chair... You mean old braggart... You egomaniac who can't even run.* Maybe something like that. It would come to him, he thought, as the doors parted to deposit him on the second floor.

The texture of the walls here made Pasha uncomfortable. Tiny bumps of paint like little pimples. He could feel them on the backs of his arms and his palms. He spotted the gang at the far end of the hall, where Donald's door was open. The others seemed shocked and amazed by whatever they saw inside. Pasha was shuffling down to get a closer look when out came my father. His shoes were laced, his hair wild and white. He wore his pine-green highly decorated military jacket over a baby-blue nightgown. The gang tried to pat him on the back, but he was too fast for them. He ruffled Terrance's hair, pinched Ane's chin, and saluted Oliver. Then he offered Darla a deeply respectful and enigmatic bow that made her blush. He took the lead and hoofed it down the hall. The others followed, a mob headed straight toward Pasha.

It's too soon, Pasha thought. He lost his grip on what he was going to say, how he was going to make his move. Maybe if he stood very still Donald might mistake him for a mural. *No, let him come.* Words took shape in Pasha's mind, curt and scathing; words to rival Marx, Churchill, and Wilde. But wait—*why is Donald Victoria Estringi walking? Why is he out of his chair?* How could Pasha crack wise about a cripple if that cripple was strolling—no, dancing—toward him.

Donald slapped Pasha on the shoulder. "Evenin', Chuck! You coming with us?" and strolled on by. The gang bounced happily after him. Pasha didn't follow. The elevator swallowed his enemy, and Pasha was left alone.

When Donald Victoria Estringi first opened the door of his new second-floor room and found Terrance, Darla, Oliver, and Ane, he knew for sure that his plans were blessed by the gods. He took the initiative. "We're getting out of here. Who's with me?" Now in the elevator, Donald had one floor's worth of descent to explain his plan. "It's simple," he said. "We walk out the front door and all these doctors and their prescription deaths can kiss our collective ass goodbye."

None of the others fully registered Donald's intentions for some time. It excited them to see him standing on his own two feet and they simply allowed themselves to get caught up in his robust momentum. It was only at 8:15, when they'd left the elevator and made their way down the long hall to the main lobby, where Donald brought them to a hidden halt behind a bronze sculpture of two entangled Renaissance lovers, and shushed them with a look of complete and total seriousness, that they realized just how serious his serious business was.

"Where will you go?" Terrance asked.

"Nicaragua," my father said.

"Do you think Denny's is still open?" Darla asked.

"It isn't wise to go too far," said Oliver. He caught himself glaring at the back of my father's head. How did a man that age manage to keep so much hair? Darla, caught in Donald's magnetism, continued to inch closer and closer to him until their shoulders touched.

Donald said, "Those doors are gonna be locked. Any ideas?"

"Everything's automated and timed to the local clock," Terrance said. "I just have to convince the system that it's the middle of the day and we're home free."

"What about the nurses?"

The evening staff could be seen behind a pane of glass near the doors. Jen was putting down her trashy novel to answer my call and the redheaded nurse was messing around on the computer. As soon as the gang reached the doors there would be no way of getting by without alerting them. Walking out of Chestnut Homes wasn't illegal, but it was officially prohibited without prior authorization, so Donald knew they wouldn't let him go just like that. And now that he was on his feet he suspected they would want to keep him for science. Like that time in Bucharest when he'd infiltrated the maple factory only to find his brothers in arms undergoing hideous experiments for the advancement of Soviet warfare technology. He'd only managed to rescue one, a regret that would never cease to haunt him.

"Just get me in there," Terrance said.

"There's no way," Darla said. She put a hand on Donald's elbow as if to convey her point through his skin.

"One time in Berlin I drove a golf cart through a glass window," my father said. "The lacerations were negligible."

8:21 was when it finally happened. The moment that led to what I'm seeing now. Oliver was watching Jen leave her post. It was now or never, he decided. He took a good long look at his feelings—his jealousy of Donald, his lust for Darla—and ran it all up against the odds of him being dead before next spring. As soon as Jen was gone Oliver stepped into the open. Donald almost reached for him, but the confidence in the bald old man's movements defied consultation. Oliver's left hand locked around Darla's fingers and he pulled her out with him. The clock hit 8:22. Oliver's combined feeling of loyalty to the mission and a dread that Donald Victoria Estringi was about to steal away his girl forever drove him on. He swept Darla into his arms and struck up a geriatric waltz across the lobby floor, humming a tuneless hybrid of Strauss's *Emperor* and Tchaikovsky's *Piano Concerto Number One* as loudly as he could. Startled and brittle, Darla gazed into his eyes.

And where was Pasha during all this? After his failure to tell

Donald off, it took him another five minutes to settle his nerves. He found his resolve again on the return elevator ride and there he formulated the ultimate insult. He formulated it in his head, he transcribed it into moans, and then he announced it with words to the elevator doors. This was a real zinger. If only Donald had been there to hear it. The elevator spit Pasha back out onto the first floor, and he made his way wall by wall toward his room in the east wing. He figured he'd missed his chance, and was just thinking about how nice his warm bed would feel against his cold, revenge-robbed heart, when he heard the commotion from the lobby. He followed the sound and he found the waltzing couple waltzing, and the panicked redhead fleeing the nurse's station, and Terrance catching the door to slip inside behind her. Pasha saw my father's long, impossible strides toward the front doors, and he followed.

The nurse did what she could to extinguish the amours of Oliver and Darla. She said things like, "Mr. Spoonbowl, please, this is quite inappropriate."

Pasha slipped around the corner and took quick and tiny steps toward Donald. His heart thundered. He'd been rehearsing his great elevator insult in his head all the way down the hall. Now he would say it. Boy would he say it. He stopped where Ane was drawing equations on the walls, and she backed off to let Pasha slide past.

That's when my father noticed him. "Chuck, what are you doing?" Donald kept stepping up and down on the floor mat, which, during daylight hours, would have made the glass doors open.

Pasha was closing in. Fifteen feet away. Ten feet. Five. It was 8:24, the very moment Jen was opening the back door to let me in. Donald craned his neck to see how Terrance was coming along through the sliver of glass not entirely blotted out by Oliver and Darla's writing make-out session.

"Donald," Pasha said. He probably didn't say it as loudly as he wanted to, his voice just kind of creaking and moaning around the word.

Donald's feet stopped tapping and slapping, and for a second Pasha thought he'd captured the old man's attention. But then he saw my father's spindly knees tremble behind the hem of his nightgown. Blue tugboats on the fabric shook as if facing a tsunami. Donald looked at Pasha with horror. His legs gave out and he collapsed to the floor.

At 8:25 a high-pitched ringtone went off deep within the labyrinth of Chestnut Homes, calling the security crew to action, forcing them to suspend their game of poker. Within seconds, frantic footsteps were echoing down the main hall.

Back near the lobby's entrance Pasha clung to the wall, looming over my father, whose crumpled body covered a large portion of Chestnut Homes' interior doormat. Donald looked up and smiled. "Chuck, you old Wallflower. I'm done for, but you can still make it. Don't die here, Chuck. You've got what it takes."

Three security attendants with pale cheeks and desperate eyes run into the room, their shoes slapping on the plastic floor, wheelchairs thrust before them. One ran to the nurse's station and tried to get in. The other two stopped when they saw Ane and her graffiti. Feeling a responsibility to put a stop to the desecration of property, they let go of the chairs, both of which continued rolling toward the front doors. One slipped right between Pasha and Donald, bumping into the glass, and that's when the door finally opened. Terrance gave the thumbs up through the window just as the third security guard managed to get in.

Cool night air teased Pasha's skin. He felt a pull from the outside, a gentle suction. He clung to the doorframe, standing half-in and half-out. The first wheelchair slipped through the open door and vanished. The other was just stalling out on the edge of the rug next to Donald. Without so much as a single instant of conscious intention, Pasha pushed himself away from the glass wall. He felt suddenly as if he were floating free in space. The world seemed to lunge at him from all directions and the only thing he could do to remain stable was continue onward and downward, kneeling and reaching, tugging and lifting, holding up and clinging as if for his very life to the fluttering frame of Donald Victoria Estringi.

Pasha grips my father's shoulders, half to tuck him into the drooping blue seat of the wheelchair, and half to have something, anything to hold onto. It's 8:26 when I walk into the room, feeling everything that had ever happened and everything that would ever happen converge on this unlikely instant. Pasha looks up and catches my eye. He knows exactly why I'm here, and we're connected now through some link of thought and intention. I feel his memories from before he became a slave to the walls, going back to the days when he used to stand unaided on his own two feet. The memory surges like the shattering of an ancient spell. Pasha lets go of Donald, holding his hands up in surrender. He looks back into the room at nothing in particular, gazing into the invisible. The breeze tugs on his thin shirt, its sleeves flapping like ghosts, and I watch him stumble backward through the doors and out into the parking lot. His hands flail for something solid and familiar, and as soon as he's past the threshold the front doors close.

Pasha stands alone in the night, nothing around him but open space, closed off from the chaos in here, which isn't showing any sign of calming down. Oliver has grabbed Darla's ass and she has returned the favor. Four more hands, Jen's joining the redhead's, mingle clumsily between them. Ane draws a pentagram on the forehead of one of the guards. I run to Donald Victoria Estringi and touch his hand. "Dad?" His body is paralyzed but his eyes are vigorous. He points over my shoulder and I turn to see the black and yellow striped emergency door lever on the doorjamb by the far wall.

I watch Pasha through the window. He remembers cradling his grandson's tiny body in the hospital on the boy's very first day on the planet, and in those days he did not float away or lose his footing. He had lived once as a man.

When Pasha turns away, vanishing into the darkness, I can no longer feel his thoughts. Donald's pointing finger is wagging now. I jump back and grab the emergency lever and rip it out of the wall and the doors open again. This time they stay that way. I hear the alarm clattering along the walls of the Home. My father smiles at me. I kiss him on the forehead and run outside. The alarm is louder out here, but it can't drown out the horrified banshee squeal of Derwin's old truck, which Brooks drives around the corner to find out just what the fuck I've done now.

In the dark street Pasha's hands stretch to the sky. Finding nothing to cling to, they can only grasp the night air itself. Something drags him and he tumbles farther on. He sees the long black road like a gaping throat into the belly of the universe. His legs feel strong. His heartbeat roars in his ears. Headlights move slowly toward him behind a suffocating engine that turns the intensifying rain to steam.

Brooks pulls up beside Pasha. The old man stumbles into the door. His fingers thrill at contact. The steel handle is cold and slippery on his skin.

19

"I THOUGHT I TOLD YOU I was joking."

Brooks isn't exactly glaring at me across the shoulders of the old man hunched between us, blinking in time with the windshield wipers.

"This just happened." I don't know what else to say. What else is there to say? *Now what,* I guess, would be a good start. There are two ways in and out of the grounds of Chestnut Homes. We call the back lot the service entrance, and it's locked up at night behind a gate. The main entrance is always open, just a quick turn off Chestnut Avenue, but there's no way around it because a hedge of trees grows on either side and the wall starts where the lawn meets the sidewalk. We're all jammed in, Pasha squeezed between me and Gabe and it's a good thing he's so skinny. Pasha rests his hands on the dashboard, then removes them, then puts them back again. "It's okay," I tell him. He relaxes and sinks into the seat. Gabe touches his elbow and says, "Once, the Buddha was a monkey."

Our headlights hit the sidewalk between the trees and it becomes clear we're not going anywhere. Two night watchmen stand in the rain holding out their hands, blocking our way. One of them looks familiar. A guy named Daryl, now on his radio.

The other one walks toward the truck. He goes to Brooks' side, gestures for him to roll down the window. Brooks cracks it just enough to talk, not out of fear of the guards, but because he doesn't want to get wet.

"You old enough to drive, son?" asks the guard. I can't make out the name on his name tag, but I see his employee number clear enough: 00062.

Another pair of headlights cuts off the conversation as a green Subaru rolls up behind Daryl. He turns and tells the car to stop, but it doesn't even slow down. Comes right at him. Not real fast, but enough to make Daryl jump to get out of the way before the bumper hits him. The other guard steps back and reaches for his hip. They don't have guns or anything, just utility belts with canisters of pepper spray. The car pulls up beside us. Luis is driving. Nate hops out of the passenger side and walks up to Daryl.

"Just hold it right there, kid," Daryl says. "Cops are on their way."

"Good," Nate says. "Been meaning to get arrested tonight." Daryl pulls out his pepper spray and aims it at Nate's face, but Nate doesn't stop and Daryl doesn't spray. He maneuvers Daryl backward until we have a clear shot at the street. Luis pulls up by my broken window, so I crack open the door.

"Who's the old guy?" Bre asks from the back seat.

"Matthew Craig's granddad," I say. Pasha lights up at the mention of his grandson's name. "Pasha Luski. You know," and I pantomime like I'm guzzling a quart of booze.

"This is *that* guy?"

Pasha mimics my pantomime.

"That shit's all just rumors," Bre says.

"You never saw it?"

"Did you?"

"With these very eyes," I say.

The second guard starts rapping on Brooks' window. He tries the handle without any luck.

"You guys better beat it," Bre says.

"You came here for us?" I ask.

"Nate's pissed," says Bre, "but I made him come. We'll keep these guys busy until you're long gone. Probably no way to not get busted at this point."

I give her one of those looks like they do in the movies that means thanks without actually saying the word. I go to close the door, but she says, "Hold on," and steps out of their car. The rain drizzles down spears of her hair. "How long since he's had a drink?"

"I don't know. Three years maybe?"

"Here." She hands me something cold and hard. A corroding brass key. "You thirsty, old man?"

Pasha nods vigorously.

"That's brilliant," I say.

"What is?" Bre says.

"Hard to explain."

"Hard to 'splain!" Gabe squeals.

"Um," Brooks interrupts, clearly doubting the ethics of my plan. But Pasha smiles. He won't stop nodding until I physically hold his head in place.

Bre shuts my door for me and gets back in the Subaru. Brooks lets off the brake and rolls toward the street. Guard Number Two tries to stop us by literally holding the side of the truck with his hands. Nate keeps backing Daryl up step after step. I wave to him. He flips us off. We turn left onto Chestnut and head north.

"You're crazy," Brooks says.

"It's perfect," I say.

"What's the angle here?"

"The return of Miss Pasha Luski. Talk about a distraction."

"He's a hundred years old," Brooks says.

"He has super powers. We need him. This is his time to shine."

There's nothing mounting about the storm. It comes and goes with indecision, as if there's a giant hose up there that some valkyrie has got it into her head to play the pinch-and-release game with. As we cross town I see the number 62 everywhere, on the license plates of parked cars and cars that pass us by, on the windows of business office, and the odometer and billboards and electric marquees. And where I don't see it I see variations like 26, 602, or 611. I keep getting melodramatic texts from Pender, who's losing his mind looking for Derwin. Brooks put him on the job an hour ago and the little nutsack seems like he's actually doing his best. Pasha never once stops staring through the windshield and into the random bursts of raindrops that these shitty wipers struggle to destroy.

When we stop at the next red light Pasha pulls his lower lip away from his face and examines it along the side of his nose. He lets it slap back into his mouth. Gabe tries to mimic this maneuver without much success. A black sedan pulls up beside us. The driver rolls down his window and signals me to do the same. I make a face and point to the sky. The driver takes off his dorky orange shades and gives me a look that I think is supposed to represent sincerity and trust, but to me it's like he's trying to show off some very special and misunderstood cold sore.

"Fucker, three o'clock," I tell Brooks.

Brooks leans forward. "You've got to be kidding me," he says.

The light changes and Brooks pulls into a Dairy Queen parking lot. The sedan follows and stops beside us, on Brooks' side this time. Windows descend. The passenger in the sedan is like the older, uglier brother of the driver. Both of them look like they keep live-in hairdressers. Brown roots and blonde tips, two fuzzy beds of twisted nails. "You're not Derwin," he says.

"You know these guys?" I say.

Brooks leans his whole torso out his window and into the rain. The guys in the sedan have surely sworn a blood oath to keep their hair unsullied by water. "Nope," Brooks says. "I'm not."

"That's his truck," the driver says. "Wait, you're the little brother, aren't you? All grown up like a champ."

"I'm Todd," the passenger yells, "this is Tony. We got a call."

"Now's not really a great time," Brooks says.

"That's the best time, from our perspective. I know it's been a while. We brought the contracts along in case you want to dispute anything."

"I've read the contract." Brooks turns back to me. "God, I hate my mom sometimes."

"What's the deal?" I am genuinely confused.

"They're from F.I.—uh, Free Incarnation."

A *Life Swap* camera crew? Here and now? I really want to interpret this as a good sign.

"Can we outrun them?" I say.

"What do you think?"

"Bring 'em along, I guess."

"They are *not* recording this."

"Who cares? It's not like we're breaking any actual laws. I'm probably sure."

"I can think of a couple," Brooks says.

Pasha and Gabe are oblivious to it all. They're at one with the slow jigsaw raindrops stuttering down the glass.

"Follow us," Brooks sighs.

"I'll follow," says the driver. "Todd rides with you."

"There's no room."

"Swap me with the girl. Sooner we start rolling the sooner we're out of your hair."

Ever since Chestnut Homes I've been riding this steadily building surge of power. Without hesitation I jump out of the truck and hop into the sedan. Todd has a camera bag in one hand, and high-fives me with the other as we cross paths.

The slam of a sedan door is so sweet. "What up, Tony?"

"What're you, like twelve?" he says.

"Eat me." I buckle my seat belt.

Like most people in this town, Nate leaves his apartment unlocked. Which means I'm not breaking, just entering. I keep a good grip on Pasha's arm as we go down the steps. Todd's got his camera out and rolling in the face of Brooks, who's got Gabe on his shoulders. Tony way back on his phone. I push on the door and lead Pasha to the couch.

"Vodka, Apple Pucker, and Jagermeister for starters. Someone grab me shot glasses."

Todd sets the camera down and checks out the room's lighting. "I'll need to bring in a 3-piece for some sit-down interviews."

Brooks sets Gabe down and he sits in the middle of the room in like the most adorable little meditation pose. I slide the key into the antique lock on Nate's old chest. The lid creaks as it rises. This is an alcoholic's ark of the covenant.

"I think you might be kind of a bad person," Brooks tells me.

I open one very fine bottle of vodka, rinse out a shot glass, and we get to work. As expected, Pasha drinks like a machine. I supervise the liquor list while Todd gets coverage of everything he can and Brooks watches out the window for an unscheduled GSB return. Tony takes notes, plays fetch for Todd, and drinks a beer. He keeps teasing me. I can't tell if he's hitting on me or just living the douchey dream. When it gets too annoying I send him out to the store for two cans of Guinness because Nate doesn't consider anything with a pop top fit for his collection.

Pender checks in. *I can't find him,* he says, meaning Derwin.

Great. *Any news on Mirielle?* I type.

Pender says she's definitely with Matthew Craig, maybe on the move, driving around in his prissy Prius somewhere. I tell him we've got Pasha, like, in a basement. He demands photographic evidence.

While we wait for Tony I play with Gabe a little. I show him the interlinking loop puzzle and he tells me it's already solved. Todd gets some footage of Gabe, who just grins into the lens and never answers any questions.

Fifteen minutes later Tony drops the Guinness and his receipt on the table. I glance at the total. $2.60. Pasha's a blank page on the couch. His fist wraps around a rocks glass. He doesn't look any different. Cheeks a bit rosier, I guess.

"He won't drink the schnapps," says Brooks.

"Oh, Pasha." I sit beside him and take the glass gently from his hand. I smell it. "It's kind of gross, huh?"

Pasha nods.

"Rather have a beer?"

Of course he would. Brooks grabs three bottles of porter from the fridge as per specifications. Pasha takes one, smiles at me, and chokes down the peach schnapps before diving in.

My lack of all doubt in this moment expands to the surface of my skin. My arms feel as if they're covered with a million tiny candles. I'm ready to bark orders at the T brothers. "You guys hooked up?" I say.

"Looking for weed?" asks Todd.

"No. Information."

When the last can of Guinness slips from Pasha's fingers he slumps deeper into the couch corner, half asleep. I'm watching him relentlessly, waiting for some sign of transformation that does not involve drool. Gabe insists on sitting on his lap, which perks Pasha up a bit, but I have to separate them when he almost drops the kid.

"He doesn't look great," Brooks says from the plush blue chair in the corner where Todd has spent the last twenty minutes setting up lights. Tony's still out on the porch trying to dig up a way to track Mirielle's cell phone or something. My faith in him is staggeringly nonexistent, but it's nice that he's trying.

"Pretty much the opposite of great," Todd affirms. "What's this for, some kind of art project?"

"We should take him back to the Home," says Brooks.

Have I seriously just poisoned an old man?

"Pasha? Can you hear me?"

He turns his head. His eyes are young and full of fire, two vibrating coals trapped inside a sluggish old tomb. He holds up his hands, feels the air, touches my face.

"So overall, how would you characterize your *Life Swap* experience up to this point?" Todd asks. His eyes are arctic blue in the viewfinder's LCD display.

Through these last hours I've been running on pure instinct, less in control of my body than ever. Somehow I manage to get Pasha on his feet. He strokes my hair, then launches himself off the side of the couch, slamming into the wall by the little hallway that leads to the bedrooms.

Today is the second of June.

"Lexie," says Brooks.

"Give it time," I say, faking confidence.

Pasha draws new strength from the walls. He drags himself along with his hands and vanishes down the hall.

"Where's he going?"

"What would you say is one thing you've found in your new life that was totally missing from your old life but you never knew it until you found it here?"

"What if he dies? Then what?"

I grab Brooks' sleeve, tugging on it like the rope tied to a church bell. "We did everything right!"

"You think maybe all this has something to do with wanting a woman you can't have?" Brooks asks.

Tony comes back inside, holding up his phone and doing like this fist pump thing with it. Walks right up to me and pushes it in front of my face. "Got it."

Terrance, who never was successful in hacking Mirielle's email, would be livid to find out that this reject from Jersey Shore has just delivered a readout of her last ten texts. "Unbelievable," I say, taking the phone out of his hands.

"LA connections, yo."

"With what, the NSA?"

Todd turns the camera on me. "You're into chicks?"

I stare at the tiny screen. "She's with Matthew Craig right now," I say. "They're going for coffee somewhere."

"That narrows it down."

"It's a small town, Todd. We're looking at no more than three options this time of night."

"Should we check on the old guy?" Tony says.

I get a text from Pender: *No D... MC spotted at Denny's holding Mirielle's hand in a mostly desperate way.*

"Location," I scream. I run around the house corking bottles and filing them back in the liquor chest.

"Is someone gonna check on the old guy?"

"Start the car. We're going to Denny's."

Brooks says, "We have to take Pasha back to the Home. Or a hospital."

"He's got to be so fucked up," says Todd.

"I bet he's puking his guts out," says Tony.

"You guys, you don't even—" I give up. "I'll get him."

Standing in the fulcrum between two bedrooms on the threshold of the crooked line where the kitchen light invades the narrow hall, I know exactly what I am about to discover. Pasha has found his way into Bre's room and he is not lying on the bed or the floor. He's facing the door, sitting upright in the desk chair, straddling it and watching me over the wooden spine, long arms crossed in front of him like railroad tracks, with wrists so lax that even the outlines of his fingernails are visible, backlit by a small red reading lamp. The rest of Pasha is a smoky silhouette, proud bare shoulders swaying like a pair of cobras. I beckon him without a word, offering my hand. He manages to swing his right foot in one sweeping straight-legged arc over the back of the chair and push himself upright as his heel touches the floor. His swagger reveals no hint of intoxication. He's all hips and legs and thrusting shoulders, and the moment that he enters the light I do not see the ancient wrinkled body of Pasha Luski shoved like a wilted carrot into the dress of a young girl nowhere near his size. I see the intrepid force of feminine power. Her makeup is flawless, blending with the false eyelashes until they look almost real.

"You need a wig, sugar," I say.

"Damn right, you sweet little thang," Pasha's whisper is melodic. She bends over to trace a fingertip down my cheek. In her raid of Bre's closet she discovered the one and only dress, probably buried in the back: a long, tight-fitting satin green slipover that must be some sort of prom legacy or ill-conceived Christmas gift from an oblivious grandparent. Pasha's legs don't look half bad in her lacy nylons, though, supported by three-inch black heels at least two sizes too small for him. I catch a glimpse of the strap of what is most definitely a leopard-print bra.

The camera is on and rolling as we walk back down the hall toward Brooks' inscrutable expression.

"Whoa." Tony's eyes distend.

"Best episode ever," Todd says.

"Skandha is Ātman," Gabe says.

"Denny's?" I say.

Pasha sashays up to Tony and plants a weird kiss on his cheek. "Can't speak for you boys," she says, "but I feel like dancing."

I can see Matthew Craig through the Denny's window. He leans over a cup of coffee or possibly his bloody heart on a plate, motionless and alone. I lead the way with Pasha on my heels, camera glued to Brooks who walks a pace or two behind with Gabe back on his shoulders. We all strut past the pie rack and the "Please Wait to be Seated" sign and the service counter and the chalkboard specials announcing two mini turkey pot pies for six bucks and the flat rectangular view into the kitchen and a table of drugged-out wastrels and an old truck driver half asleep over some bacon and eggs, and then right on up to Matthew Craig, where we stand for a reasonable period of time waiting for him to look up. I have no clue what to expect and definitely no plan on how to make this moment—let's call it point A—lead to the clear but elusive point B. I've alerted Pender that things are moving now and he really needs to find Derwin or all this chaos will be for nothing. Right now I'm kind of just hanging onto the hem of Fate's skirt to see where she leads me.

When Matthew Craig finally notices us, his eyes scan right by me and lock onto his grandfather in all her glory. "Paps?" he says, sounding almost like a lost little boy. "What the fuck?"

"Watch your mouth, son." Pasha slides into the booth. She grabs the boy's cup and tips it toward herself. "Ever try coffee with your cream?" Staring at Matthew Craig's slack jaw, I can pretend Pasha's own laughter comes from somewhere down inside his grandson's shell-shocked center. "I feel like a new man," she says.

"What's going on?" Matthew Craig whispers, as if his own diminished volume will counteract his granddad's booming voice.

Todd sticks the camera in Matthew Craig's face. "Can we get your name, for the record?"

A teapot-shaped waitress of about fifty, whose wiry grey is like bursting out of her hairnet, comes by to see if we need anything. "Coffee, my dear," says Pasha. "Black as the womb."

"Y'all need a bigger table?" she asks.

I shake my head and swivel around until I get the bathroom door in my periphery. As soon as Mirielle comes out I'm going to have to do or say something. I text Pender that we need Derwin like right now. Now is the time. Not every moment is now. Only this. This is as now as it gets.

"I realized something tonight, Matty," Pasha is saying. "We don't have to die."

I get a text back from Pender that Eric Anderson just heard from Charlotta Woosher that she saw Derwin's bike pull into the Town Pump.

Pasha's hands float in the space between her and her grandson. Matthew Craig looks like he's about to weep. "We are all luminiferous beings," says Pasha, "ricocheting off of each other in a fabulous cosmic dance."

"Where is she?" I say.

Matthew Craig sees me for the first time. "You're the girl with the sword."

"Mirielle. Is she here?"

"She's done with me."

He looks so broken, glossy eyes and all, but there's no time for empathy.

"Okay, but where exactly does that put her now?"

He glances up to the window. I follow his eyes toward a covered bus stop on the street and a pair of white shoes just barely visible under the bench. "There's no buses this late," I say.

"That's what I told her," Matthew Craig moans.

"If you'd seen what I saw tonight," Pasha says. "In the hall. The joy in their little faces..."

I pull Brooks aside. "How much longer are these guys going to tail you?"

"A couple more hours tops," says Todd.

"The mountain will be worn away before the kalpa ends," Gabe says.

"…their gentle hands peeling me from the walls."

I point to everyone.

"Don't follow me."

20

STANDING IN THE RAIN THREE feet behind the bus stop, staring at the pale anklets of skin between the backs of Mirielle's flats and the upturned fold of her jeans, I wrestle with a feeling both familiar and impossible to pin down. How many times have I come this close, crept up on her with intentions to say hi or compliment her skirt or whatever, only to back down—giving in to whatever excuse seemed most convenient at the time for covering up the fact that I was really just afraid to talk to her?

Here I go. I'm drenched. My hair looks like scraps of washcloth soaking in a bucket. Thank god I don't wear mascara. Here I go. Go say hi. If the word hi was any longer I might never start a human conversation. Mirielle scratches her ankle with a toe. Her feet settle. The limp rain falls. Here I go.

"Hi," I say to the faded poster for new orange scented dryer sheets behind the bus stop's Plexiglass back side.

When I walk over and stand in front of her she's staring at the palm of her hand, holding it up close to her eyes. Her index finger's unpolished nail attacks her flesh, scratching at a pinpoint spot just off the intersection between head line and fate line.

She's sitting on the bench's right end. I realize standing can be creepy, so I sit on the left. "Hi," I say.

Mirielle doesn't look away from her hand, but she says, "And then on top of everything else I get this sliver thing." She says it to her hand. Shakes her head at it like she should've known this would happen all along.

"Does it hurt?"

"Only when I scratch it, it does. But it's like as long as it's there it's going to bug me, you know? Fuck, I don't even know what it is. It's not wood. Whatever the bench is made out of. Some kind of plastic, I guess? All I did was put my hand down. It's really in there."

She smells like rosewater and gingersnaps.

"If I start crying, I'm sorry," she says. "I've been weepy off and on all day. No reason. Right now I'm mad. Mad is better."

"I cried today, too," I say.

She laughs. "Men, you know?"

I don't, actually. Did I just say that out loud? Because now she looks up. And she tries to share a conspiratorial grin, but I can't smile. I can't move at all.

"Oh hi," she says. "Layla, right?"

It's the name I gave her by accident in the Yard. My tongue-tied fake name that I still have no idea where it came from—I've never even met a Layla.

"Yeah," I say. She can have it. This is how I want her to remember me.

"I'm Mirielle." I know. "I'd shake hands, but I'm in the middle of this. Self-inflicted. The pain is starting to make my skin warm."

"Splinters suck," I say.

"You know there's no buses this late."

"My mom's picking me up."

"Kicking it in Denny's?"

"Kind of."

*

"Me too." She's looking into the rain now, her fingernail still scraping. "With this guy actually. Really sweet. Kind of. Too sweet, maybe? Do you ever get that? They're too nice, but you can tell they really aren't nice at all. Just this side of crazy. No, I don't know. That's probably not fair. I guess love fucks you up."

"Yes."

"But then if they aren't psycho for you then they're just assholes. God, I am so done with men."

I've heard her say those exact words in a dream.

"Are you waiting for someone?" I ask.

She says, "No, not really."

A motorcycle passes us on the street, kicking up a thin hedge of stale water in the rain. The dead hiding among the living.

"Here, let me see," I say. I reach for her and she offers me her hand. Her middle knuckle rests on the tip of my index finger. The splinter is perfectly centered in her palm, just peeking over her skin. I pinch at it with my raw, chewed nails.

"Schools out," she says. "Cool, huh?" I'm reaching into my pocket, digging around for the little knife I sometimes carry, shaking so much my hand gets stuck. "Any plans?"

"Not really."

Trying to get the knife open with three fingers, eyes fused on the speck stuck in her skin. My enemy, my only friend.

"Have you ever kissed a girl?" she says. There are so many ways I should be answering that question. "I was just thinking maybe I should give women a try. Guys are a total waste of time."

"You don't want kids?" I say.

"Yeah, I do. But there's always adoption, right?"

Her hand is still in my hand. If I let go I'll never get it back.

Mirielle, I love you and I'm sorry I made up all this shit about you and Derwin. I take it all back. I just want you. You and me and this bus stop forever. I'll show you how it can feel.

"Have you heard of Haploidization?" I say. I touch the tip of the blade to her hand and feel her involuntary flinch. "They make an artificial sperm cell out of your bone marrow. Then use that to fertilize your partner."

"That's a thing?"

"They're working on it."

"Yeah okay, but who gets to carry the child?" she says. "Who gets pickles and ice cream at 2am?" I can't bring myself to make eye contact, but I picture her winking at me.

"You could both do it at the same time."

"That sounds like a dangerous adventure."

"The thing is the child would always be a girl. No Y chromosome."

The tip of my knife indents her stratum corneum, pushing up against the splinter.

"How do you know this stuff?"

"My mother wants me to be a doctor."

"Is she pushy about it?"

"I guess, if you consider making me learn the name of every bone in the body by the time I was six 'pushy'. She's always sending me links to weird medical articles. Does that hurt?"

"No," Mirielle says and leans into me. Our shoulders touch. Her hair falls over my arm. I can feel her breath. "I was thinking about going into radiology," she says, "but I'm not very good at school. I'll probably just be a stripper." I look at her and she smirks in the most seductive way possible. "I'm kidding," she says. "Not about the school thing. I am, though. Bad at it. Math mostly. I don't know what I want to do."

"I think you'd make a great stripper," I say, and her laugh is soft, more gentle than the rain.

"You have pretty eyes, Layla," she says. I put the knife on my knee and pinch her hand. The green splinter sticks to my fingertip.

"There," I show her. She rubs her palm with her thumb, but leaves her hand where it was. In mine. We don't say anything for thousands of years. We're both just staring at the splinter, almost caressing. Then I start to talk. It's either that or leave. I consider leaving. Get up and go. Instead I talk. "Three weeks ago after school I followed you to the gift shop on Euker. You bought a birthday card for your cousin and a thing of body lotion. Then you got a hamburger at Loche's and only ate half of it. Your favorite poet is e.e. cummings. You never drink soda and sometimes you bring a water bottle to school full of lemon wedges. The same blue Nalgine bottle you've used all year. There's a Paramore sticker on it, but you aren't really a fan. You listen to Jay Z and One Republic, but you love Led Zeppelin and Cake because your brother was so into them."

I don't go on. There's so much more I could say. But then I realize I haven't actually said anything. I've just been staring at her like a dope, silent, unable to get the words out. My lips hanging slack. Her head is cocked like a curious puppy. I hope I wasn't making idiot moaning sounds or something. But now I have to speak. Say anything. "You have pretty eyebrows," is what I say.

I stop breathing. She doesn't even seem surprised.

Then she moves into me and puts her lips on my cheek. Resting there, breathing through her nose. Her hair on my ear.

She leans back, but only a couple inches. Inside I'm dissolving, my body releasing weird chemicals at impossible rates of production. She doesn't stop looking at me. She doesn't get up and leave.

"Derwin loves you," I say. "He's like, in love with you."

I let go of her hand and put mine in my lap. I'm no longer touching her in any sort of way and the absence comes with an unbearable emptiness there aren't enough drugs in the world to fill. Take her, grab her, kiss her. Her lips are right there. Right there.

"I have to go," I say. She's still searching out my eyes, looking more puzzled than rejected.

"You're Brooks' friend, right?" she asks.

I'm nodding, clearing my throat, reaching around for my knife.

"You should call him," I say. "I mean if you want to."

"How do you know?"

Everyone knows everything, all the time.

"I don't know," I say.

The lights are out in the park down the street, but there's a small playground castle where I can sit and stay dry and bang my head against the concave plastic window. I left her on the bench staring after me like some sort of nutcase, which is exactly how I feel right now. I can still smell her. Should've just gone for it, let her take me home, melted into her body. What difference would it have made? Derwin's probably not even in the state. He isn't answering his calls or his texts. Probably just got on his bike and got out.

When I scream in the little cubby, its Plexiglass rattles against the wood. It's a long, distended, shuddering sound. When I stop, my breathing is ragged. I remember once years ago when I heard someone scream out in the streets in the middle of the night and I imagined it was an attack. I never thought it might just be something like this.

＊

And here's the part where I sort of fall asleep in the play fort. The part where I can't for anything keep the emotional drain from shutting my body down. I lay there and listen to the rain and I have no idea how much time goes by. My thoughts dwindle and evaporate, but my eyes never close. They stare without seeing through the scratched and blurry window until a figure emerges on the far side. Her movement brings my awareness slowly back into focus. It's just me, of course, coming closer, cupping my hands like parentheses around my eyes, peering in to see why I'm no longer in the dry quiet tunnel, but out here again in the rain. My phone buzzes. I don't answer it. The storm has let up for a minute, but it's getting colder and I have to move fast to stay warm.

Which I guess is how I end up on Sussex Street wandering around blind for a few dark blocks, and when a bus pulls up ahead of me I run to catch it. Weird because I didn't think there were any buses this late. I have no idea where it's heading. I wish I could ride off after Derwin, chase him across the country, drag him home.

I wonder if her splinter is still on my finger.

The lights inside the bus turn human skin orange and pale. It's mostly empty except for an older woman with groceries, two college kids in the back drawing on each other's hands, and then this guy maybe in his thirties with short ashy hair and an orange sweater. He's the one I zero in on, and I sit kitty-corner so I can watch him. His body slumps forward like he's about to fall asleep, but his eyes are locked on the empty seat beside him, a tear clinging to his cheek, suspended on the peak of the bone. The damp trail back up to the corner of his eye gleams when the bus jostles and the fluorescence hits his face.

At first all I know is he's sad, and all I want now is to figure out his sadness. He lost someone. It's a lonely sorrow. My only clue is the way he's looking at that empty seat like someone should be there who isn't. That and the way his tears seem to float on top of his skin like he's not even aware he's been crying. He's that far outside of his body. What is it? Of all the horrible things that can happen to a man. The possibilities spin me back to my own problems, reflected in the life of this stranger. I remember losing Charlie and how I felt then and now it all comes back so I feel it all over again. I haven't missed her like this in a long time. With her I was never brittle. Suffocating in the warm sarcasm of her breath. My heart only breaks for me, but I can tell his is breaking in the same way, and in my mind this guy and I compare the pieces and we understand each other. I know him. I imagine him riding the circuit of this route for hours, never looking away from the empty seat. I feel actual pain and I want it to go away—for him, not me. For me this pain is the sweet sting of her absence. I almost enjoy it. You could call this enjoying it, when I get a reason to think about her again. But his pain is acute: recent, maybe only a few hours old. I need it to stop. After everything I've fucked up right now—if I could just find some way to take the pain away from him before he gets so lost in it that there's no way back.

All I have in my pockets is the Guinness receipt. I borrow a pen from the bus driver and write a note. It's nothing special, just some crappy words of encouragement about today's sorrow being the source of tomorrow's strength. The thing is I believe it, at least while I'm writing it. Total platitudes is what it would sound like if I said it out loud, but for him—just for him, in just this moment—it's the truth. It's true on this scrap of paper, on this bus, for this guy.

We hit a few more stops while I sit with the note folded up

in my hand. My heart is going apeshit. Maybe I won't give him the note after all. What good will it do anyway? It's just some stupid words. And then what, do I hand it over and run away? We're on bus number 62, I'm pretty sure.

Then at a certain stop I don't even know where we are this guy he drags himself up and wipes his face. I follow him off the bus. I run after him and tap him on the shoulder and say here take it. At first he looks confused but then he reaches out. Automatic trust. I smile and he smiles back a little, but it's not a happy smile—just an instinctive reflection of my own. As soon as he takes the note I run the other way. I don't even know where I am. After a few blocks I start walking, but not in a straight line. I go ten or twenty steps, then turn around. Then I turn back, change my mind, and turn again. Rising out of all this alternating momentum comes a surprising and immense and just as immediately subsiding terror. Something warm and extravagant is happening inside me that at first feels like total panic and then expands like a bubble until it bursts through my skin and now I'm completely covered in chills and my scalp floods with light. For ten blissful seconds I am released from all desire, all sense of self. Only waves of elation remain in the shape of my body. My heart is still dropping the bass all the way down to my quickening footsteps, but everything in-between goes weightless. I feel like I could start taking steps up and up and up without having to touch the ground ever again, and this crazy sort of energy surges along the insides of my arms forcing me to raise them up and spin in circles until whatever this feeling is comes radiating out of my fingertips in these like parabolic arcs. A rapturous warmth covers me and every bit of it has everything to do with the way I just emotionally connected with a total stranger. I have jacked into the switchboard of empathy on some sort of cosmic compassion network that I never knew existed; something that now I can see has always been present and open and available to me, everywhere I go, every time I meet another person.

When I calm down and finally look around I know where I am. I've seen these trees before. I'm two blocks away from Mirielle's house. I remember my phone. Three texts from Brooks. *I found D. On his way to Loche's,* followed by two more where-the-heck-are-you's. Okay. Here I go. I see myself walking right through her front door, flying upstairs and into her room, looking her in the eye, grabbing some part of her clothing, and all I will say is, "He loves you. He loves you. He loves you."

Her house is dark, and I don't see her car on the street. No cars anywhere that I recognize. Her room is upstairs but I don't know which window is hers. Should I start throwing pebbles? A rickety trellis tacked to the wall and covered in hops rises out of a white lilac bush. A drainpipe runs along one side where the trellis and the corner of the house meet. Maybe the flimsy wood will hold me. It's my only chance. I crawl through the bushes and start to climb.

I'm no longer cold, and I think maybe the rain has stopped. I should just tell her the truth. Every last bit of it. The vision, everything. Either that or ask her out for french fries. Who knows what I want anymore. I'm as responsible for the things I don't do as I am for the things I do. But I no longer see myself as a cause in all of this, only as another effect in a long chain of effects. The hops smell pungent and wild, vaguely sweet, with buds that look like tiny glowing pinecones. A few steps up. The wood seems strong enough so far. I will never again be someone who just turns around and goes home. I will act, I will fail, and I will fail beautifully. I will pass random notes out to strangers for the rest of my life. My ears vibrate with the surging sound of bees and I imagine this lattice crawling with insects on hot summer days. There's a hive in here somewhere, hidden behind the vines. I once read that at night they fan the honey with their wings to dry it out. I keep my body pressed close, clinging to the thin wooden slats held in place with only tack nails and hope. With every step I expect it to rip out of the wall and send me crashing to the ground, taking the bees with me. Maybe it's the strength of the vines keeping us all up here. This is a slow, deliberate crawl. Not gonna look back. I spot a rectangular aluminum tag tacked into the wall, embossed with the number 04062862 ...*her face veiled in vines...* Each step takes longer than the last. The higher I climb the more certain I am of my own mortality and impending death. A headline: *Teenage Girl Breaks Neck Stalking Homosexual Love Interest.* My mother would be so pleased.

I locate the hive, finding it with my ears before spotting the slats of honeycomb that droop down behind the lattice. When she comes to me I'll beg for forgiveness. I'm careful not to get my hands anywhere near the hive and I try to nudge myself over to a better vantage. The bees move slowly on the vines, mostly just their wings. Some of them circle my head, buzzing in whispers. Bees know how to coordinate immense populations in very small spaces without getting in each other's way. There's no director ordering them around or micromanaging traffic. But somehow they maintain a perfectly honed self-awareness that results in the equivalent of some like psychic group perception. Like each individual bee follows its own unique invisible song in its own little brain, a song that is genetically synchronized to every other little brain, and then what you get is a social organization based on each bee going all-out to express its own bee-ness. Absolute trust that if each bee just follows its inner song, the whole system can't help but function.

I know these vines. They're guiding me down to the beach and onto the Tongue and into the cave, where thousands of small green lights swarm the room. Some land on the walls and crawl over the rocks. Some fly together forming funnels and clouds that hover in the air. I walk into them but they don't touch me. They carry me to the back of the cave where their light illuminates the body of a woman hanging naked on the wall, tangled in a cocoon of chains. Her wrists are bound above her head. Her neck is swollen with vines. Her face cradled by damp spirals of hair. Bees crawl over her skin and swim past her eyes. Her fingers twitch like antennae picking up on fields of distant time, triggering jigsaws of mantic babble. Honey drips down from her hair onto her shoulders and rolls off her skin in long golden threads. The tiny lights swarm around my arm and drag me toward her. They lift my hand to her chest. Honey drips onto my fingers. I finds no resistance in her skin and I submerge deeper and deeper into her viscous flesh, absorbing, melting, fusing into her. The sticky sweetness is all around me. Faint green flashes on and off in my periphery. I can feel my memories draining out through my ears, my nose, my eyes. With each breath some violent machine siphons out impressions of everything I have ever seen or felt. My body dissolves. My awareness courses from axillary to brachial to ulnar and radial arteries, and then into a capillary mesh and out through fingertips to penetrate her and diffuse, advancing toward her core. A familiar smell of oil and freshly shaved metal. It's my perception she wants. It's my eyes through which to behold the world in a brand new way. The future is not mine to see, but it is partially mine to make. The cave evaporates and she shields me from the sun, which cascades through the honey in long golden spears. The saltwater washes sugar off her skin. Snug inside a tiny pulsing chamber, my palm rests on my cheeks, my elbows touch my knees. I have never felt so full, so enveloped, so everlasting.

I must be twenty feet off the ground. If this turns out to be Mirielle's parents' window the odds are pretty good that I'll panic and fall. I let go of the lattice with one hand and reach for the ledge, shuffling to the edge of the vines, keeping my feet locked between the diamond slats as my body leans toward the glass. I face my reflection in total darkness until my eyes adjust and I can look inside. All I can make out at first is the shape of a muddled bed. Do I bang on the window or try to open it? I wonder which is least likely to get me shot. I watch and wait. The stillness of the room becomes something on which I can focus and balance. I see her vanity and her closet door and a small bookshelf. There's a red guitar in the corner of the room. Not a single poster anywhere. A headless mannequin wearing half a blouse. Small sculptures of half-finished owls everywhere. An empty wine bottle turned over on the floor next to a skirt, a pair of jeans, cowboy boots, and a bra that by this light looks the same color as the discarded knee brace beneath it.

One bare foot sticks out under the blanket. A head of dark hair sunken into a white pillow on the far side of the bed. Dark, curly, rough hair. Not Mirielle's. *My champion.* I watch him roll over until his mouth falls open, then he lies still again. The covers consume Mirielle's head and I can see the scrunch of cloth where her fist clings for warmth, trying to burrow deeper. But the foot is hers, and not just the foot, but the calf, too. When he rolled he pulled the blanket off her leg all the way up to her knee, which looks back at me now like a marble sculpture on a sarcophagus lid.

21

IT'S NOT THAT I DON'T notice the old people, it's just that at this point nothing really surprises me.

I've been wandering more or less aimlessly through town for who knows how long. An hour? The rain is on-again-off-again background noise that I've tuned out. When it comes it never seems to be quite enough to get me wet. Brooks texts me that he ran into Maggie Andrews, who told him that earlier she saw Mirielle get onto the back of Derwin's motorbike. I can't decide if this makes me feel more vindicated or more insane. Did I do this? Did he get my text? Do I even want to know? I'm shaking. I'm skinless and tender. Did she lash out, hit him, scream at him, blame him and unload all the reasons she hated him until the only thing left was some impossible wanting that they couldn't unwant? I can't believe I made it back down the vines with how fast my heart was going. I don't even remember the climb now, almost like I blacked out. Just suddenly I was standing at the bottom staring at my hands, the image of her bed still in my brain. I felt like someone struck a tuning fork and stabbed it into my heart, where it resonated and expanded into a whole new cosmic universe of suffering I never knew was possible.

After a few seconds it was gone. It feels like someone else's pain now, like it accidentally fell into the wrong body and then realized its mistake.

Drawing my sleeves down over my hands I clench the hems in my fists and wish I'd brought a jacket. I'm on Williams Street, I think. Someone's moving toward me on the sidewalk: a bald old mustache of a man who looks vaguely familiar. He walks slowly but there's some pride in those footsteps. He stops me before I can slip by him. "Have you seen them?" he says.

"Huh?"

"They're leading us home."

"Right on, buddy," I say, and get the heck away from crazy. But one block later I pass another pair of gents trailed by an old lady on a walker. One of these I recognize for sure. They don't say a word but their eyes stick to me and they're shivering and I can totally understand for the first time how occasionally people feel like strangers might want to eat them. The next old lady I come across might as well be choking herself with her shawl. Her lips glossy with rain. Then I see three more across the road—Marvin Wise and Gladys Brilz, and another I don't recognize—passing in and out of the pools of streetlight, not moving in any particular direction as far as I can tell. One old woman all alone rests against a mailbox, working her gums and gesturing to her ears. She's talking to someone who isn't there.

A familiar red Chevy pulls up beside me, passenger window down. Gabe leans out and touches my face. "Night of the living geezers," Brooks says.

"How'd you fix the window?"

"It was broken?"

Safe inside, we cruise down Main Street. I tell him what I saw in Mirielle's room. He listens without comment. He's thinking, concentrating. Gabe pokes my leg like he's typing a letter.

"I haven't been dreaming," Brooks says to the windshield.

On every block we find more and more ancient figures wandering baffled through the rain. It's so fine a mist that Brooks doesn't need to use his windshield wipers, but he does anyway, on the lowest setting. I start recognizing more and more of these people. Terrance and Ane Lopez Lopez stare into a shop window on Main. In my imagination they smash it open with a trash can. I don't even try to figure what might have happened after we left Chestnut Homes. Who cares. Things happen in this world. I'm numb to the possibilities.

"Where are we going?"

Brooks doesn't answer. He turns down 9th Street where the old high school building wastes away like the century it was once a part of. He flips off the lights and glides up into the alley that cuts between the two main buildings. We hop out of the truck and Brooks takes us down to where a bunch of kids dressed in black kick it next to a blue dumpster.

Only when we're close enough for me to realize it's GSB do I notice how they're all sitting on the concrete, paying a surreal level of attention to Donald Victoria Estringi, who wheels back and forth in front of them, conforming to a tight runway, occasionally shaking a fist in the air. Todd and Tony are here, too, both with cameras pointed at my father. I already know he's talking about the Wall. And they're listening.

"Hitting it with whatever was handy," he says, "sledgehammers, crowbars, tire irons, pieces of concrete that had already broken off. Clawing at the cracks with their fingers, kicking it with steel boots. I told my commanding officer that if there hadn't been a wall it would've been the soldiers."

I stand next to Bre until she sees me. There is so much I could say right now, but I go with, "My dad. Sorry." Her look is like, shush we're in a library, and she goes back to ignoring me.

"You little fuckers need to understand why this sort of thing happens. As spawn of the new age, you need to know where you came from. Someday the 20th century is going to look like ancient history. For all our advances my time is going to go down as more brutal and insane than the middle ages. So you have to understand. You need to be prepared to avoid the mistakes we made. In the 50's there was a malaria outbreak in Borneo. Their solution was bomb the shit out of the land with DDT. Kill off all the mosquitoes. No more malaria. Well it worked. Oh boy how it worked. But what then? Now you've got a billion other insects flying around kamikaze-style, all pumped up with DDT-poisoning. Geckoes eat the bugs, and then cats eat the geckoes. Before you know it the cats start dying off in droves. And where there's no more cats the rodents take over. A boom in rat population. Which leads to widespread typhus and plague. The cure returns to the disease. You got me?"

After a chilly silence during which I can actually hear a vagabond gust of wind push an empty chip bag from one side of the alley to the other, Luis says, "The fuck?"

Nate leans back, head on a string. His laughter comes from deep inside his body and doesn't make a sound.

Donald's eyes swivel like spotlights toward me. No, he's looking at Bre, whose hand is raised.

"What did they do?" she asks. "About the plague."

He nods to affirm the question, seems amused with himself. "They dropped fresh cats from airplanes into the cities. Cats on parachutes. Tens of thousands of cats. If you'd been there what would you have done? Taken a picture on your goddamn mobile phone, is what. I see legions of humans marching lock step across a withering world, lenses out, filming everything in their line of sight, seeing nothing with their own eyes, trampling the miracle below their feet."

I cross the eye line of every GSB member to take Donald's hand. "You wanna go home?"

It's still a little like he doesn't even see me. "I long for the woods," he whispers.

Bre helps me get my father in the truck and Luis throws the wheelchair in the back. I give Nate back the key to his liquor chest and his parting glance is not anger or annoyance, but mystery, maybe even the mystery of approval. Maybe even the kind of mystery of approval that will transform into forgiveness and acceptance in a few weeks. I force myself not to hold my breath. Brooks drives us up the canyon. I ask him where Pasha is and Gabe says, "He's with the lady." Donald says it's going to snow—which is crazy but not unheard of even late in the summer. Not in these mountains. I ask him how it felt to walk again.

"What are you talking about?" he says.

"When you led them out," I say.

"I didn't lead anyone. It was Pasha. He finished his book, he brought us downstairs. He told us it was time to go."

"No," I shake my head. "You led them. You walked. I saw it."

"You saw wrong."

The part of me that wants, wants to leap right over the contradiction as if he'd never said, or I'd never thought, or that the voice and the thought never met. Other parts of me keep reaching up like hands through floorboards to draw me back down into what I already know to be true. I know, and yet I go. I couldn't look it in the face if I wanted to. It feels like one night a few years ago, just after Brooks and I started hanging out. We'd built a fort out of all the blankets in my mother's closet, using the couch and chairs for structure, pinning down and tying off corners of blankets. When the whole thing collapsed I was in the middle and Brooks was outside. Laughing, tangled in blankets, holding each other back, unable to find the way out but always with his body and breath nearby until neither of us could tell who was in and who was out, or which side we'd be on if either of us managed to find the other. All I can do in the glare of this light is to peel back more and more of the folds. I finally ask him the question. It just comes out, tumbling. "When you tried to kill yourself in Budapest, who was the angel that saved you?"

"She was an old woman named Ezster," he says. "Worked with the poor. She told me I was not destined to die among civilized men."

And in the clutch of his own voice this feels far more true than the answer I always imagined I would hear. Muffled from out beyond my quilted cocoon.

It's okay, I think. *You can still be my father.*

Brooks' hands clench at ten and two, knuckles drained of blood, his body tilted forward. Gabe resumes his typing, this time on Donald's leg. He tells him, "Those with good eyes are inclined to fall into a deep well." We climb the gravel switchback and pass the turnoff to the campground and further on by where Derwin showed me the bear. "Brooks, slow down." He's already going about as slow as humanly possible. We creep toward the hairpin turn and I scan the woods until I see the boulder, but the bear is gone, his throne abandoned. I guess it had to happen sometime.

"How far are we going?"

We go farther, climbing the kind of narrow jostling road that reminds you just how big mountains really are.

The first snowflake hits the windshield, splattering like the guts of an interstellar insect. Then another, and another.

"Stop here," I say. "Up at that turnout."

We park where the woods fade into a little canyon crevice above the pinch of the road and sit there in the dark as the snow comes down.

"You know," Donald says, "now that you mention it, I do feel like I could walk out here." He cracks open the door.

"Maybe that's not such a good idea," I say.

Donald swivels on his ass and pushes the door open. I crawl over Brooks and climb in the back where we both scramble for the chair, which is heavier than it looks. Donald puts his feet down and leans against the hood of the truck. Then he pushes off and takes a couple steps toward the side of the road, legs trembling. I forget about the wheelchair and jump down to catch him when he falls. He doesn't, though. Sways and teeters, but stays upright. Gives me a look like *I told you so.* I can no longer grasp who told who. Across the road the cliff drops off into the valley and I can see tiny streetlights way off through the trees. The snow melts on contact with my skin. I'm shivering now. The sky is only about half clouds and I can't tell the difference between the stars and the snowflakes. Every dark patch of forest, from the space between trees to the shadows in the leaves, feels like a tunnel or a cave where death keeps a branch office. My father once told me he'd rather be consumed by wolves than cancer—by something that understands hunger, something he could look in the eye. I belong here, in this space, vulnerable to all the proper ways to die. Where everything is exactly as fucked up as it's supposed to be.

"I think I'd make a pretty okay god," Brooks says, staring away at a patch of nothing in the air like he's talking to someone else. I guess the truth is Brooks has had his own train of thought this whole time, living his own story as his own main character all these days and years, in which I'm just the weird friend only marginally allied with the complex and ineffable facets of what I could never hope to understand, except in that it brought him here, right now, to those words.

Donald puts a hand on my shoulder. It's the most fatherly thing he's ever done. He says, "When you're out wandering in the hills and you come across a lone tree, a tree that's the only tree for miles, know that these trees have power. They are citadels —spiritual antennae for the ant and spider, the prairie dog, the blackbird, deer, coyote, slug, wasp, elk, fox and bear; in fact, for any other vibrating, digesting, metabolizing organism in and on the nearby earth. If you're lost, you may find a rock at the base of one of these trees. You almost always will. Sit there and take a few deep breaths. Listen. It's good to share some of your water with the roots. Then find the longest branch and walk in whatever direction the branch points, even if it's the direction you just came from."

I don't have it in me to wonder why my commie-bashing ultra-conservative ex-military father has decided it's time to start talking like a hippie. Still trying to wrap my head around his sudden decision to walk again, and whether or not that has any meaning in light of my deluded vision of him walking earlier. A snowflake hits my tongue. My stomach tightens and knots drill into my lower back. My body informs me for no particular reason that I am in the presence of the bear.

My insides are on fire.

And with one shudder of pain my consciousness tumbles

down the canyon, skipping out past high school and into the future. I am nineteen years old, joining a post-rock band with Rae Stryker of all people and a guy I've never met who won't stop claiming to be in love with me and another girl who is anorexic and tries to kill herself with pills, but I manage to remember this is going to happen and get her to a hospital in time. Mirielle sticks around town until her daughter becomes quite the little lady, and now they're moving away in a car Derwin fixed up for them, and before they leave I give the little one the Tongue as a going away present. I kiss Mirielle on the forehead like a grandmother or something. They're moving out east. I do not become a famous musician, although I try like hell in college. I play a few house parties and a lot of people seem to think I'll make it big, but something has changed. I stop feeling the music. Gradually I leave off composing and fall in love with silence. I graduate with a BA in psychology after acing A&P in my sleep, and I move to Newport where I get a job in a bakery. I almost marry a tall, wealthy man who covers my car with crushed beer cans after we break up.

When I turn thirty I start writing the story of my life, but I will never let anyone read it. Long, boring, pretentious paragraphs about the beautiful girls who broke my heart and a few women with ugly dying souls who almost destroyed me, and about the sort of things I was feeling when I crashed my car into the side of a building after my mother's death. I reunite with Brooks and Derwin when I'm thirty-six. Gabe has been playing professional baseball for three years. Brooks tells me Mirielle married a linguistics professor and has been living in Vermont. Derwin's daughter is there, all grown up and about to start a scholarship to a university in Indonesia. I get a few minutes alone with her and talk about how I held her when she was only a few hours old, how her dad brought me and Brooks to the hospital and Mirielle dreamily called me Layla even though by then she had my real name figured out. "I held you up to the window and tried to show you what outside was like," I say, and she smiles and says, "That was nice." I tell her how she looked me in the eyes, which is not something newborns often do. "We're connected you and me," I say, but I don't tell her why and she doesn't ask. It's the last time I see her face-to-face. I develop a hyperthyroid condition and go on levothyroxine for the rest of my life. Every year or so I try to move a little closer to the coast, drifting toward the tide a few blocks at a time.

In my forties I spend six years with a woman who decides to leave me for no reason she can explain. The only thing I can find to throw at her is my mother's urn: a waspish ceramic Grecian with a smoky red glaze and cobalt accents, painted on one side with a nest of violet orchids. It glances off my lover's cheek and hits the wall. The impact chips her tooth. The chip falls into the pile of ash and shards on the floor. We salvage what we can and sweep it up and put it all in a mahogany box with a sleeping Buddha carved onto the lid. She stays with me one more year and then she's gone.

I recover by going back to school. I'm halfway through an MFA in music composition when the city is evacuated. We're relocated and taken care of more or less for six months in crowded housing before I'm handed a packet full of options, none of which include or require a degree. I pick an office job in a small mountain town but quit the next year and move back near the sea. I'm poor, scraping by as an attendant at a big-box-store-themed amusement park where my job is to provide polite small talk and run items over refurbished scanning plates for visitors who want to experience the old ways. I wake up everyday wondering if she's done it. I'm certain neither of us will ever know. Maybe she'll meet the man who would have become the next Hitler, and shows him a kindness that changes his path. Or maybe it'll be something that seems totally useless and random —a little thing like taking the wrong turn or choosing apple pie instead of chocolate cake; and whatever it is will start a chain reaction leading to the right place at the right time, the right this instead of the wrong that, a button that never got pushed, a friendship that would never have been made, a death or a birth that no one will even remember or recognize the value of.

A month after my fiftieth birthday I run into Charlie at random in a gas station on my way to spend the weekend in Canada with a woman who thinks she's in love with me. I'm buying sunflower seeds and she's getting cigarettes and my girlfriend is filling the tank. We don't speak. We look at each other and both make enough of an effort to be close enough to be sure that we end up almost touching. She leaves first, and after she walks out the door I watch without staring. The bell chimes and the door closes and when she passes by the window what I see is Mirielle as she was at eighteen, back straight, chin to the sun. Two steps and she's gone, her profile seared into my eyes. Everything bubbles and floods, the aching and longing rushes up from deep memory in one brief kindling crippling moment and I cannot even hear the attendant asking me, "Ma'am can I help you?" and I walk out with the sunflower seeds unpaid for, looking for a girl who isn't there, standing in an empty parking lot where my travel date, whatever her name is I forget, waves at me that she's ready to roll.

Sometimes Brooks brings Derwin's grandchildren to visit me. I don't need to ask what their mother is up to. It doesn't matter. She's living the life that makes sense to her. The older I get the harder it becomes to differentiate between what has already happened and what sort of comets are on a return pass. I cruise right past 62 with no incident, but the next year I finally start to mellow out and I start to think a place like Chestnut Homes might be nice someday. Thirteen wars have come and gone in the span of a decade. I take up micro-gardening and hydroponics until the tremors become too strong and I can no longer control my fingers. Billions of people are born and die. I live now as close to the tide as a foundation can legally or physically stand.

Everything comes in jump cuts like this, working into a blurry concourse where fifteen years old starts to feel strangely like yesterday. All the flashes of my youth attain a crisp lucidity and unity, undifferentiated by clocks; each year a new aspect of myself branches out along a fixed middle. I identify this feeling with moving backward in time rather than forward, and it strikes me that I can no longer tell the difference. I balance on the fulcrum where a young girl foreseeing her future is indistinguishable from an old woman recalling her past. At 89 I lie on the most comfortable velvet couch in the middle of a scorching tropical beach. I'm cold. Like winter's-out-there cold. I look around and think perhaps none of this is real. I can still feel the snow falling on my bare neck. "This is it," I think. The end of light in my eyes. The end of this luminous flesh. There are somewhere around nine million different species of life on the planet, from Wolbachia to the Blue Whale. Enough species where we can speak in terms of how many hundreds go extinct every year. Nine million different shapes for the sunlight to take. Nine million different ways light slows itself down to experience time. I can't tell if what I'm feeling now is time slowing down or speeding up. The last word that trickles through my brain is a name.

No longer able to breathe, or blink, or wiggle my toes. No longer able to think. No more autonomic functions in process. Metabolism is old news. My cells unravel, splitting and seeping: organs collapse like failing cake. As brain cells burst from lactic acidosis I suddenly realize that this is a rising rather than a falling curtain. My mind has been a studio all these years: recording, analyzing, mastering the mix. The decomposition process is the final playback. This is how it begins. As each cell dies it releases trace chemicals that transmit indeterminate semitones of quantum information to various interconnected agencies that ultimately converge like a projection onto a screen or like light cast through a holographic plate or a filmstrip.

They've put me in the ground where thank god Brooks has made sure I'm not in a box or anything, just a canvas bag that will disintegrate and leave my body to the hungry critters. I continue falling to pieces. The process feels endless. There is nothing to compare the sensation, except maybe it's a little like peeling off a scab or sunburned skin. The molecules that remain, like husks of corn thrown to mulch, wait for new processes to scavenge them. I become this flower, that weed, this worm, that tree. The experience does not drag on. Time accelerates to a blur. For each new infusion my perspective fractures and multiplies exponentially, and I experience so many points of view and so many timelines that centuries start pouring out in seconds as eons unfurl, and it takes all my attention to track where this is headed. Eternity can be overwhelming, but we don't have to do it all at once. The generations emerge and dissolve in fluttering instants until I can only follow this equable thread millennia by millennia—a thread that unwinds the world until one solar system collides with another and our galaxy smears out into a million tiny explosions on a black horizon that separates one universe from the next in heat death's starlit race against chrysalis. I can no longer make out something from nothing as I lunge into the infinitesimal blip where being and non-being coexist that some people refer to as the end and others as the beginning of the universe, at which point I find myself living this same life all over again. Lexie again. Fifteen again. Doing and feeling everything in exactly the same way. And even though I am fully aware of this I decide that I won't change a thing—or maybe I can't change a thing because I knew it the last time around too, and every alteration I make only ends up being precisely whatever it is I've already done. Here I am again, compounding this realization time after unquantifiable time until the starfield and the snowfall diverge and I am only beholden to one space, to this single moment. Donald Victoria Estringi is gone. His footprints trail off in the snow, between the trees and out of sight. The bear has taken his place, standing upright on hind legs, mouth shut. A quiet moment in a hush before the wind swells. Staring over the canyon from the side of this road.

You could say I never loved Mirielle but your words would be like sign language to the blind. And it's not that I can't see, but fingers can't move fast enough for my eyes. Our hearts live in a space that is no space, where all four dimensions burned up long ago inside an exploding star. We wait now under open skies for the new morning of the ageless radiating background song. Our skin interpreting the braille of cosmic rays. You could say I never loved her but even this weird, lonely, unrequited longing is real, and it's still mine. Other loves will never know purity like this, fueled by the gap between desire and fulfillment, our fire dwindling and renewed, decaying into germination until it's only a blurry wing inside the clouded swarm. We linger and ache and grow in the dark. Something comes for us, eclipsing the sad, thermodynamic equilibrium of stagnant marriages and hideous divorce. It rides on currents of invisible, unsullied passions, encrypted inside each disembodied sound, each passing touch, each secret flash in the crooks of our eyes. We know what waiting means. We are not bound by light. When we let go we burn. Our fingers uncurl and breath rushes in.

The truck's dome light catches my eye and I see Brooks back there in the driver's seat. On his phone. Wiping his eyes. Crying maybe? The wind drills into me from above, the same wind stirring up pine branches to splash into each other until their tips sway like the masts of plodding vessels. I feel something warm and wet between my legs. My life is about to begin.

Behind me the bear exhales, deep and musical. Vapor drifts out between his nostrils. He's staring across my shoulder, hardly noticing me, looking into the valley and the thistles of golden lights, where he starts to get a notion that maybe somewhere down there a community of bears has gathered, waking up to surprising new ideas, developing notions of electricity and central heating and dance parties and conspiracy theories and precision machinery and cultural anthropology and optical networking. Of jealousy and gender studies and campaign promises and quantum computing and polyamory. Of mania, artificial flavors, structural analysis, and social responsibility. His ear twitches, scattering a teaspoon of snow. His paws limp at his sides.

Soon I will hear my mother's voice.

ACKNOWLEDGEMENTS

To my core: Jasmine Hopkins, Katie Ludwick, Brad Wilson, Kiva Singh, Heather Miller, Adryan Taylor Miller-Gorder, Joel Vogt, Jenna Berg, Josh Ludwick, Josh Cudinski, Mike Wagner, Alexis Wagner, Al and Sis Smith, Buzz and Ruth Wagner. You are the people I'd be nothing without.

Thanks to Carl Codor, Shawn Mihalik, Skye Grace Bennett, Helen Magart, Efrem Carlin, David Gates, Rick Bass, Kevin Canty, Megan Schneeberger, Aurora Darling, Valerie Rinder, Robert Isaac Brown and Sarah Jennings who provided valuable feedback in part or full during the three years of this book's development. To Mikey Winn, Diemkieu Ngo, and Sarina Hart —who made it possible for me to spend a peaceful summer in paradise finishing the first draft. And to Tommy Pertis for easing me into Budapest.

To my most brutal editors: Nelly Tobias and Karinya Funsett Topping— I'm endlessly grateful for your bluntness and insight. And to Asymmetrical's excellent editorial team: Samuel Engelen, Tahlia Meredith, and Trisha Suhr.

To Asymmetrical Press: Ryan Nicodemus, Joshua Fields Millburn, and Colin Wright—thank you for being more than just publishers.

To everyone who has gone out of their way to support my books over the years, a hopelessly incomplete list: Kay and Dean Ludwick, Alyssa English, John Nilles, Lindsay Zachariasen, Curt Jacobson, Steve Wilcox, Cory Fay, Shane Hickey, Jeff Keuber, Lauren Perry, Melanie Childress, Jan Richter, Jan Napiorkowski, Josh Hagler, Francesco Murrone, Skyla McCord, Theo Ellsworth, Jon Aaseng, Andy Shirtliff, Erika Fredrickson, Kate Morris, Rebecca Schaffer, Daniel Scott Morris, Aaron Jennings, Reid Reimers, Steve Saunders, Susan Akey, Anthony Gregori, Matty & Kimberly McCullough, Spencer O'Bryant, Dan Lair, Colin Westcott, Cab Tran, Jason Miller, Tim and Cheryl Martin, John Pennington, Andrew Rizzo, Dave Baxter, Clare Edgerton, Skye Steele, Myke Lacy, Steve and Melissa Wax, Ian Schoneman, Bruce Gordan, Craig Wareham, Josh Higham, Javier Ryan, John Hunt, Ashby Kinch, Katie Kane, Casey Charles, Karin Schalm, Bob Baker, Brian Buckbee, and so many more.

ABOUT THE AUTHOR

Josh Wagner was living in the middle of the desert with his dog Lucyfurr in 2008 when Ape Entertainment released his first graphic novel, Fiction Clemens. Since then he's traveled all over the planet, spinning stories out of what he finds.

Josh is the author of five books (Shapes the Sunlight Takes, Mystery Mark, Smashing Laptops, Deadwind Sea, and The Adventures of the Imagination of Periphery Stowe) and nearly a dozen plays (Including Ringing Out, Bleach Bone, This Illusionment, Salep & Silk, and Pit Girl). In his spare moments he reads too much, gets lost in the woods, and dances until they kick him out of the bar.

He blogs and promotes the arts at NothingInMind.com.

OTHER WORKS BY JOSH WAGNER

Fiction

Mystery Mark

Smashing Laptops

Deadwind Sea

*The Adventures of the Imagination
of Periphery Stowe*

Plays

Salep & Silk

Bleached Bones

Comics and Graphic Novels

Fiction Clemens